PINNED DOWN

Footsteps approaching. Slade could hear them plain as day—except it *wasn't* day, and even with the sounds to guide him, he still couldn't see a damned thing in the dark. He would be ready when the sniper closed to killing range, but for the moment, Slade's best bet was staying put and keeping deathly still.

With emphasis on *death*.

He waited, felt his enemy approaching, peered along the barrel of his Winchester at darkness. Was there movement just ahead? Ten paces, maybe less? Slade's index finger started taking up the trigger slack—and then his world exploded in a pyrotechnic flash, immediately plummeting to black.

TRACKDOWN

— THE LAWMAN —

LYLE BRANDT

BERKLEY BOOKS, NEW YORK

THE BERKLEY PUBLISHING GROUP
Published by the Penguin Group
Penguin Group (USA)
375 Hudson Street, New York, New York 10014, USA

USA • Canada • UK • Ireland • Australia • New Zealand • India • South Africa • China

penguin.com

A Penguin Random House Company

TRACKDOWN

A Berkley Book / published by arrangement with the author

For information, address: The Berkley Publishing Group,
a division of Penguin Group (USA) LLC,
375 Hudson Street, New York, New York 10014.

ISBN: 978-0-425-25918-4

PUBLISHING HISTORY
Berkley mass-market edition / April 2014

PRINTED IN THE UNITED STATES OF AMERICA

10 9 8 7 6 5 4 3 2 1

Cover illustration by Bruce Emmett.

For Warren Oates

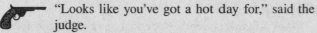 "Looks like you've got a hot day for," said the judge.

"Looks like," Jack Slade agreed. He didn't think Judge Dennison had called him into chambers for a chat about the weather, when they had four convicts waiting in the basement cell block, ready for their transport.

"You'll be careful with this lot, I hope," said Dennison.

Slade nodded. "Like I always am."

"That Mayfield's probably the worst, but all of them are dangerous."

"Good thing they're locked up."

"I'd have hanged Mayfield," said Dennison, "if there was solid evidence of anything besides attempted murder and the robberies. I *know* he's murdered half a dozen men, at least. But proving it . . ."

Slade knew the rules. Fergus Mayfield had been lucky, though he likely didn't think so, looking forward to a twenty-five-year stretch at Leavenworth. He would be well past sixty when he breathed free air again, assuming he got out alive.

Some didn't.

"Mind you," Dennison was saying, "if I had to pick amongst the four you're carrying, it's just a matter of degree that makes me call Mayfield the worst. Reese Dawkins, now . . ."

Another hard case, facing fifteen years for robbery and rustling livestock. As with Mayfield, he was known to be a killer, but there was a world of difference between knowing and proving the matter in court. Slade had arrested Dawkins personally but had missed the chance to end him when the outlaw chose surrender over gambling on his fast draw.

Slade wondered if there had been something in his manner or his eyes. A silent warning that he didn't care if Dawkins lived or died.

"Dan Kilgore is another one that got away," said Dennison.

Not quite, since he was caged downstairs and heading off to twelve years in a slightly larger cage, but Dennison meant that he had escaped the gallows by a whisper. Once again, it was *attempted* murder, paired with smuggling liquor to the reservations, and he would have stretched rope if his aim was better. Both the deputies he'd shot survived their wounds, although Jeb Thomas still had bullet fragments in his hip and would be feeling them with every step he took until the day he died.

"Can't hang 'em all, sir."

"Isn't that a pity?" Dennison considered what he'd said, frowning, and backed it up. "I don't mean that, of course. Some crimes—*most* crimes—don't rate a rope. But when I think about the lockups and what happens there, the kind of people they give back after the poor damned souls have done their time, I wonder sometimes why we bother."

"Some go straight," Slade said. "Joe Marley."

Settled down and farming now, after he'd served the best part of a year for moonshining. Married with one child, and another on the way.

A baby on the way . . .

"Marley, of course," said Dennison. "But who else can you think of, Jack?"

Slade tried, halfheartedly, then gave it up, distracted.

"An exception to the rule. Now, Orville Washington . . ."

"The odd man out," Slade said.

"And then some," Dennison agreed. "He's murdered no one that we know of, but armed robbery implies a willingness to kill. Don't take him lightly, Jack."

"No worries there."

"You think Guy's ready for a ten-day turnaround?"

They had to travel some two hundred fifty miles from Enid, up to Leavenworth in Kansas, at an easy walking pace, two horses hauling the tall prison wagon with one marshal driving, the other mounted on his own horse, free to scout ahead.

"Guy's fine," Slade said.

Guy Hampton was the new boy, twenty-one or -two, a little damp behind the ears. He hadn't grown into his badge yet, but Slade reckoned he was getting there. The long run up to Leavenworth and back would reinforce the rookie's understanding that a U.S. marshal's job involved long hours of routine, with precious little romance or adventure on the side.

Romance, Slade thought and pictured Faith. *Too late for that, damn it!*

"You'll have to watch for trouble in the wagon, Orville being colored," Dennison reminded him, unnecessarily.

"We're keeping them in shackles," Slade replied. "Not much that they can do, except insult each other."

"Still."

"I'll keep an eye peeled."

"You'll have rest stops. Nine nights camping on the road," said Dennison.

"They'll be in irons the whole time, under guard."

The judge frowned. Heaved a sigh. "All right," he said at last. "I'll let you go. We're burning daylight."

The goddamned manacles were chafing Mayfield's wrists already, making their infernal rattling noise to match the shackles on his legs and the connecting chain between them. Forced to shuffle as he walked, smelling the reek of sweat soaked into his striped prison uniform, with black thoughts churning in his head, Mayfield eyeballed the jailers who'd been sent to take him out and up into the daylight. Stubby shotguns meant they wouldn't even have to aim if he tried anything.

As if he could, chained up the way he was.

"You boys look scared," he told them, putting on a sneer. "Like you're about to wet yourselves."

The taller of them answered back, "Twenty-five years. I'm betting you don't get through half of that."

"You could be right," Mayfield replied and went off chuckling down the cell block, stopping when they told him to.

The next one out was Orville Washington, chained up the same, his skin almost the same shade as the black stripes on his uniform. He looked through Mayfield and the guards, the same blank stare that he'd been showing white men all his life, and fell in line under the guns. More clanking, shuffling as they moved along a few more yards, then stopped again.

Reese Dawkins was a wiry weasel of a man, stoop-shouldered, with a mop of hair no brush had ever tamed. Like all of them, he could have used a shave but wasn't getting near a razor till they reached their final destination, and he might not get one then.

Not if the guards had any common sense.

Dawkins nodded to Mayfield, a brief acknowledgment, but kept his mouth shut. There was nothing to be said about their present situation. They were on their way to Hell ahead of time, without the courtesy of burial.

Last up, Dan Kilgore, with his potbelly and thinning sandy hair. He'd lost a little weight in jail, but not enough to make you think that he could run a hundred yards without a breather. Mayfield pegged him as a back shooter, but there was nothing wrong with that. Why give someone a chance to kill you if you saw an opportunity to take him down without a fight?

A few more yards along the dank stone corridor, walls sprouting algae blooms, they reached a flight of stairs with daylight spilling through an open door above. Another lawman had the doorway covered, not one Mayfield recognized— but then, why should he? Focused on the badge, the Winchester, the holstered Colt, he clanked upstairs and out into the morning's glare.

Still early, but the dead air in the courtyard told him it would be a scorcher. Riding in the steel box of the prison transport wagon, Mayfield and his fellow cons were going to be sweated dry by noon, if not before. The canvas water bags hanging outside the cage on wheels clearly weren't large enough to see them through the trip. Of course, he'd known that they would have to stop along the way, if only for the horses' sake.

Mayfield was counting on it.

At his so-called trial, when he was sentenced, Mayfield hadn't threatened, fumed, or blustered. Hadn't boasted that no jail would ever hold him. It was better, in his personal experience, to let the law think you were beaten down and broken. That way, when you proved them wrong, it came as a surprise.

He needed all the edge that he could get, this time. Because, if he was on the prison wagon when it rumbled into Leavenworth, his life was well and truly over. He'd be gray and feeble by the time they let him out again, assuming that he didn't get time added to his sentence for some misbehavior in the lockup—or some other convict didn't slit his throat.

Now he saw a face he recognized: Jack Slade, one of the lawmen who had marched him back and forth to court during his trial, standing beside the wagon with a lever-action shotgun in his hands. The cage's door stood open, with a stepstool on the ground in front of it. That was a challenge, with the shackles on, but Mayfield made it up and in without embarrassing himself.

A younger marshal waited in the wagon, holding shorter lengths of chain, four padlocks hanging from his gunbelt. He directed Mayfield to the left-hand bench, stepped back to let him sit, then ducked and used one of the short chains to secure his shackles to an iron loop on the wagon's floor. Snapped on a padlock, then stood up and beckoned to the second man in line.

Damn, if he wasn't riding with the colored boy beside him.

Never mind, thought Mayfield. *Keep your mouth shut. Bide your time.*

"All set," Guy Hampton said, as he secured the final padlock on the prison wagon's door. "Ready when you are, Jack."

The wagon was an iron box, painted black but showing rust in spots where paint had chipped or flaked away. It had a wooden floorboard over iron, and inch-thick bars along each side, with two-inch gaps between them. A breeze could whisper in one side and out the other, if you met one on a day like this. Tarpaulins strapped atop the iron roof could be lowered on a rainy day to keep the prisoners from getting soaked, if anybody cared.

There was no food or water in the wagon's cage, no bucket for relief until the scheduled rest stops. Jailers had advised the four men bound for Leavenworth to do their business prior to leaving, or to hold it otherwise. The penalty for answering a call of nature in the wagon was a long, foul ride.

Already mounted on his roan mare, covering the convicts and their keepers as they were secured inside the wagon, Slade relaxed and answered Hampton. "Roll it, then."

His partner for the ten-day journey scrambled to the driver's seat, picked up the reins, and flicked them lightly at the two draft horses harnessed to the wagon. They took off, an easy walking pace that should devour something like four miles per hour through flat country, which was mostly what they had to navigate. Behind the wagon, trailing by its bridle, Hampton's sorrel gelding matched the easy pace.

Ten days. *At least* ten days.

Slade wished that he could stay in Enid, keep an eye on Faith, if only from a distance, but he had a job to do. He had to keep those paychecks coming now, be ready to support the child they'd made together when it came into the world. Of course, he wasn't sure that Faith would let him *see* the baby, much less be a father to it, after all the grief he had inflicted on her. Unintentional, of course, but suffering and danger seemed to haunt him like a pack of mangy scavengers trailing a wounded buck, sniffing along its trail and wishing it would die.

He wasn't dead yet, but it had been close, a time or two. For him *and* Faith, the last time, shot down on what should have been their wedding day. Slade had prepared to lose her then, and had hammered his grief into a bitter rage and wielded it against the men who had destroyed the only dream he'd ever treasured. Returning from that vengeance ride, he'd learned that Faith would live, recover fully—and that she was leaving, selling up and heading East.

Her choice, of course, and there was nothing Slade could say to say to change her mind, no decent argument for staying put and placing everything she had at risk, time after time. What kind of life was that for anyone?

He'd been prepared to lose her then, to close the door on "normal" life, rethink his options—when Faith had dropped another bombshell. She was pregnant, bearing his child, but she wouldn't talk about a life together, wouldn't say if the discovery had changed her plans for getting out of Oklahoma Territory.

Now, Slade had twenty days to think about it on the road, watching four convicts simmer in the heat.

Just what I need, he thought and urged his roan to catch the prison wagon as it rumbled out of town.

"I don't believe we're spendin' two weeks in this goddamn box," Reese Dawkins said. He kept his voice down, nothing that would make the law dogs snap at him, but there was venom in his tone.

"Neither can I," Fergus Mayfield answered, managing a thin-lipped smile.

"It ain't two weeks," Dan Kilgore chimed in, facing Dawkins from the bench directly opposite. "More like ten days, the jailers said, in town."

"Ten days, two weeks," sneered Dawkins. "What'n hell's the difference?"

"Four days," suggested Orville Washington.

"Oh, you a smart boy, is you?" Dawkins challenged.

"I can count."

"Mebbe you can," Dawkins replied. "But that don't mean you *do* count. Unnerstan' me, nig—"

"Shut up, the two of you!" hissed Mayfield. "We're already locked up, as it is. Don't make things any worse."

"Just how'n hell could it get *worse*?" Dawkins demanded.

"They could leave us chained in here the whole damn time," said Mayfield. "Tell 'em at the other end that we were fightin' and they couldn't take a chance unhooking us, when it was two to one against 'em. Do you want to spend the whole trip wearin' out your ass on this plank, sittin' in your own damn mess?"

"They wouldn't do that," Dawkins said, not sounding sure.

"Why not? Makes life a whole lot easier on them. They wouldn't have to sleep in shifts. We hit the pen, first job they give us would be cleanin' out the wagon for their trip back home."

"They gotta stop and feed us, don't they?" Dawkins offered.

"Poke some hardtack through the bars," Mayfield replied. "The hell do they care if we lose some weight along the way?"

"They gotta give us water," Dawkins told them. "That's the law."

"You see that siphon on the water bag behind you?" Mayfield asked him. "They can let you drink all day and never budge from where you sit. Just means more pissin' in your trousers."

"Jesus, that ain't right."

"Just think about it," Mayfield said. "And if you feel like killin' one another, bear in mind you've both got ten or twenty years to do it, once we get to Leavenworth."

"And you got twenty-five," Dawkins replied. "So why'n hell do you keep smilin'?"

"Just my sunny disposition, I suppose."

"Sunny? That what you call it when you're robbin' folks?" asked Washington.

"You've done your share of that," Mayfield retorted. "Did it make you sad?"

"I never felt no way about it. Jus' stood up and did my bidness," Washington explained.

"And when you killed a white man," Mayfield pressed him. "How'd that feel?"

"Who sayin' I killed anybody?" Washington displayed a deadpan face. "Nothin' like that was proved against me. Same as you, boss."

"Boss. I like that."

Now the dark face smiled at him. "Jus' don't get used to it."

"You *are* a smart boy."

"Kept myself alive this long," said Washington. "I ain't done yet."

"May be a little different in the pen," said Mayfield.

"Differ'nt than a bunch of white men tellin' me what I should do? I've had that all my life."

"Don't guess it took, though," Dawkins said.

"An' never will," said Washington.

Dawkins put on his weasel smile. "I guess ten days ain't all that long to wait," he said.

"Ten days, ten years," said Washington. "You come at me, bring ever'thing you got the first time out."

"I always do," Dawkins assured him.

"Because I don't give nobody a second chance."

"Big talk, when I'm chained up."

"Don't guess I'll lose much sleep over a horse thief comin' after me. I ain't a gelding."

"Yet," said Dawkins.

Mayfield gave up. The squabbling was tiresome, fruitless, but he'd done his best to calm the idiots down. When it came time for him to make his move, they'd have a bare split second to decide whether they lived or died. Their call. And in the moment, sweating in his rolling cage, he didn't give a tinker's damn.

Their route of travel took them east of Faith Connover's ranch. Slade wouldn't have a chance to glimpse the house, but he could picture it, imagine Faith moving around the rooms where they had been together, once upon a happy time. A bitter pang of loss added to Slade's discomfort from the morning's heat, making him wish he could forget about the whole damned thing. Maybe fall off the roan and hit his head, and if he lived through that, enjoy a nice bout of amnesia.

For the longest time, he'd been a drifter, living by his wits and talent with a deck of cards, until his brother's death had brought him into Oklahoma Territory. He'd been looking for revenge then, too, but found another life entirely—and the unexpected promise of a future with his late twin's fiancée.

All gone, now. Shot to hell.

But there was still his job, as long as he stuck with it. At the moment, that meant shepherding four losers who would likely kill him without thinking twice about it, and be glad when it was done. The law and common decency required that he take proper care of them along the way, but he and Hampton would decide what that entailed, based on the way their prisoners behaved.

The muttering he heard while riding on the left flank of the wagon didn't trouble Slade. He'd known some deputies who wouldn't let cons speak while they were traveling, but Slade had always thought that trying to enforce the rule of silence was an extra headache that he didn't need. It made no difference to him what a group of prisoners discussed, as long as they were physically restrained. Whether they prayed or raged at one another, sang a hymn or cursed him up one side and down the other, Slade controlled their movements, told them when they were allowed to eat, drink, and relieve themselves.

It was the most he could expect with captive beasts.

He knew Bible thumpers and reformers who would argue on behalf of rehabilitation or salvation, call it what you like. Slade rarely gave a thought to souls or what became of people in the afterlife, assuming that there was one. For the moment—while he kept his badge, at least—his sole concern was discipline. If someone broke the law, he either brought them in for trial or left them with the nearest undertaker, if they called him out. Once they were judged and sentenced, he delivered them to prison or the gallows.

Simple, on the face of it. But every time he faced another shady character, his life was riding on the line.

If you could call that living.

And it was, of course. You bought into the game when you were born, like it or not, and played the hands as they were dealt. Win some, lose some. If things got too bad, you could always fold. He'd known a few who took the so-called easy route and left a stinking mess for someone else to clean up after him. That wasn't Slade's style. He had never been a quitter, though he'd left a town or two—well, four or five was closer to the truth—when he'd run out of luck and time. A part of him still hoped that he could patch things up with Faith, somehow, but while he worked on that, Slade didn't plan to hold his breath.

A red-tailed hawk swept out of nowhere, dipping past the prison wagon to his left and pouncing on some little furry thing that squealed before the bird took off again and carried it away. One of the convicts in the wagon hooted, cheering on the predator, or maybe just relieved to see a creature of the wild still free to fly.

It would be years before the men he was escorting had another chance to spread their wings. Call that a lucky break for civilized society, for what it might be worth. There was no shortage of replacements when it came to human predators and parasites—the reason Slade would always have another job to do, as long as he was working for the law.

And if Fate decreed that he should do the job alone, without a wife and son or daughter . . . well, what of it? There were worse things in the world than being on your own.

He rode the next five miles trying to think of one.

2

They stopped at noon to let the prisoners relieve themselves and have a rationed drink of water, plus a couple of corn dodgers each. Slade stood off to one side, covering Guy Hampton with his Winchester Model 1873, in case any of the cons tried something. His lever-action Model 1887 might have been a more intimidating choice, but if he had to fire, Slade didn't want the buckshot pellets hitting Hampton by mistake.

Guy took it slow and easy, like they'd talked about. Removed his gunbelt first and left it on the driver's seat, so no one could disarm him at close quarters and start blasting with his Schofield .45. Four prisoners to deal with, and he took them clockwise, starting nearest to the cage's door. Unlock the chain that kept the inmate's shackles fastened to the floorboard, then clear out and let him exit. Point him toward the nearest roadside bush, to do his business while Slade covered him, then dole him out a cup of water, put corn dodgers in his hand, and do the whole thing in reverse.

Four times they did the little dance, none of the convicts saying much. Slade figured Mayfield was the one who needed watching most, but any of them, given half a chance, would crack his skull with anything that came to hand and light out for another taste of freedom, even knowing it would be their last.

Being a gambler, then a marshal, meant he'd had to learn the ins and outs of human nature: when a man was bluffing or about to go for broke. Often, you saw it in the eyes or twitchy hands. There was a time to strike first and be done with it, knowing that if you let the other guy complete whatever move his mind was cooking up, you were as good as dead.

With convicts, now, he took for granted that they lied whenever they were speaking, and they'd flee if given any chance at all. There didn't have to be a thought-out plan; for many, just the simple act of running was enough. And if they had a chance to kill one of their keepers first, why not?

When Hampton had the prisoners all watered, fed, and locked down in their proper places, he resumed the driver's seat. Slade mounted up and rode in close to say, "I'll take the next round, if you want."

Guy thought about it for a second, shook his head, and answered, "Honestly, I'd rather have you covering if anything goes wrong."

Slade understood and nodded. "Suits me fine," he said.

His rookie partner hadn't shot a man, so far as anybody knew, and it was always better to be cautious, handling inmates. Longtime prison personnel who let their guard down could be gutted just as easily as any greenhorn on his first day in the pen. There'd likely come a time when Hampton had to drop the hammer on a fugitive or rowdy prisoner, but there was no point risking both their lives unnecessarily his first time out with cons.

Besides, watching a youngster do the work was easier on Slade.

He checked his pocket watch. "Camp in about five hours?" he asked Hampton.

"Good enough."

They'd make it up tomorrow, with a start at sunrise. The cons might miss some of their beauty sleep, but that was tough. Slade didn't care much what they thought about accommodations or amenities along the road to Leavenworth. He simply wanted to deliver them, then get back home alive.

If asked, Guy Hampton wouldn't have admitted he was nervous. Sure, the prisoners were dangerous, but that was part of what had drawn him to the marshal's job: adventure—which, of course, included danger. Getting paid to travel was another factor that he'd had in mind while filling out his application. Marshals rode for days or weeks, sometimes, in search of fugitives or witnesses, and he had always been more comfortable under stars than underneath a roof.

Hampton was too young to consider his mortality in any but an abstract way. He'd seen dead men, attended public hangings, and had never come up squeamish yet. He was a crack shot and a decent fast draw with the Schofield, though admittedly he'd never faced a man who planned on killing him. When that day came—not *if*, he thought, unless he left the marshals service first—Hampton believed he'd hold his own, but who could ever really say?

Jack Slade had shot a slew of men, from what Guy understood, and had been shot himself. Shot on his wedding day, in fact, which had to be about the worst luck ever. Hampton only knew that story from the gossip he'd picked up in Enid, being too new on the job himself for any firsthand knowledge, but he'd heard that Slade had tracked the men who nearly killed him and his bride-to-be from Oklahoma Territory down to Mexico. Killed all but one of them, and brought that one back north to hang.

Whatever problems might arise while they were on their way to Leavenworth, Hampton felt better knowing Slade was there to back him up. The trick, though, was to do his job efficiently and make damn sure there were no problems.

Camping out nine nights was something that concerned him. He'd agreed with Slade to let the cons out, shackle one of them to each of the four wagon wheels and let them sleep that way, but privately, he would've liked it better if they all stayed in the cage. Give them another chance to stretch their legs, of course, then lock them down and give each one a plate of beans before they slept hunched over on the wagon's benches. Comfort didn't enter into it.

No matter. If he had to take a shift watching the cons sleep, that was part of what he'd signed up for. He might be tired tomorrow or the next day, in the driver's seat or riding out ahead to scout the trail, but he was young and fit. Late nights were nothing new, nothing he'd ever shied away from in his life.

Late afternoon, Slade rode ahead and came back twenty minutes later with the word that he'd picked out a campsite for the night, with running water for the horses, decent grass for them to graze on, and a shallow swale where they could build a fire without announcing to world for miles around where they were bedding down. Hampton was grateful for the first day's ending and decided that he'd use one of the convicts' designated blankets—maybe two, the more he thought about it—as a cushion for the wagon seat, next time it was his turn to drive the team.

Nine days to go, and then the ride back home from Leavenworth—almost a paid vacation with the wagon empty and no chores to do, aside from caring for the horses. Back to find out what came next: a manhunt or a hanging, maybe even doing some detective work. Hampton looked forward to it, grateful that he'd picked a job where there was something different to deal with every day, instead of plowing fields or adding columns in a ledger while the boss breathed down his neck.

He was a lawman now, and it felt fine.

The beans smelled fair, a little fatback in them adding to the scent and flavor. Fergus Mayfield felt his empty stomach grumbling and cursed it silently, a sign of weakness he was disinclined to tolerate. He shifted on the grass, tried for a posture that would be more comfortable, but the way his shackles had been fastened to the left-rear wagon wheel he only had two choices: lying down or sitting with his knees up to his chest, his back turned toward the camp fire.

It was better than inside the wagon, though, that bench chafing his ass.

And if his plan worked out, it wouldn't be for long.

He hadn't told the other convicts what he had in mind. Why would he? Mayfield barely knew them, and he didn't need their help. If he succeeded, they would have a choice of going with him or proceeding on to Leavenworth.

For all he cared, the three of them could roll on straight to hell.

Judge Dennison had strict security around his jail in Enid, but convicted prisoners were granted time with family, to say good-bye before they climbed the scaffold or were carted off to prison. Mayfield's solitary visitor had been a cousin who impressed most people as an idiot, but who could follow and remember simple orders if you drilled them into him.

In this case, Mayfield's orders had been *very* simple. Watch the prison wagon. Trail it from a distance. Pick your time.

Ten days and nine nights on the road. Plenty of opportunity.

And if his cousin failed?

The idiot had better pray he died before the law set Mayfield free to call on him.

One of the deputies—the younger one—was coming with two plates of pork and beans, a spoon for each of them. He handed one to Mayfield, told him, "Fifteen minutes," and moved on to feed Reese Dawkins, shackled to the wagon's left-front wheel. Then back for two more plates to feed the others, chained where Mayfield couldn't see them with the wagon in his way.

That didn't matter. He had nothing to communicate and had already seen enough of them to last a lifetime. If they declined to join him when he made his break, he'd never have to look at them again.

The beans were better than he had expected. Mayfield wolfed them down, belatedly remembering to chew, so that his stomach wouldn't cramp him all night long. If he had fifteen minutes for the meal, why not use every second of it?

This was when the worry started eating at him, when he started counting all the things that could go wrong. His cousin wouldn't let him down on purpose, but he might get waylaid somehow—if his horse went lame, for instance, or somebody picked a fight with him and got the both of them locked up. He also liked the fancy ladies, when he had the cash to buy their time, but Mayfield had impressed upon him the urgency of focusing on business for the time it took to do his job.

Now he could only wait, and hope that would be good enough.

Slade took his time eating the beans and corn dodgers, watching the convicts in their places, far enough apart that any conversation would require raised voices. It was primitive security, but ought to be sufficient for his purposes, as long as someone kept an eye on them all night.

He had first watch, had won a coin toss for it. Hampton didn't seem to mind. He was the easygoing type and took things as they came, was generally cheerful, but not flighty, like some youngsters. Old enough to understand the rigors of the job he'd chosen, even if the full weight of it hadn't hit him yet.

And when it did hit, would he stick?

Slade didn't know, figured it wasn't his concern in any case. Hampton would stay or go, whatever he decided. Slade already had enough to think about with Faith, their unborn child, and what *she* might be planning that he didn't know about. She could be packing up her things right now, might list the ranch for sale tomorrow and be gone before he made his slow way back from Leavenworth.

What, then?

Nothing.

The choice was hers; apparently, Slade's feelings didn't enter into it. If she took off, he couldn't search the forty-four United States, plus its southwestern territories, asking after her in every town along the way. Faith had some semi-distant relatives in Philadelphia, but that was no help. Last he'd heard, more than a million people lived on top of one another in the so-called City of Brotherly Love. It sounded like an anthill, and he knew he'd have no chance of scouring its streets to find one woman and her child.

Not if she wanted to conceal herself from him.

And what would be the point in chasing after her, if she was done with him? Suppose he tracked her down somehow and begged her for another chance. What was the likely upshot?

Further misery for both of them.

The wise thing, he supposed, was just to let it go. Whatever Faith decided, whether she informed him of her final choice or not, Slade reckoned he could live with it. He'd lived alone most of his life, survived the murder of his twin and being gunned down at the altar. How hard could it be to live without a child he'd never even see?

Another question that he couldn't answer, sitting on the prairie, watching convicts shackled to a wagon eating beans.

First watch meant he'd be sitting up till midnight, covering their four reluctant passengers. The night was warm enough that he could let the fire burn down and shave the odds that any passersby would notice them. The swale they'd camped in did its part to hide the fire, but in the pitch-black of an Oklahoma prairie night it didn't take much light to draw attention.

Or draw scavengers.

There shouldn't be a lot of traffic passing by at night, and they had camped well off the road, but you could never tell who might be out and roaming in the dark. Slade wasn't worried about predators of the four-legged kind, who'd shy away from human smells and sounds after they had a peek to satisfy their curiosity. It was the human sort, aside from those already shackled to the prison wagon's wheels, that made him keep his weapons handy while he ate his beans.

Something about the great wide-open spaces, he'd decided, that could tip a man over the edge. Leave him in town, he'd likely go about his daily business, stick to the routine, maybe engage in petty theft or some embezzlement if he was short on conscience. City trouble came from liquor, lust, and grudges. On the prairie, though, a man could go insane, do anything that struck his fancy more or less, and ride away from it when he was done.

Not many, granted, but enough to keep the marshals service working overtime, spread thin.

One problem at a time, Slade thought and tried to focus on his meal.

•

"It's them," Tad Mayfield hissed.

"O' course it's them," his brother whispered back. "Who else was you expectin'?"

"I'm just sayin'."

"Never mind that. Keep them horses quiet."

They were both afoot and well back from the marshals' camp, Tad leading his bay mare, while Earl had charge of his perlino gelding and the red dun stallion they had brought along for Fergus, saddled up and ready. There was precious little to be seen from where they'd stopped, afraid of tipping off the lawmen prematurely if they went much closer, sizing up the situation.

"You see 'em?"

"Got 'em hooked up to the wagon wheels somehow, looks like," Earl offered, squinting in the night.

"Two guns, you said."

"Two *marshals*," Earl corrected Tad. "Don't know how many guns they got."

"Same difference," Tad muttered, sounding sulky now. "So, how's this gonna work, again?"

"Same way as what I told you last time, dummy."

"I'm so dumb, maybe you ought do it by your lonesome."

"And tell Fergus you wouldn't help me cuz you're poutin'? How you think he's gonna like that, little brother?"

"Never mind. Just go back through the first part, will ya?"

Jesus wept. "Awright, now, listen good. You hold the horses here, while I go into camp and tell 'em—"

Tad stood nodding while Earl spelled it out, wearing that crooked smile of his that told you he was either soaking up the information or had wandered off somewhere inside his head, distracted by something he'd seen last week, maybe last month. You never knew with Tad until the chips were down. He normally came through all right, but it was never guaranteed

"And you do nothin' till I tip you off," Earl finished. "Have you got it, now?"

"I got it," Tad replied. "It's all up here." Tapping his temple with an index finger as he spoke, Earl thinking it was a relief he didn't hear a hollow ringing sound.

"And what about your pistol?"

"I don't pull it till you call me," Tad replied, pleased with himself.

"Or cock it, either," Earl reminded him. "Don't wanna shoot your own damn foot off."

"No."

"Okay." Earl gave another squint, hunched forward, as a shadow moved across the firelight. "Pickin' up the supper things, I'd say. They'll start to bed down purty soon."

"Be easier to come up on 'em while they's sleepin'," Tad suggested.

"Sure it would, if both of 'em were sleepin' at the same time."

"Oh, right."

"Let's just do it like we planned."

"Just like we planned," Tad echoed.

"Now, shut up."

"I'm shuttin' up."

"Goddamn it, Tad!"

"Sorry."

Earl needed time to think, never his strong suit, but he reckoned that he'd covered everything. He couldn't plan for how the marshals would react, of course. They might decide to play along when they were covered, or they could start blasting every which way. Four cons in the camp, and Tad was only pledged to keeping one of them alive. Whatever happened to the rest—and to the lawmen—he'd just have to wait and see.

Slade rinsed their tin plates and utensils in the stream beside their campsite, counting spoons twice over, to make sure that none had vanished up a convict's sleeve. Hampton covered the prisoners while Slade was washing up, then spread his blanket on the grass near where their horses grazed, with tethers long enough to let them drink at will.

They hadn't talked much over supper, just some speculation over how much distance they could make tomorrow, whether there was any chance of rain to break the heat a bit. Slade was prepared to drive the wagon, take his rightful turn, while Hampton did the scouting. Neither job demanded any special expertise. Escorting prisoners came down to equal parts tedium and watchfulness, waiting for something to go wrong. Most times, it went without a hitch.

Most times.

They did a final round of visits to the bushes, warning each con that he wouldn't be unchained again until they broke camp at the crack of daylight, moving on. No trouble there, with Hampton on the escort duty, Slade on backup with his rifle following each prisoner in turn. It seemed as if the jostling, baking ride had worn them out, and that was fine with Slade.

Let sleeping convicts lie.

From past experience, he knew that each day on their journey, drawing closer to their destination, would increase his inner tension. Just like winding up a watch spring, he'd start reading more into the looks he got from their unhappy passengers, the whispers passed among them, any little movement that suggested a potential mutiny. Slade didn't want to share that mood with Hampton, but he trusted that the younger deputy was smart enough to stay alert, not let himself be lulled into complacency by passing days and miles.

If it appeared that Guy was slacking off, he'd mention it. But otherwise . . .

A sound pricked up Slade's ears, not something he expected, like the whistling of a night bird, but an equine whickering. Not one of their four horses; it had come from farther off, beyond the rim of fading firelight, possibly from southward.

Hampton was beside him, asking, "Did you hear that?"

"Heard it," Slade agreed, lifting his rifle.

"Someone passing by, you think?"

"I couldn't say."

If it was just a harmless traveler, and he had seen their

fire, the odds were even that he'd stop, looking for company. Safety in numbers on the prairie was a rule of thumb, but every stranger was a wild card in the game.

"If he comes in—"

"We'll need to send him packing," Slade finished the thought. "Be civil, but we can't have any hangers-on."

"Agreed."

That said, there was a limit to their handling of a stranger passing in the night. They could refuse him hospitality and send him on his way, but he could set up camp a hundred yards away and there was nothing they could do about it, legally. Worst case, a drifter with a screw loose might be prone to take offense. Ride off, but circle back and try his hand at stalking them. In that event, they'd use whatever force was necessary to protect themselves and keep their prisoners secure.

"Maybe they'll just ride on," said Hampton.

"Maybe." Slade was skeptical.

As if in answer to his doubt, a reedy voice called out, "Hello the camp!"

3

Fergus Mayfield heard his cousin's voice call from the darkness, shifting toward its sound the same way anybody else would, if they were in his position. He was careful not to smile or look expectant; he didn't want to tip the marshals off to anything amiss.

"Hello the camp?" Earl called again, making the shout a question this time.

Across the fire from where he lay chained to the wagon, Mayfield saw the law dogs separating, putting space between themselves to make it harder for a single shooter, backing off from firelight so they weren't shown up in silhouette. Good thinking, there.

"Who's that?" Slade asked the darkness.

"Just a traveler," Earl's voice came back. "My horse went lame a few miles back, and when I seen your fire . . . well . . ."

"Sorry," Slade called back, "but we can't help you. We're transporting prisoners."

"That so? Well, I swan," Earl responded, sounding closer. "Me, I'm headin' for a job in Enid. Maybe you could spare a cup of coffee and a plate of somethin', just to get me through the night?"

Mayfield saw Slade and the young marshal trading glances, and the youngster shrugging, saying, "Up to you."

Slade muttered something Mayfield didn't catch, holding his rifle steady as he answered. "Come on in. Both hands where we can see them."

"Sure thing," Earl said, advancing until he was visible by firelight, empty hands held well out from his sides. "I'm grateful for your hospitality, and that's a fact."

Earl's eyes were darting here and there around the camp. They lit on Mayfield's face, but only for a second, then moved on to spot the other cons like anyone might do, on seeing four men in striped uniforms, chained up to wagon wheels.

"So, where's your horse?" asked Slade.

"I had to shoot him," Earl replied. "Stepped into a hole and broke his leg."

"How long ago was this?" the younger marshal asked.

Earl seemed to think about it, screwing up his face the way he always did when asked a question that involved some kind of calculation. "Couple hours after noon, I'd guess. Don't have no watch, and never woulda thought to check it, if I did."

"And you've been walking all the time since then," Slade said.

"Not *all* the time," Earl told him, grinning. "Damn hot as it was, I stopped wherever I could find a bit of shade, you know?"

"Just left your tack and saddle," said the younger marshal.

"How's that?"

"When you shot your horse. Just left your tack and saddle on the body, there? Whatever else you had along with it?"

"Hey, now—"

"He's curious," Slade said, "because it's strange. Also because we heard a horse's whinny just before you called out to us."

"Musta been the wind," Earl answered feebly, clearly not believing it himself.

Goddamn it! Mayfield thought. *You stupid peckerwood!*

"First thing you want to do," Slade said, "is take your gunbelt off and drop it. Nice and slow."

"Damn cup of coffee's all I wanted, but if you—"

"Drop it!"

"Okay, okay! I'm droppin' it!" Earl fumbled with the belt buckle, all thumbs, then dropped as if someone had yanked his skinny legs right out from under him, shouting into the night, "Now, Tad!"

A gunshot followed instantly, ringing in Mayfield's ears. It missed both marshals, and they dived for cover, leaving Earl out in the open as all hell broke loose.

Slade didn't know where the first bullet went, and didn't care once it was clear the shot had wounded no one. Number two rang off the iron cage of the prison wagon, making all the convicts shackled to it duck and grovel for their lives. Slade risked a glance around the oak tree where he'd gone to ground and couldn't spot the skinny weasel who had walked into their camp, right off, then saw him snaking on his belly toward the wagon, six-gun in his fist.

My own damn fault, Slade thought, ducking another, closer rifle shot, but what alternative should he have chosen?

Run into the darkness, hunting, when they'd heard the horse's whicker? There had been no time.

Refuse to let the guy walk in? In that case, they would have *two* shooters firing at them from the shadows, maybe dropping him and Hampton, both.

They should've killed us first, instead of talking, he considered, but it didn't matter now. Edging around the big oak to his right, more rifle fire echoing through the night, Slade angled for a clear shot at the target he could see. Couldn't get one, since the weasel had crawled underneath the wagon, screened from view by Orville Washington, his wagon wheel, and shadows.

Slade tried anyway, though it meant switching off to fire his Winchester left-handed. It was awkward, but he drew a bead on where he thought the creeper's head should be and let one fly, rewarded with the *spang!* of lead on iron and a demented-sounding squeal from Washington.

Across the camp, Guy Hampton was dueling with the invisible sniper, matching him shot for shot, tracking the shooter's muzzle-flashes as he moved around out there. Horses were whinnying, inside the camp and out, their noise annoying Slade, but there was nothing he could do about it. He was trying to decide which prisoner the gunmen hoped to liberate, prepared to kill the bastard where he sat in irons before he'd let their plan succeed.

Not Washington, that much was obvious. The weasel had crawled past him, and Slade frankly couldn't picture a white desperado risking life and limb to save a colored convict. That left three to choose from, only one of whom was clearly visible from where he'd gone to ground.

Shoot Kilgore, just to play it safe? Not yet. There should

be time enough for that if someone tried to free him from his chains. Meanwhile, Slade thought the gunman underneath the wagon must be angling toward one of the others.

Dawkins? Mayfield? Both had worked with various confederates who might try springing them from custody before they disappeared for good behind the walls at Leavenworth. Security around the Enid lockup was supposed to be airtight, but Slade knew that was wishful thinking. Visitors came in and out, guards talked to friends—or even strangers, when they'd had a few at the saloon. It could be something innocent, Hampton remarking to a lady friend that he'd be out of town for ten days, give or take. Nothing you'd give a second thought to, never wondering if it would be passed on.

Forget it.

All that mattered was the here and now of it, taking the shooters down before they scored a lucky hit or managed to release one of the cons. To do that, Slade would have to move, give up his cover for a better vantage point. A cleaner shot. Take out the one under the wagon first, while Hampton kept the other busy, then team up to flank him in the dark and finish it.

Right now.

Guy Hampton wriggled backward from the campfire, seeking cover in the shadows. He'd already snagged his saddlebags in passing, with the extra ammunition that he'd packed, and needed somewhere he could make a decent stand.

Last stand?

He shrugged that notion off, refusing to believe that their position was a hopeless one. They only had two raiders to contend with: one pinned underneath the prison wagon at the moment, and the other prowling outer darkness, taking potshots as he went. If there had been more guns outside the camp, they would be chipping in by now, making the swale a cross-fire slaughterhouse.

So it was two-on-two, as long as the intruder over by the wagon didn't manage to release the prisoners. He hadn't started shooting at the padlocks yet—still hadn't used his gun at all, in fact—and Hampton would have heard him if he'd started grinding with a hacksaw that they hadn't seen when he walked into camp.

The minute that it looked like any of the cons were getting loose, he was prepared to kill all four of them. Cold-blooded it might be, but he was under strictest orders to prevent any escape attempts, by laying down his life if need be for the public safety. The reverse side of that coin was an official understanding that he'd stop them cold, by any means required. And if that meant cold *dead*, well, better them than him.

It hadn't reached that point, but Hampton figured he could pull the trigger on an unarmed man, given the present circumstances. Felons under sentence, trying to escape from custody—which would, of course, mean further vicious crimes until somebody locked them up again or put them down for good. It might as well be him, and if that cost him any sleep, Hampton imagined he'd get over it.

Right now, the trick was just to stay alive.

He'd fired eight shots so far from his Winchester's fifteen-round tubular magazine, without hitting anything other than shadows. Guy knew that he ought to reload soon, and started the process by opening one of his saddlebags, groping inside for an ammo box there, while his eyes kept tracking the night, his ears pricked for any stray sound of a shooter advancing. It wouldn't be easy to hear someone coming, with gunfire still echoing inside his head, but he'd do what he could.

Hampton found a cardboard box of cartridges and pulled it clear, glanced quickly at its label to make sure he'd grabbed the rifle ammo, then managed to open it one-handed, spilling brass and lead onto the ground in front of him. Reloading wasn't difficult, pushing each cartridge through the elliptical gate on the right-hand side of the rifle's receiver, but he had to stay alert in case the sniper tried to rush him from the darkness and he had to fire back in a hurry.

As if in answer to his silent thought, another shot cracked through the camp, peeling a strip of bark off of the tree where Slade was hunkered down. Guy saw the muzzle flash and rapid-fired two shots as close as he could put them to the spot where it had flared, hoping he hear something—a yelp of pain, whatever—that would indicate a hit.

Nothing.

At this rate, how long could they stay pinned down and still survive? They had another seven, maybe eight hours till daylight, but if he kept trading shots with ghosts, he'd be damned low on ammo by the time daylight exposed him to his enemies. Better to finish it in darkness if he could.

And that meant getting off his belly, carrying the fight to his opponent.

Easier if I could see the sumbitch, Hampton thought, but he could only work with the conditions that existed. When the next shot came, instead of lying where he was and firing back, he'd rush the spot, pump half a magazine out if he had to, covering himself, until he had a target he could nail.

"Come on," he muttered to the night. "Just give me one more chance."

And it was time for Slade to move, as well. He knew there was no future in remaining where he'd gone to ground, giving the mobile sniper time to creep around and plug him from behind. He hated leaving one intruder underneath the wagon, with the prisoners, but if he shifted now, he just might get a clear shot at the weasel on his way to bag his helper.

Nothing ventured . . .

Keeping to the shadows, Slade moved out. He circled to his left, in the direction of the prison wagon, taking care to make no noise along the way. That might not matter much, with Hampton and the unseen shooter swapping fire, but why take chances?

Slade could not have said exactly what he had in mind, beyond the urge to *do something.* Ideally, he could pot the creeper underneath their wagon, then move on to overtake the sniper, drop him in his tracks, and finish it. But since he'd rarely seen a plan succeed precisely as devised, Slade was prepared to compromise.

Nail down the weasel, maybe, then flush out the sniper so that Guy could deal with him. Or spook the wagon lurker out of cover, into firelight, where he'd be an easy mark for Hampton on the other side. That done, the two of them could leave their convicts chained and hunt the second shooter in a more concerted manner.

Failing all of that, the rescue party still had horses somewhere in the darkness, south of camp. If Slade could spook them, run them off, he'd leave his enemies afoot and make it that much easier to hunt them down in daylight.

If he lived that long.

He caught a mental flash of Faith, sitting at home—alone?—and pushed it out of mind. Any distraction, at the moment, was as deadly as a pistol pressed against his head. Slade had to concentrate, to do a dirty job as quickly and efficiently as possible, if he was ever going to lay eyes on Faith again.

Or even if he wasn't.

Tired of living yet? Not even close.

He was edging closer to the wagon, heard some kind of muttering. Fergus Mayfield, maybe, talking to the creeper?

Slade was crouching, leaning forward for a better look—a better shot—when rifle fire exploded once more, on the far side of the camp. He turned in that direction, picked out muzzle flashes from the dark, then saw his partner rising, rushing toward the site, pumping the lever on his Winchester and spitting sharp-edged thunder as he ran.

Slade had his mouth open, a warning on his tongue, when Guy went down. He hit the turf, rolled over on his side, and brought his knees up like a man will when he's taken a punch to the gut. He clutched himself with one hand, while the other gripped his Winchester, and when his fingers came away, Slade saw them glinting scarlet in the dim light from the fire.

"C'mon, for Christ's sake, will ya, Earl?"

Fergus Mayfield felt as if his life was slipping through his fingers, every passing second pushing him a little closer to the grave. His brain felt raw, and it was getting on his last nerve, watching while his cousin fiddled with the padlock that secured his shackles to the wagon wheel.

"You mighta noticed I ain't got no key," Earl answered back.

"So, what is that you're usin', then?"

"Hairpin," his cousin said. "I got it off a whore in Enid, t'other night. Said she could pick a lock with one a these, no problem."

"Guess you shoulda brought her with you," Fergus sneered. "Just shoot the goddamn thing, why don'tcha?"

"I could do that," Earl replied. "Might blow one a your feet off, while I'm at it. Split a bullet on that padlock, I might get 'em both."

More rifle fire, across the camp. Fergus leaned back and craned his neck, trying to see if cousin Tad was making any progress with the law dogs, and he noticed Slade had disappeared. Rolling around to his left side, he scanned the darkness, looking for the marshal, worried that he might appear at any second with his Winchester.

"Hol' still!" Earl hissed at him. "I can't do nothin' with you wigglin' all around."

"You can't do nothin', anyhow," Fegus spat back at him. "Gimme your Colt."

"What for?"

"To scratch me ass with, dummy! Hand it over!"

"If you're gonna shoot the padlock, lemme outta here."

"Give. Me. Your. Colt." No room for arguement when Fergus used that tone.

"Awright, awright." Earl drew the gun and passed it over. "I just need a minute to get out—"

"Stay put! Keep workin' on that goddamn lock!" He cocked the six-gun, peering into shadow as he said, "One of them laws is on the move."

"Damn it!"

Earl bent back to his task, as Tad cut loose across the camp. Fergus allowed himself to peer in that direction, saw the younger of the deputies leap up and rush the night, then drop and curl up like an armadillo trying to protect its belly.

Was he hit? By God, he was!

A whoop of triumph died in Mayfield's throat, strangled by fear of drawing more attention to himself. With any luck, Slade would have seen his partner fall and would run off to help him, maybe leave himself exposed while he was at it. Tad could shoot him from the front, or Fergus from behind—maybe the both of them together, just to make it stick.

He hadn't planned to kill the law dogs, not exactly, though it stood to reason they would go down fighting for their prisoners. Not that it mattered, either way, except that next time Fergus found himself in custody, he would be looking at the gallows, rather than a term of years inside a cage.

Which only mattered if there *was* a next time—and he didn't plan on that. If he could beat the odds and skip that ride to Leavenworth, Fergus would swear an oath on any so-called "holy book" available that he would never go to jail again.

A graveyard, doubtless, when his time came. But a cell? Forget it.

"Come *on*!" he snarled at Earl.

"Gimme another second, here. I almost got it!"

Slade put the wagon weasel and the convicts out of mind, focused on Hampton and the job of keeping him alive. It might already be too late for that, but doing nothing guaranteed it. What he had to do was *move*, start cleaning up the mess they'd stumbled into, doing everything he could to help the younger deputy.

Step one: take out the sniper.

Step two: turn around and kill his sidekick, if he wouldn't shinny out from underneath the wagon on command.

Step three: examine Hampton's wound and try to judge how bad it was, how long he had.

Step four: if there was time, load up the convicts; otherwise, take Guy and leave them where they were, chained to the wagon's wheels.

Step five: head back to Enid, hoping Hampton didn't die along the way.

Maybe reverse the first two steps, since he could see the wagon weasel, more or less? That would expose Slade to the sniper's fire, but it appeared the man who'd walked into their camp was trying to unlock the chain securing Fergus Mayfield to his wheel. If he succeeded there . . .

Slade swung around, shouldered his Winchester, and fired a shot under the wagon. Knew he'd missed the second it struck sparks from iron and sang the high note of a ricochet. The weasel bawled, "Son of a bitch!" before a pistol flashed down there and sent Slade rolling to his left.

Who had the gun? Mayfield? His little helper? Either way, it made the game more dangerous.

Slade pumped the rifle's lever action, fired another shot, and heard another clank that told him it was wasted powder. Maybe he could wound one of his targets with a fragment of a slug, but stopping one of them for good that way would stretch dumb luck in the direction of a miracle.

And Slade didn't believe in miracles.

A rifle shot rang out behind him, coming close enough to tell Slade that he ought to move again. The middle of a cross fire was the last place he desired to be. If Hampton was alive and had the strength to raise his rifle, maybe he could help. Pick off the sniper, possibly, if he revealed himself to get a better shot at Slade. Without that help . . . well, he'd just have to do the job alone.

Slade pushed off from the ground, bracing to turn and run back to the cover of the tree where he'd begun his dead-end trek. It wasn't good, retreating to his starting point, but neither did it mean that he was finished, necessarily. Once he had decent cover, he could seek another path or let the shooters come to him, expose themselves if they were bent on killing him.

And if they simply tried to flee, hell, he would shoot them in the back.

No rules for fugitives or murderers, at least until they got to court and stood before Judge Dennison. Lawyers could help them then, but in the meantime, they belonged to Slade.

Funny it didn't feel that way.

In fact, he thought it just might be the other way around.

Footsteps approaching. Slade could hear them plain as day—except it *wasn't* day, and even with the sounds to guide him, he still couldn't see a damned thing in the dark. He would be ready when the sniper closed to killing range, but for the moment, Slade's best bet was staying put and keeping deathly still.

With emphasis on *death*.

He waited, felt his enemy approaching, peered along the barrel of his Winchester at darkness. Was there movement just ahead? Ten paces, maybe less? Slade's index finger started taking up the trigger slack—and then his world exploded in a pyrotechnic flash, immediately plummeting to black.

4

Slade wondered whether he was dead, and if it ought to hurt this much. It was a question he had asked himself before, after the massacre that spoiled his wedding day, and now he wondered whether he was doomed to keep repeating that experience in slightly altered form, forever, as his private little slice of Hell.

He tried to move, rode out a savage wave of pain that made him feel as if his head was going to explode—or maybe had, already. Thinking that brought back an avalanche of jumbled memories: the stranger in their camp, the sniper firing on them, Slade and Hampton firing back until . . .

Someone had shot him in the head.

Slowly, experimentally, Slade raised his right arm to explore the wound that throbbed and burned above his ear on that side. He was trying to imagine what his brain might feel like, oozing from his skull, and how he'd cope with that.

Just lie here, he decided. *Let it go and hope I'm dead before the buzzards find me.*

Grimacing with pain, be probed the bloody track that seemed to run across his scalp for two, maybe three inches. He felt nothing that reminded him of calves' brains he had seen in butcher shops, and probing harder, cursing from the jolts of agony it cost him, Slade felt reasonably sure his skull had not been fractured.

Just a graze, then? Bad enough to knock him down and out of action, and the blood caked on the right side of his face—now sticking to his fingertips—had likely tricked whoever shot him into thinking he was dead. Rising to all fours brought his supper up, a greasy spew, but Slade felt slightly better after that.

Until he thought of Hampton.

Turning to survey the camp, Slade thought his pounding head might topple from his shoulders, almost wished it would. The prison wagon stood where they had parked it, chains puddled around its wheels where the four convicts had been freed. Long gone now, and apparently with all four horses. Facing toward the spot where he'd seen Hampton fall, Slade felt a fleeting hiccough that he took for hope, seeing the younger marshal wasn't lying there.

He knew Guy had been wounded, but he might have had the strength to crawl away somewhere, find cover and continue firing while the convicts and their rescuers made off without a chance to finish him. It wouldn't be the first time someone had survived a major wound and kept on fighting for his life against tall odds.

Slade struggled to his feet, dizzy and reeling from what now felt like the worst hangover of his life. The bleeding from his scalp had slowed to something more like seepage, and he mastered standing up after a minute, maybe less. His new height let him scan a wider area around the camp and dashed his hope of Hampton getting clear.

The youngster lay beneath and partially behind a willow, farther down the swale where they had camped, with one foot in the burbling stream. His shirt was blood-soaked from the stomach wound, but Guy *had* traveled some and fought at least a little longer, before someone shot him through the left eye, blowing out the whole back of his skull.

There was no sign of Hampton's rifle, or the gunbelt he'd been wearing when Slade saw him last. Reflexively, Slade reached down for his Colt and found his pistol belt was gone, as well, together with his pocket watch. Bastards had robbed him without noticing that he was still alive, somehow. He took it as a lucky break, then wondered what to do with it.

First thing, take stock of what they left behind.

It wasn't much. No guns remained in camp, and some-one had been through the saddlebags, taking spare ammu-nition, food, whatever clothing they could find to swap for prison stripes. Slade lost a shirt and wasn't sure what Hampton had been carrying. The cons had taken both of their canteens, but he could wash and drink some water from the spring before he started walking.

Going where? A long trek back to Enid, or perhaps some homestead he might find along the way?

Before he left, Slade knew he had to do something for Guy. He couldn't leave the youngster out for scavengers to dine on, but he didn't have a shovel or the strength to dig a decent grave by hand. He had begun to curse his impotence when something drew his eyes back to the prison wagon, one big cage on wheels, and Slade had an idea.

Sometimes a man's life turned around on a five-cent piece. Last night, he had been wearing stripes and chains; now

Fergus Mayfield was a free man with a pistol on his hip, a horse beneath him, and the makings of a gang riding his dust. He'd also shot a law dog, but he didn't count that as a negative—nor had it been his first.

His cousins, Tad and Earl, had done all right for dunderheads, all things considered. They'd remembered clothes for Mayfield, and the whiskey he had asked for. Fergus couldn't fault them for not bringing extra duds along, since he'd had no idea, himself, if they'd be bringing any of the other convicts with them. Naturally, all were anxious to be free, and with a choice of druthers, all had stuck with Mayfield.

Maybe one too many, he considered.

Orville Washington was back there muttering again, whining about the slug he'd caught while they were scrambling around in camp. Mayfield had been surprised to see the younger marshal up and fighting, after Tad gut-shot him with the Winchester '92 carbine he'd picked up somewhere, but the kid obviously had some sand. They'd let it out of him, but not before he put a lucky round in Washington, low down on his left side.

"I gotta stop awhile," the wounded man called out. "Y'all go on widout me if ya hafta."

Fergus tugged the reins to stop his red dun stallion. Turned and saw the others stop, as if he'd given a command to halt. So far, so good.

"We leave you now," he cautioned Washington, "the chances are you won't catch up to us."

"You care 'bout that?" the wounded convict asked him, thick lips twitching in what might have been a smile or grimace. "It ain't exac'ly like I fit in with the rest a y'all."

"You wanna go off on your own, then?" Mayfield asked him. "That the plan?"

"Mebbe."

"That's if you don't bleed out," Reese Dawkins offered.

"Take ma chances," Washington replied.

"Thing is," said Fergus, "that it ain't just *you* takin' the chance, here."

"How you figger that?"

"Hey, think about it. You get caught, draggin' your ass across the prairie, goin' Christ knows where. What happens then?"

"Go back to jail, I reckon."

"And?"

"An' what?" asked Washington.

"You don't think some law dog is gonna ask you where *we* went?"

"What if they does? You gone your own way. I can't tell 'em nothin' I don't know."

"That sounds all well and good, until you think about it," Mayfield said.

"How's that?"

"C'mon, boy. Don't play stupid with me. You could tell 'em where we were last time you saw us. Show 'em which way we were headed."

"I ain't doin' that," said Washington.

"I know you ain't," Mayfield replied.

And drew the Colt he'd lifted from the head-shot marshal back in camp, raised it, and fired as steady as you please. The .45 slug traveled thirty feet to drill the wounded convict's chest and knock him backward from the draft horse he'd been riding with a blanket in the place of saddle leather. Maybe he was dead before he hit the ground, or maybe it would take a minute.

Fergus Mayfield wasn't worried, either way.

"So, anybody else feel like desertin' me?" he asked the other startled faces ranged around him.

No one answered, and he took that for a vote of confidence. It was important to affirm the power he'd exerted back in camp, when he'd told Earl to free the other cons and let them tag along. There'd be no doubt in anybody's mind, from this point on, concerning who was boss.

"Okay, then," Mayfield said. "Now that we cleared the air a bit, I wanna tell you where I'm headed, and for what."

Red ants had gotten to Hampton overnight. Slade found his bloodied hat, filled it with water from the stream, and sluiced them off the best he could. He guessed that Guy had weighed around one-eighty, but it felt like twice that when he took the youngster's wrists and started dragging him from where he'd fallen, toward the prison wagon. Every yard along the way, Slade cursed himself for having the idea, but it possessed him now.

The ants would be back soon enough, but he was pledged to keep the larger scavengers away from Hampton while he went for help. Whoever came to fetch the corpse would find Guy more or less intact.

Slade cursed each step along the way, cursed Hampton, cursed the morning heat, and cursed himself. For what? He couldn't answer that or think of anything specific he'd done wrong the previous night. Clearly, the gunmen had been trailing them and looking for a chance to strike. If he had paid better attention to their back trail, maybe spotted someone following, would it have made a difference?

Slade didn't think so, but he cursed himself for failing, anyway.

They'd reached the wagon. How was he supposed to get Guy up and into it?

The way his head was hammering to beat the band, Slade knew he couldn't pick the youngster up as he had planned to carry Faith across the threshold of their married home. He'd likely pass out in the process and wake up—*if* he woke up—with coyotes gnawing on the both of them.

But maybe . . .

Slade left Hampton on the ground, retrieved one of the chains the fleeing convicts had abandoned, and came back to loop it underneath the dead man's arms. There was enough behind him for a hand grip, and he used a padlock to secure it, keep the loose ends from escaping, during the maneuver that he had in mind.

First thing, he crawled into the wagon, turned around, and reached down for the loop of chain encircling Hampton's chest. A tidal wave of dizziness washed over Slade, his consciousness a bobbing cork that nearly slipped away from him, but then it passed and he was hanging on to Hampton like some giant fish he'd caught.

The rest was grunt work, hauling up and backward, dragging Guy's dead weight into the wagon, while a hornet swarm of black spots blotted out Slade's vision, strangled respiration wheezing in and out of him. At last, they lay together like two dead men, side by side. Slade didn't know how long he stayed there, but the tickling of a fly on his left eyelid brought him jolting out of it.

Not me! he thought. *No free meals here!*

He tumble-slid out of the prison wagon, closed the door, and locked it. Bugs would have a field day, nothing Slade could do about it, but at least his partner would be safe from rending beaks and teeth, until somebody came to take him home.

Not Slade.

He would report the killing and escape, of course, but after that, his job was tracking down the cons and their accomplices. Either returning them to hang for Hampton's murder or, if they resisted, leaving *them* for buzzard bait.

His first step, cleaning up. Slade trudged back to the stream and drank his fill, then drank some more, knowing he couldn't carry any water with him on the trek ahead. Next, braced for pain, he plunged his face into the stream, head turned so that its rippling water washed the crusted blood away. Instead of hurting him, it soothed his throbbing wound a little. Slade would happily have stayed there, half submerged, but his survival and his duty both depended on him getting up and out of there.

He put his hat on, had to wear it at a cocky angle to avoid chafing his wound, then scanned the campsite one last time, searching for anything of any value that he might have overlooked. The convicts had been thorough in their looting. Slade guessed he was lucky that they hadn't left him nude and barefoot on the prairie. Luckier, indeed, that they'd mistaken him for dead.

Their worst mistake.

Maybe their last.

"A hunnerd miles or so northwest of here," said Fergus Mayfield, "there's a little town called Gilead. I think that's somethin' from the Bible. It's a small town, like I say. Maybe two hundred people all together, last time I was through there, if you don't count farmers livin' off a ways and comin' in on Saturdays to shop or Sunday go to meetin'."

"So what?" Dawkins asked. "We need to stay away

from people for a while, not ride for three, four days to be right in the middle of 'em."

Mayfield met his eyes and answered, "No one's askin' you to come along. Me and my cousins will be headin' up to Gilead. Right, boys?"

"Tha's right," said Earl.

"Uh-huh," Tad grunted.

"Mebbe if we knew the point of goin'," Kilgore said and left it hanging there.

"The point," Fergus replied, "is sweet revenge. I never woulda met you fellas in the dungeon, back in Enid, if it weren't for all the happy little folk in Gilead."

The others sat and waited for him to continue, even Earl and Tad, who knew the story, more or less. When Fergus knew he had their full attention, he went on.

"You see this town, you know it's easy pickin's," he explained. "Nice little shops with money in the till. Fat little constable who doesn't wear a pistol half the time—or didn't, anyhow, first time I went in there. He might be packin' now, he knows what's good for 'im."

"Get on with it," urged Dawkins. "We need to be makin' tracks."

"Long story short, then," Mayfield said. "I rode in there with two of my best friends, Deke Hagenmaier and Lennie Stovall. Looked around the place and thought we'd take their tidy little bank. Why not? They didn't have a guard or nothin'."

"But?" asked Kilgore.

"But, somebody looked in through the window while we's at it, cleanin' out the place, and when we hit the sidewalk they was waitin' for us. Deke and Lennie got the hell shot outta them. They kilt our horses. Nothin' I could do but let 'em take me."

"Coulda fought it out there, like the others," Kilgore said.

"And I'd be worm food, just like them," said Mayfield. "hell with that."

"So, lemme get this straight," said Dawkins. "People in this town already caught you once, and killed your two best pals. Now you want *us* to follow you back there and get our ass shot off?"

"Don't make much sense to me," Kilgore agreed.

"And as I said, you're free to go," Mayfield replied. "But if you think I'm ridin' in without a plan, the two of you are dumber than you look."

"My mama thinks I'm handsome," Dawkins told him. "Rest her soul."

"Blind, was she?" Fergus asked him.

"Listen, now—"

"*You* listen, now. I got a plan that don't involve nobody gettin' kilt. Well, nobody on *our* side, anyhow. It's sneaky, just the way you prob'ly like it. Slip in there, all quiet like. First thing the townies know, we got their little piece of heaven all sewed up. That's when the fun starts, and I pay 'em back for all the grief they caused me."

"I dunno," said Kilgore.

"Pick a compass point and ride," said Fergus. "Any way except northwest. If you ain't with us, I don't want you followin' along behind."

"I didn't say I *wasn't* comin'," Kilgore said.

"Make up your mind. Right now."

"Well, shit. I guess I'm in."

"You, Reese?"

Dawkins looked weary. "What the hell," he said, at last. "It ain't like I got somewhere else to go."

"Is that a yes, or what?"

"Goddamn it, *yes!*"

"Guess we oughta move out, then. We're burnin' daylight, like you said," Fergus allowed.

"And Washington?" asked Kilgore.

"What about him?" Mayfield countered, without glancing at the convict's corpse. "I reckon buzzards like the dark meat, well as anything."

Leading the way toward Gilead, still three or four days distant, Mayfield knew he'd have to keep an eye on Dawkins and Kilgore. Maybe his cousins, too, although he thought their childlike awe of him would hold them true.

The plan he had in mind for Gilead required at least two other men. With four, he thought, it should be relatively simple. Dwelling on the details he'd imagined since his capture helped to pass the time and miles. A pleasant, lurid fantasy for now, but soon to be a flesh-and-blood reality.

With emphasis on blood.

Slade started walking south, the long road back to Enid. If he met somebody headed in the right direction, maybe he could use his badge to get a ride, but they'd seen no one on the outward journey yesterday, so he was short on hope in that regard. A normal walking pace, if he could keep it up, should get him back to town sometime that night, but with the way his head felt, "normal" didn't seem like it was in the cards.

Sometime tomorrow, then, if he was lucky. That meant sleeping in the open, hungry, unprotected, though he had some matches in his pocket that would let him start a fire—assuming he could find sufficient fuel. If not, then he'd be *cold*, hungry, and unprotected. Food was one thing, but Slade knew he'd wind up missing water most, before he finished walking.

Or the walking finished him.

That would be one way to resolve his break with Faith. Drop dead and wait till someone found him—how long afterward? They'd be expecting him at Leavenworth, but not for four or five more days. Add on a couple more, allowing for odd problems on the road—a thrown shoe, maybe, or a wobbly wagon wheel—and it could be a week or more before the warden's office wired Judge Dennison in Enid, asking where their convicts were. Another day to organize a search party and get it on the trail, if there were deputies to spare, and they'd still have to find him. If they could, assuming that he didn't lose his way and wander off the beaten track.

Slade wondered whether Faith would shed a tear for him or if she'd be relieved that he was gone. For all he knew, she could be packed and on her way to brighter days before he was reported missing. She might never even know, and maybe that was best for all concerned.

Without Slade breathing down her neck, she could describe him any way she chose to their prospective son or daughter. Build him up into a hero, or dismiss him as a fool. Slade thought the latter category fit him better, but he wasn't qualified to cast a ballot in his present addled state. Putting one foot before the other was about as much as he could manage, staying upright more or less, with something of a tilt in the direction of his wound.

A mile or so from camp, Slade thought a rattlesnake had crossed his path, but later wasn't sure. He might have been seeing things and wouldn't know the difference unless it bit him—which it didn't, in this case.

The sun beat down on Slade, dried out his hat, and seemed to shrink it somehow, tightening like rawhide drying. That was an illusion, he discovered, fussing with the hat and finding that in truth, it was no tighter than the day before, or any other day since he had purchased it. The wound above his ear was playing with his senses, making him imagine things. Scabbed over now, but possibly infected.

Gangrenous?

What could a doctor do for him, in that case? They could lop off arms and legs to save a patient, but the head was mandatory for survival. Would he die outright, or simply be a raving lunatic, caged up somewhere out of the public eye?

Another out for Faith. Telling their child, "Your dad was crazy about me. Of course, now that I think about it, he was crazy about *everything*."

And so what if she did? Nothing she said to anyone could hurt him, once his bones were planted or picked clean and sun-bleached on the prairie.

Resigned to play his miserable hand, Slade plodded on. He had to tell someone what had become of Hampton and the convicts if it was the last thing that he ever did.

An hour later, maybe two or three, he saw smoke rising to his right, perhaps a mile off-course.

Try it? Why not?

With dogged, shuffling steps, he turned and left the road.

5

"Somebody's comin', Pa."

Floyd Larson looked up from the hoof that he was trimming on a splashed white mare, off to the northeast where his son, Albert, was pointing. He could see a speck on the horizon, heat haze causing it to dance and waver, but the size seemed wrong somehow.

"Not riding," he decided.

"Walkin' in," Albert agreed.

"Half mile or so?"

"I'd say."

It felt like trouble. Larson couldn't think of any reason for a man to be afoot out there, a half day's ride from Enid. The McCandles family, his closest neighbors, lived ten miles away, due west. A man on foot, on a day like this— or any other day, for that matter—was either being hunted or had found himself in grievous need.

And either one spelled danger for Floyd Larson and his family.

"Reckon you'd better fetch my rifle," he told Albert.

"Yes, sir!" Off and running like his life depended on it. Which it might.

A glance back at the house, tracking his boy, showed Larson what had beckoned the dismounted stranger. Chimney smoke, from Katherine and Emma working on the midday meal. Larson could smell it cooking, knew the stranger couldn't, but the smoke would have been visible for miles.

The walking man had closed the gap a bit when Larson heard his son returning. Walking now, though briskly, since he had been cautioned against running with a firearm in his hands. Behind the boy, his younger sister and their mother followed closely, drawn away from cooking by the possible emergency.

"Who is it, Floyd?" asked Katherine.

"Can't say. Still too far out."

"Not from the Goodsons."

"No."

Ira Goodson, Mary, and their four sons lived twelve miles or so away, off to the east. This wasn't one of them, unless he'd lost both his horse and his sense of direction.

"Must be comin' off the road," Albert suggested.

"Just might be," Floyd granted. "Got that rifle?"

"Here, Pa."

Larson took the Winchester Model 1866 from his son, knew the chamber was empty because he had left it that way, with a full magazine. He liked the old "Yellow Boy"—so called for the bronze gunmetal alloy used to manufacture its receiver—for its accuracy, durability, and stopping power. This one was chambered for .45-75-caliber rounds, Winchester's variation on the .45-70 Government cartridge, using a shorter case. On the receiving end, you wouldn't notice any loss of power between one slug and the other.

Larson hoped he wouldn't have to kill the walking man, who'd closed the gap between them to a quarter mile with steady, dogged steps. He'd never shot a man before, or even *at* one, but if danger threatened any member of his little family, he wouldn't hesitate.

Not ever for a sliver of a second.

"Kathy, you and Emma need to get back in the house," he said.

"Now, Floyd—"

"I mean it. We don't know this fella. I don't want him seein' any womenfolk until I find out who he is and what he's after."

"Well . . ." She didn't like it, but went back inside the farmhouse, leading Emma by the hand.

"Want me to go in, too?" asked Albert.

"Nope," Larson replied. "I might need help." And he could almost feel his son swelling with pride.

"I oughta have a gun, too," Albert said.

"All right. Go in and get your twenty-two. But careful-like."

"Yes, sir!"

Another whirlwind in the dooryard, gone and back in nothing flat, toting the Winchester Model 1890 slide-action rifle Floyd and Katherine had given him when he turned nine, two years before. Its tubular magazine held twenty-two .22 Short cartridges, and it could fire up a storm if you needed it to.

Which, Larson prayed, would not be necessary on his threshold, with his wife and daughter doubtless peering through the shutters.

When the stranger closed to fifty yards, Larson saw

sunlight glinting off a badge, pinned to the vest he wore over a sweat-soaked shirt. Albert had seen it, too, asking, "Is he a lawman, Pa?"

"Don't know."

A badge could come from anywhere—including the dead body of a constable or sheriff murdered by the man who'd pinned it on. The tin alone was nothing but a decoration. Or it could be a disguise.

"He doesn't have a gun, Pa."

"None that we can see," Larson corrected Albert.

There could be a pistol, maybe even two of them, tucked underneath the stranger's belt, around in back. Maybe a derringer inside his vest, if he had pockets there.

"Watch close, in case he starts to reach behind his back."

"I'm watchin', Pa."

"Or toward his boots." A knife could be concealed there, just as easily.

"Yes, sir."

"That's close enough," he told the stranger, when they stood some thirty feet apart. "I'll have your name and business."

"Slade," a parched voice croaked out, in reply. "Deputy U.S. marshal, out of Enid. What I need's a horse and something that'll shoot."

"Smoke over there," Earl said, to no one in particular.

"I see it," Fergus told him.

"Vittles cookin'," Kilgore said.

"'Bout goddamn time," Dawkins chimed in.

"We goin' over, cousin Ferg?" asked Tad.

"Be right ungrateful if we didn't," Fergus said, "after they went to all that trouble for us."

"S'pose they ain't expectin' visitors," Earl said. "What, then?"

"Turn on that charm you're famous for," Fergus replied. "They won't be able to resist you."

"Nor the five of us," said Kilgore.

Riding toward the dark smudge on the skyline, Fergus Mayfield figured that it had to be a homestead. There was no town out this way, between Enid and Gilead, and Fergus didn't think a campfire would raise smoke enough to mark the sky like that. It took a chimney, or at least a good-sized stovepipe, which meant settlers, food, other supplies.

And maybe women.

They had a mile or more to plan their moves, and Fergus wasted no time spelling out what would and wouldn't do. "Go easy, when we're ridin' in," he said. "No cutting didoes that'll get their backs up. Keep it easy, or they'll barricade the place and make a fight of it. Last thing we need."

"Still five of us," said Kilgore.

"And there could be ten of them," Fergus replied. "Could be a goddamn barn-raising, for all we know, and ever' man amongst 'em with a Winchester."

"You scairt?"

He turned on Kilgore, let his hand rest on the curved butt of his Colt, responding with a question of his own. "You stupid?"

Kilgore stiffened, but made no move toward the shotgun that he'd taken from the marshals' camp. "I wouldn't say so," came the surly answer.

"You may wanna reconsider that," said Fergus, then dismissed him, turning back to focus on their target. "Lemme do the talkin' when we ride in. And if that don't suit you, strike off in a new direction now, before you spoil it for the rest of us."

"I hears ya, massuh," Kilgore told him, putting on an imitation of a field hand's voice.

"Recall what happened to the last one," Fergus warned him, without looking back.

Riding in, no hurry, Fergus strained his eyes to pick out details of the spread while they were still well out of rifle range. He saw a house and barn, a privy, chicken coops, and a corral, two horses circling clockwise in it. What he didn't see was people, causing him to wonder if they'd spotted riders coming or were sitting down to eat.

He pictured simple people saying grace, as if they had a friend upstairs protecting them.

I guess we'll see.

"How long, you think, before they find the wagon and them deputies?" asked Dawkins.

"All depends," said Fergus. "If our luck holds, nobody'll miss 'em till they're overdue at Leavenworth. Then you got telegrams, decidin' who should start to look for 'em, from which end of the trail."

"And if our luck *don't* hold?"

"Somebody comes along and sees the buzzards pickin' over them. Rides on to Enid with the news. They could be found already, come to that."

"Don't matter," Kilgore said. "They don't know where we's goin'."

"Ever heard of trackers?" Dawkins asked him. "And we left Orville to mark the trail."

"Forget about that, now," Fergus advised, "and put your best face on. We're havin' lunch with friends we ain't met yet."

When he'd told his story, shown he was unarmed, the farmer's family took Slade inside their house and sat him at a

handmade kitchen table while the missus—Katherine—
tried tending to his head wound. Dabbing at it with a warm,
wet cloth revived the headache that had settled into something like a dull and distant memory of pain while Slade
was walking underneath the sun, and somehow helped to
clarify his thoughts.

"This calls for stitching, Marshal," she advised him.

"Going back to see the doc in Enid means they gain
another day on me."

"Unless I sew you up right here."

"How long would that take?" Slade inquired.

She smiled at him and said, "Depends on whether you
hold still or thrash around."

He thought about infection setting in while he was on
the trail, and maybe finishing the job one of the cons had
started. "All right, ma'am. I'd be obliged."

"You need something to eat, first," she suggested. "We
were just about to have some stew."

"Well . . ."

"We've got plenty, I suppose," her husband—Floyd—
said, grudgingly.

"Of course we do."

With a steaming plate that smelled like heaven set in
front of him, Slade realized that he was close to starving.
On his long walk from the camp, his headache and the misery of staying upright, taking one step at a time, had can-
celed out the minor pangs of hunger. Thirst had dogged
him, quenched by gulping from the farmer's pump once
they decided not to shoot him, and his stomach rumbled
loud enough to be embarrassing.

Slade had his mouth full when the boy—Albert—chirped
up to ask, "How are you gonna run them outlaws down?"

"*Those* outlaws," Katherine corrected him.

"Depends on what I work out with your pa," Slade answered.

Floyd was eating with determination, focused on his food, but the exchange forced him to pause. "You being hurt and all," he said, "the wise thing seems to be returning where you came from, getting up a posse. I don't like your odds against—how many was it?"

"Six I'm sure of," Slade replied.

"Nope. I don't like those odds at all."

Who would? Slade asked himself. "You're right. That *is* the wiser course. But if somebody else could warn Judge Dennison on my behalf, the men I'm after wouldn't gain a day—or two, if it takes time to organize the hunt. I run a decent risk of losing them already. Every minute wasted is another burr under my saddle."

"You don't *have* a saddle," said the farmer. "Nor a horse to put it on. No guns or ammunition, either."

"That's all true," Slade granted. "And there's two ways I can remedy that situation."

"One of which is going back to Enid," Floyd observed. "The other calls for me to let you have a horse, saddle and tack, a firearm, ammunition—plus, I guess, more food and water in the bargain?"

"All of which I'd itemize in writing," Slade replied, "for compensation from the court, when you present it to the judge."

"So, after getting you set up to hunt these fellas, *then* I lose a day of work and leave my family alone to go in town, palaver with the judge, and hope for—what? You think full compensation's likely?"

"Floyd, what's wrong with you?" the missus chided him. "There's killers on the loose. They could be coming here!"

"No, ma'am," Slade quickly interjected, seeing the alarm she'd raised on two young faces. "They'll be lighting out and covering as much ground as they can. If they were headed this way, they'd have come before me."

"Oh. Well, thank the Lord for that!"

"Now, Mr. Larson . . ."

"Mind you, Marshal, I can spare the things you need. A good horse, extra saddle. As for guns, I've got a Springfield carbine, Model 1886, that I can spare on loan. It's single-shot, of course, but it'll do the job for someone with a steady hand."

"All much appreciated," Slade assured him. "And you *will* be paid, no matter if I have to do it out of pocket when I come back."

"*If* you come back."

"Floyd!"

"The marshal understands he's bucking bad odds."

Nodding, Slade acknowledged, "Yes, I do."

"But going into Enid, now—"

"Floyd, we'll be fine without you for a few short hours. Albert here can keep us safe."

The boy was beaming, but his father said, "It hasn't been a minute since you said the outlaws might be coming here."

"And that was a mistake. I stand corrected. Do your duty, husband!"

"Hmmf."

"Now, Marshal Slade," the missus said. "About that stitching . . ."

"Damn nice of you to make us feel at home," said Fergus Mayfield, talking with his mouth full.

"They's real Christians," Kilgore said. "I seen that, right away."

"Honest ta *God*, real Christians," Dawkins echoed, sniggering, heedless of gravy dripping down his chin.

Across from Fergus, well back from the table where he and his men had taken five of the six chairs available, their hosts were huddled in a line against one wall: the father, mother, and three daughters ranging from about fifteen, down to a weepy six or seven years. The man was red-faced, hard-eyed in his hatred of the strangers who had barged into his home at gunpoint, but he wasn't fighting back. Not yet, at least, with all his womenfolk at risk.

His womenfolk . . .

"Must be a grave temptation, even for a Christian man," Fergus surmised, thinking aloud. "Bein' alone out here, with all this quim around. Don't know if I'd get much work done around the place."

He watched the farmer grind his teeth, afraid to answer back. The wife and oldest daughter blushed in unison, the younger girls not following his words or train of thought. Tad was a little quicker, speaking up to say, "Good thinkin', ain't it? Breed your own and keep 'em close-like."

Fergus imagined that the farmer's face was hot enough to melt snow off the roof, if there'd been any falling. Wind him up a little more, maybe they'd see steam rising off the dumb sodbuster's scalp.

"I reckon it's like raisin' any other kinda stock," said Fergus, following Tad's lead. "You try'n keep the bloodline pure, and when they're old enough, you break 'em in."

"Figger you need some help in that department, mister?" Kilgore asked the farmer, while his eyes passed up and down the line of frightened females. "I'd be glad to lend a hand, or somethin'."

"Spare the rod an' spoil the child," Dawkins said. "I read that in the Bible."

"Read, my ass," Kilgore shot back at him. "You know damn well you're illegitimate."

"Somebody read it to me, then," said Dawkins, glowering. "It's in there, one way or t'other."

"See there? Y'all made a Christian outta Reese, now, with your hospitality," said Fergus. "That's nigh on a miracle, itse'f."

"Reckon I owe 'em somethin' for it," Dawkins said, his smile revived. "Like, mebbe helpin' Mr. Sodbuster break in his stock."

"I'm thinkin' we could all help," Fergus said. "Be good Samaritans."

The farmer vaulted to his feet then, with a roar that would have done a mountain lion proud, and hurled himself across the room toward Mayfield, hands outstretched, their fingers hooked like talons. Fergus drew his stolen Colt, cocked it, and slammed a shot into the farmer's chest. He was a tad off-center for the heart, but with a .45 it hardly mattered. Impact pitched the farmer back among his little ladies, thrashing like a hooked trout while he died.

All kinds of sobby screaming, then, the younger voices shrill and grating on the ear, but Fergus didn't mind. In fact, he liked the sounds of panic he'd evoked. He sat still while the others kicked their chairs back, moving in to silence it, and thought of how much better it would be to hear the cries of terror waft through Gilead.

Fergus had heard the saying that revenge was best served cold, but he felt bound to disagree. Granted, a little planning didn't hurt, beforehand, just to keep things running smooth, but he preferred his vengeance hot and wet.

Like raw meat, dripping blood.

Putting the Colt away, he rose and walked around the table, reaching down to drag Reese Dawkins off the oldest daughter, shoving him away.

"Me, first," Mayfield demanded. "Lemme show ya how it's done."

The horse Floyd Larson loaned him was a gelding, dapple gray. The saddle wasn't new, by any means, but didn't chafe Slade's backside, either. He'd have gladly swapped the Springfield carbine for a Winchester repeater, but the single-shooter with its trapdoor action chambered .45-70 Government rounds, with an effective killing range of something like a thousand yards. The weapon's sights were calibrated out to fourteen hundred yards, but Slade didn't delude himself into believing he could recognize a target at that range.

With luck, maybe some practice, he could fire ten rounds per minute from the Springfield, but his host could only offer twenty-seven cartridges, so there would be no practice, and he'd have to make his first shot—*each* shot— count. Take down a couple of the fugitives, by one means or another, and retrieve the weapons they had stolen. Level out the playing field.

Unless they slipped away from him—or killed him, first.

Katherine Larson stocked him up on day-old biscuits, some with bacon stuffed inside them, and her husband parted with an old canteen to wet Slade's whistle on the trail. While they were getting all of that together, Slade wrote out a brief report of what had happened, for Judge Dennison, and listed all the items that the Larsons should be compensated for. He hoped to bring the horse, saddle, and carbine back, at least, but if he didn't make it, Slade had every confidence the judge would make things right.

And Faith?

He tried to think of a postscript for her, but nothing suitable came forward from his groggy brain. She likely wouldn't want to read it, anyway, or hear from him at all. In Slade's experience, a woman's mind, once closed, beat any bank vault he had ever seen.

Leaving, he thanked the Larsons all around and felt them watching as he rode out of their dooryard, back the way he'd come, two hours earlier. How far had the escapees traveled while he stuffed his face and Mrs. Larson stitched his scalp? Twelve miles or so, he thought, assuming that the runners planned to keep their stolen animals alive. Twice that, perhaps, if they were being run to death.

And which direction had they gone?

Slade couldn't work that out until he got back to the site of last night's camp, checked Hampton in his coffin-cage, and started out from there, looking for tracks. With any luck, he'd find some fit to follow. If he didn't . . . well, then, he was done. Defeated. Useless.

No.

He thought about the fugitives. Decided Fergus Mayfield had to be the brains behind the break. There'd been a vague resemblance between Mayfield and the man who'd come into their camp, the similarity between a weasel and a wolverine. That might be Slade's imagination working on him, but he noted that the weasel hadn't gone to ground by Dawkins or by Kilgore when he'd ducked under the wagon. He had run to Mayfield, straight and true.

Which helped Slade—how?

All right. He knew they wouldn't head toward Leavenworth, or back to Enid, so he scratched two compass points off his prospective list. To head for Mexico, they'd have to cross the breadth of Oklahoma Territory, avoiding Enid and the hunting parties that were bound to rally, searching for them, then push on through Texas to the Rio Grande. Eastward meant riding into Arkansas, maybe Missouri, but the telegraph would broadcast word of their escape ahead of them. Same thing if they rode westward, to New Mexico or Arizona, down toward Mexico that way, but they would run a better chance of passing unobserved that way—except, perhaps, by some Apaches on the prod.

And then, of course, there was the possibility they'd scattered to the four winds, sick of one another after weeks in jail at Enid and their long day in the prison wagon. If they split up, Slade supposed the weasel from the camp would stick with Mayfield, and the unseen sniper from the shadows, since they'd come for him originally. Slade would follow them, if possible.

Given the chance, he'd track them all the way to Hell.

6

"Awright, boys," Fergus Mayfield told them, when the midday sun had dipped at least two hours westward. "Time for us to hit the trail."

"How come?" Reese Dawkins asked. "We got a roof over our heads. Why'nt we spend the night right here?"

"Three reasons," Fergus said. "For one, these folks are gonna get ripe purty soon, and I don't fancy sleepin' with a buncha stiffs."

"So, we can put 'em in the barn," Reese said. "Hell, leave 'em in the yard, for all I care."

"The second reason," Fergus offered, "is that someone might come callin', unexpected-like, and we don't want no company."

"Could be all right," Dan Kilgore said. "Maybe they'd bring a couple more fillies for us to ride."

Dawkins joined in the laughter over that, and Fergus felt his cheeks begin to warm a little, building up a head of steam.

"The most important reason," he continued, reasonably, until he was ready to unleash the whiplash, "is because *I goddamn said so!*"

Dawkins blanched a little. "Jesus, Ferg—"

"Shut up! I'm tellin' you one goddamn final time: I run this sorry outfit, if there *is* an outfit. Anyone don't like it, go your own way, but be goddamn sure about it. If you change your mind and try to follow after me, I'll turn you into buzzard bait."

"Awright, awright," said Dawkins. "I jus' like a roof at night, is all."

"You'll have your choice of roofs, and anyone you like to keep you company beneath 'em. When we get to Gilead."

Sated with food and stolen sex, maybe remembering the fate of Orville Washington, they didn't give him any further arguments about departure from the farm. It took some time for them to finish dressing, more time to exchange some of their winded mounts for fresh ones from the farmer's stock and get them saddled up, but all of them were broken and they didn't seem to care who held the reins.

Fergus felt good. Not rested, but replenished, like their stop-off at the farm had been a kind of dress—make that *un*dress—rehearsal for the hell he planned to raise in Gilead. That would require more than an hour or two, and it would pose a vastly greater risk, but he was committed to his goal of vengeance. He owed it to Deke Hagenmaier and Lennie Stovall, rest their rotten souls.

He damn sure owed it to himself.

No one was ever putting Fergus Mayfield in a cage again. Well, maybe if they caught him sleeping off a drunk, or snuck up from behind and cold-cocked him—but otherwise, no way. He'd go down fighting first, force them to kill him on the spot. And if, by chance, they managed to disable him somehow and lock him up regardless, he would find a way to kill himself before he heard the gates of any prison close behind him.

That, he guessed, might make some people happy, but he didn't give a damn. What others thought had never meant a hoot in hell to Fergus, and it never would. His daddy used to say that there was something wrong with him, some little bit of *soul* or *conscience* that failed to take, while he was cookin' in his mama's belly, but if so, Fergus had never missed it. Why waste time pining for something that would only make you feel bad when you tried to please yourself?

Stupid.

His four mismatched companions finally got mounted up, all looking to him for the signal to proceed. He gave a silent nod and led them off to the northwest, the same direction they'd been traveling when they had come across the former happy family.

What had their names been?

Fergus shrugged it off. Who cared?

He knew some names in Gilead; knew all their faces, too. The townsfolk had trooped past his cell while he was waiting for the marshals, up from Enid. Some of them had cursed him, all of them regarding him through bars as if he were an animal from Africa or some such place, imported for their personal amusement. He recalled the little children who had laughed at him, a couple of them sticking out their small pink tongues.

And smiled, imagining their high-pitched dying screams.

Slade liked the dapple gray and was relieved that it appeared to bear him no ill will. Backtracking to the prison wagon grated on his nerves, a sense of wasted time oppressing him, but there was no alternative. To track the fugitives—if he *could* track them—Slade would have to start where they had, on their run to God alone knew where.

No, that was wrong, he thought. Wherever they were headed, as a group or scattering to make it each man for himself, the runners he was after had at least some vague idea of where they meant to go. It would have been to Slade's advantage if he knew that in advance, but lacking the supposed powers of a psychic, he'd have to do it the old-fashioned way, by eating trail dust.

If he found a trail.

There'd been no rain since he left Enid with the prisoners, which could be good or bad. If the escaping cons had left a trail for him to follow, then it wouldn't have been washed away. Conversely, if the soil and been too dry and hard to hold hoofprints, then he was out of luck. Slade couldn't sit and guess which way they'd gone and hope for any kind of satisfactory result. He needed Lady Luck to smile on him, but she'd been scowling like a witch for so long now that Slade had trouble just remembering the last time things had gone his way.

He didn't count surviving on his last two missions for Judge Dennison. Slade couldn't credit luck, per se, with his ability to use a gun. Each time, he'd come back home to hear bad news: Faith leaving, first, then telling him that she was pregnant with his child, but he would have no part in raising it. The way she'd said it, as if thinking Slade would be relieved to be left out, had stung him worse than anything she might have done.

And could he live with that? Was there another choice, once Faith made up her mind?

Slade tried to put that problem out of mind for now, assisted by his throbbing head wound and the hot, relentless sun. He kept the gelding more or less on course, not certain how far he had walked from last night's camp to reach the Larson spread, but fairly certain he could spot the prison wagon squatting on the open prairie like an ugly blot on Mother Nature's face.

Too many women in his head, Slade thought, and giggled at that notion till he heard the sharp note of hysteria and swallowed it. Couldn't afford to spook the horse and have it throw him, likely landing on his head to finish what a lucky shot had started hours earlier.

Late afternoon, according to the sun's position in the sky, and there it was. He noted something wrong about the prison wagon's silhouette, and rode another hundred yards before he figured out that there were vultures perched on top of it, eyeing the meal they couldn't reach inside the cage. It pleased Slade to frustrate them, in an odd way that he didn't fully understand, almost as if he and the youngster in the box were cheating death.

Closer, an odor on the shifting prairie wind reminded Slade that no one cheats the Reaper. Nobody got out of life alive.

He didn't check on Hampton, knowing more or less what he would find. Instead, Slade rode around the camp's perimeter, looking for tracks, and found the spot where he supposed the second shooter had been waiting, holding horses in the dark, before all hell broke loose. They made it easy on him, after all, leading his roan and Hampton's sorrel, with the dray horses, to join the rest and ride off as a group, heading northwest.

Slade frowned at that, trying to figure it. Pictured a map of Oklahoma Territory and the state of Kansas, stacked on top of it. Where did they hope to find, heading away from Mexico?

"Who cares?" he asked the dapple gray, expecting and receiving no reply.

As long as Slade could see their tracks, he'd follow them.

And if the reaper rode along beside him, that was fine.

Floyd Larson wasn't happy about riding into Enid, leaving Katherine and the kids on their own for the time that a round trip would take. Riding his strongest, fastest horse, the varnish Appaloosa stallion, it was still five hours into town, at least, and then five hours back. Adding time to tell his story, stretch his legs a little, and refresh himself, it would be well past nightfall by the time he saw his family again.

Eleven hours, anyway, with killers on the loose.

He'd almost called it off, after the marshal rode away, but Katherine wouldn't let him break his word. A promise was a promise, and the ones that didn't cost you anything were hardly worth considering. By then, it seemed her own fears had subsided—or perhaps, as Floyd suspected, she was hiding them for his sake, and the children's.

Not that Albert seemed to mind. He'd been excited by the prospect of defending hearth and home while Floyd went off to run the lawman's errand, taking care to prop his .22 beside the front door, where it would be easily accessible at need. Floyd had also left the Yellow Boy, together with his W. W. Greener twelve-gauge double-barreled shotgun, at the farmhouse, just in case. Larson himself was unarmed, except for the Colt Single Action Army revolver he wore in a holster beneath his left arm, out of sight under his duster.

Second thoughts were tricky things. He'd been an hour out from home when he began to wonder whether Jack Slade even *was* a marshal—or if that was his true name, in fact. He had a badge. So what? For all Floyd Larson knew, he could have plucked it from the marshal who had creased his scalp with lead. What if he rode just out of sight, then sat and waited until Larson left the homestead before turning back, to rob and—

Floyd had caught himself before his grim imagination ran away with him, but it had been a struggle. He had finally decided that the lawman's tale was too elaborate to be a ruse. If he was lying, why not simply say that he'd been held up on the road and left for dead? The rest of it—a prison wagon and a murdered deputy, four fleeing convicts—was superfluous, a waste of breath.

Larson had never met Judge Dennison, had never done a bit of business that involved the federal court, but he knew Dennison by reputation as a hanging judge. He couldn't fault the man for that, since written laws determined who should die or go to prison for specific crimes, and settlers like Floyd Larson benefited from the strict enforcement of those laws. It didn't always *feel* that way, when he heard stories about bandits on the loose or renegades who'd jumped the rez. He knew that deputies like Slade were few and far between in Oklahoma Territory, stretched so thin they rode a circuit over districts larger than some eastern states, and there would never be enough of them to guarantee that every ranching family lived in peace.

Another reason why he had to run the marshal's errand for him. To ensure that Marshal Slade got reinforcements in his hunt for the escaping felons and prevented them from harming anybody else.

For a change of pace, Floyd thought about the city that was waiting for him, three hours and something up ahead. There were a couple of saloons he'd had it in his mind to try, but there was never time or opportunity on market days, when the whole family rode in to buy supplies or sell their surplus vegetables. Today, though, on his own . . .

Floyd wondered if he ought to stop and drink a beer. Just one, to wet his whistle for the long ride back. He wouldn't patronize the fancy ladies—wouldn't even *look* at them, for Katherine's sake—but one beer couldn't hurt. Could it? Unless she smelled it on his breath and wondered what else he'd been up to, on his urgent errand for the law.

No beer, then, damn it.

Larson nudged his stallion to a gallop, settled in, and let him run.

An hour shy of sundown, Slade found Orville Washington. Vultures had found him first and had their way with him for hours, leaving little face to speak of, but Slade recognized his man from the prison trousers and the deep mahogany of his remaining skin. The vultures lifted off and croaked their protests when they saw that Slade was coming in to view their meal, no matter what they thought about it. Skittish, but unwilling to abandon Washington entirely, they descended in a circle thirty feet or so from Slade and the remains, waiting to see what happened next.

The stench was powerful, after a whole day in the sun, with organs opened up by probing beaks, but it was nothing Slade hadn't experienced before. His borrowed gelding didn't care for it, much less the buzzards eyeing them like something that could turn into dessert, but it stood fast as Slade dismounted, moving closer to the corpse.

Slade couldn't swear to it, but it appeared that Washington had been shot twice. Vultures begin their work on open wounds whenever possible, and Slade saw two points where they gone to town on Washington, drawn by the sight and smell of blood soaking his shirt. He'd taken one hit on his left side, down around the waistline, but it didn't have the look of something that would kill him. Number two, the kill shot, might have drilled his heart, or just come close enough to stop it while he drowned in blood. Whatever, it had done the job.

Slade pieced together what had likely happened. Knowing that he hadn't wounded Washington, during the skirmish at their camp, he guessed Guy Hampton must have done the honors. Pain and blood loss would have made it difficult for Washington to travel, and be might have been complaining, getting on the nerves of five white men who didn't give a damn about him to begin with. It had come to shooting somehow, either through an argument or as a simple means of trimming back dead wood, and now he only had five fugitives to think about.

Unfortunately, two of them were still unknown to Slade, and one of those he hadn't even seen. The sniper from the shadows could pass by him on a city sidewalk, and he wouldn't know the difference. The one who'd walked into his camp, though, that one's rodent face was burned into his memory.

"Find one, you find the other," Slade informed the dapple gray and got a wet snort in reply.

The horse had seen enough of Orville Washington, and so had Slade. He mounted up and told the waiting ring of vultures, "He's all yours." Before he'd traveled forty yards, the birds were back and busy feeding on their prize.

One down.

The other five were holding to their course, riding northwestward from the spot where they had left the odd man out. Slade calculated he could trail them for another forty minutes, give or take, before he had to camp out for the night. He couldn't follow them after the sun went down and hid their tracks, afraid of wandering off course, while they were free to ride on through the night if so inclined.

Why wouldn't they? If Slade were in their place, he knew his top priority would be escape, putting as much ground in between himself and any possible pursuers as he could. Of course, he wouldn't flee in this direction, either, so the art of second-guessing them eluded him.

He thought about the odds against him, five on one, all of them armed with good repeating weapons, while he only had the Springfield single-shot. If he could take them by surprise, drop one and grab a Colt or Winchester, he could improve his chances, but an ambush on the trail meant Slade would have to get *ahead* of them, somehow, and he was still a full half day behind the fugitives, at least.

Slade welcomed sunset with a mixture of frustration and relief, camping beside a pile of boulders thrust up from the prairie by some ancient cataclysm, with a cool spring spilling from the midst of jumbled stones. He'd sleep because he couldn't help it, clinging to the Springfield, but he would make do without a fire.

And in the first gray light of morning, he'd be on his way.

"It's gettin' cold," Kilgore complained. "I still think we should start a fire."

"Move off a half mile, then, and light your own," Fergus replied. "Give us some warnin', while the posse's killin' you."

"What posse? Who'n hell's out hunting us tonight?"

"Well, lemme think," said Fergus. "Could it be the U.S. marshals? Mebbe vigilantes, if they happened on the homestead where we had our fun?"

"It's *dark* out," Kilgore argued back. "The hell are they suppose to see our tracks?"

"Won't need to, if you light a fire, now, will they?" Fergus answered.

"Oh."

"That's why we're postin' lookouts. You can take the first two hours, Danny Boy. If your tootsies get too cold, just stomp your feet."

"But do it quiet-like," said Dawkins, "while we're sleepin'."

"You can take the second watch," Fergus informed the joker. "Y'oughta be all rested up by then."

"Goddamn it!"

"Tad, you're third up for the watch. Earl, you'll be fourth and take us through to dawn."

"I guess you won't be standin' watch, then," Kilgore said.

"You guess exac'ly right," Fergus replied. "I aim to get the best sleep that I've had in weeks, and anyone cuts in on that had better have a damn good reason why."

"You really think there'll be a posse comin', Cousin Ferg?" Earl asked him.

"Mebbe not tonight, but soon enough. We all got an appointment with the hangman, if they catch us now."

"*If* they catch us," Dawkins echoed. "Anyhow, better'n rottin' over there in Leavenworth."

"Nobody's hangin' me," Kilgore announced. "Might kill me in a stand-up fight, they send enough men for the job, but I ain't walkin' up no gallows steps. Uh-uh. No, sir."

Tough talk, and Fergus wondered whether Danny Boy could back it up if he was faced with someone other than a poor sodbuster's family. It was an idle thought, since Fergus didn't really care a whit if Kilgore lived or kicked the bucket, much less *how*. It would be helpful, having others with him when he got to Gilead, but after that, the lot of them could all go straight to hell, his idjit cousins with the rest.

Revenge was all that mattered to him at the moment. After he'd achieved it, when his thirst for blood was quenched, Fergus could think about whatever happened next. He might head west or south, whatever caught his fancy, and he wouldn't be held back by family ties. If Tad and Earl came out of Gilead alive and chose to stick with him, he might allow it.

On the other hand, he just might not.

His cousins' admiration for him boosted Mayfield's spirits, in small doses, but too much of it was cloying, like a woman hanging on his gun arm, nagging him to stay and love her when the only thing he wanted was the open road. The very minute that they started slowing Fergus down, he'd leave them in his dust. Standing or lying facedown in the dirt, their call.

But right now, what he needed was a good night's sleep.

He stretched out on the ground, a stolen saddle for his pillow, with the head-shot marshal's lever-action shotgun at his side. He left the hammer down, his right hand resting on the stock where he could cock it in a heartbeat, when the first alarm was raised. Buckshot was indiscriminate, and that was fine, if danger jarred him out of sleep. Come up and out of dreamland fighting, if the need arose.

And if it didn't, well, he hoped to dream of Gilead. The things he had in mind for the inhabitants of that self-righteous prairie town would set a standard for the fine art of revenge. Fergus would have his due, and then some. Townsfolk gloating over how they'd brought him low would have a good long opportunity to rue their foolishness.

They'd be remembered as the ones who messed with Fergus Mayfield, to their sorrow.

Gilead would be his monument, a city of the dead.

7

The sun was low and bloody-colored on Floyd Larson's right-hand side when Enid rose out of the plain before him. He'd walked the Appaloosa more than running it, given the afternoon's fierce heat, but now he nudged the stallion to a trot, relieved to have the first leg of his long ride nearly over with. Sweaty and rank, he was embarrassed to be seen on Enid's streets, but didn't figure any of the folks he met would recognize him anyway or hold the image in their memories for long.

One problem that he'd thought of, halfway in between his farm and town, was his arrival time in Enid. Larson didn't know what kind of hours judges kept, but he assumed they would clear out from work around the same time bankers did, unless they had a big trial going and they didn't want to interrupt somebody talking from the witness chair. If he arrived and found the courthouse closed, as he expected, how was he supposed to find Judge Dennison?

Big man like that, it stood to reason that most people in

the town knew where he lived, but would they share that information with a stranger, lathered from the trail, who showed up on their doorstep after sundown?

Doubtful.

He could ask at one of the saloons, and have a beer while he was at it, but that didn't strike him as the right approach, either. To find a judge, who should he ask?

A lawyer, probably, but all their offices would probably be closed by now.

Or he could try a law*man*.

That made better sense. A town the size of Enid, they were bound to have some kind of constable or deputy on duty, night and day. There ought to be an office, though he'd never noticed one on any of his other trips to town. Asking around for the police was different than trying to look up a judge at home, in Larson's estimation, something folks would understand and likely help him with. Worse come to worst, he could create some kind of minor public scene and make the townies fetch an officer to deal with him.

Smiling to think of what his Katherine would say to that, Larson crossed Enid's city limits, riding down the middle of Main Street. Contrary to his expectation, no one on the sidewalks bothered giving him a second glance, likely accustomed to the sight of strangers passing through. The shops and offices were closed, as he'd expected, and he focused on pedestrians, hoping to spot one with a badge.

Larson turned his Appaloosa toward the federal courthouse, knowing where it was, although he'd never been inside. In front of it, he tied his stallion to a hitching post beside a water trough and climbed a flight of steps to try the courthouse door.

Locked tight, of course.

He spent a moment looking up and down Main Street,

imagining how it must feel to be a lawyer or a clerk, something important in the town, then suddenly remembered that the courthouse had a jail tucked underneath it. Likely, there was someone in the cells right now, which meant there'd also be someone to guard them. Now, if he could only figure out a way to rouse them . . .

Larson found the iron-bound door, complete with small barred window, on the west side of the courthouse, down a flight of steps that left him standing six or seven feet below street level. Feeling anxious now, he knocked, then pounded louder when he got no answer. Finally, feeling a touch of desperation, Larson leaned in toward the bars and hollered through, "Is anybody home?"

"The hell do you want?" asked a gruff voice, disembodied, from the shadows on the far side of the door.

"I need to find Judge Dennison," Larson replied.

"Come back tomorrow morning, when there's court. And when you're sober."

"I'm already sober, and I've got a message for the judge," Larson shot back.

"I ain't your errand boy," the shadow man informed him.

"Then, you'd better find one," Larson answered, fuming. "Tell him that your prison wagon's done been ambushed, with a marshal killed and convicts runnin' loose."

"Jesus!" the watchman blurted out, and Larson heard his footsteps clopping off along a murky corridor.

For all his drifting through the years, and sleeping out under the stars, Jack Slade still marveled at the way a scorching day could lose its heat after the sun went down. It was the same on prairies and in deserts, where you baked all day, and shivered through the night. Worse when you couldn't risk a fire, of course, but Slade knew he would make it through, wrapped in the horse blanket he borrowed from the Larson family, along with all his other gear.

It was an odd thing, but he never felt more lonely than when he was in the presence of a happy family. Slade didn't envy them their happiness, exactly, but it brought to mind the things he didn't have—and that, it seemed to him of late, he never would.

Thinking of Faith as night fell on the prairie was a bad idea. Not that he had the power to dismiss her from his mind, but at the moment there were more important—no, more *urgent*—things for him to think about. Five killers on the run, with nothing much to lose, and who knew when he'd have a hope of reinforcements on his manhunt.

Slade imagined that the farmer, Larson, should have reached Enid by now. He'd have to find Judge Dennison somehow, relate Slade's tale—and then, what?

It would take the judge some time to organize a posse, calling in his marshals, maybe deputizing more for the emergency. But even if he got that done tonight, the posse couldn't start its search in darkness. Leaving at the crack of dawn, they'd still have given Fergus Mayfield and the other cons a full day's lead.

For now, at least, Slade reckoned it was down to him or nobody.

It was a challenge getting comfortable, with his headache and the stitches over his right ear, but Slade knew he should try to get some sleep. Tomorrow would be yet another grueling day, trying to keep his quarry's trail in sight, pushing his physical endurance to the limit, hoping that the men he hunted stuck together, so that he would have at least some vestige of a chance to bag them all.

Or that they'd have another falling-out, perhaps, and kill

each other. Do the world a favor. Slade suppose that was unlikely, but they'd set a precedent with Orville Washington. It wouldn't be the first time that a gang disintegrated, but he knew it was a lot to hope for. Still, he'd take what he could get.

Slade settled back as best he could, pulling the blanket snug around him with the Springfield at his side. He focused on the goal of sleep and hoped he wouldn't dream.

"First watch, my ass," Dan Kilgore muttered to himself. He didn't for a second think there was a posse on their trail—not yet, at least. Posting a guard was just another way of Fergus Mayfield showing who was boss, throwing his weight around. Kilgore was getting sick and tired of that, but wasn't sure exactly what to do about it.

One choice that immediately came to mind was taking off, getting to hell and gone away from there while all the others were asleep. He figured he'd take one of the horses they had stolen, lead it off a ways before he put its saddle on and mounted up. Put miles between himself and Mayfield by the time that Mr. High-and-Mighty crawled out of his bedroll in the morning.

Going where?

That was the problem. Kilgore didn't have a goal in mind, aside from staying out of custody, while Mayfield had a plan that had been cooking in his mind the whole time he was locked up waiting for his trial. Revenge was something Kilgore understood, all right, and he had nothing against rousting some hick town, even if no one in the burg meant anything to him. But on the other hand, from what he'd heard about the last time Fergus tried his luck in Gilead, sticking with Mayfield just might get him killed.

Which brought him to another possibility. He didn't have to run away from Fergus. It would be a simple thing for Kilgore to creep up on him with the six-gun he had taken from the younger marshal, put its muzzle up to Mayfield's head, and *bam!* One shot at point-blank range, and they were rid of him.

Of course, he'd likely have to kill the bastard's cousins, too. Catch them while they were foggy, jolted up from sleeping by the first shot. Drill them both before they had a chance to reach their weapons. He had never risked those kinds of odds before, but with the sharp edge of surprise—

Or, screw it, he could ride along and see what happened next. Put up with Fergus lording it over the rest of them for now. Maybe ask Dawkins how he felt about the situation, when he woke him up to take the second watch. Reese was the sort who didn't take to bosses, and if trouble came, Kilgore preferred to have at least one other shooter on his side.

He heard coyotes yodeling in the distance, agitated by the half-moon rising in the eastern sky. He thought back to the homestead they had pillaged, wishing they'd had more time with the little ladies, but he understood how dallying in daylight was a bad idea. Fergus was right about that part, at least. Sometimes it seemed to Kilgore that he'd been betrayed by dumb decisions all his life, no one to blame except himself.

Which, naturally, didn't stop him blaming others, all the same.

Kilgore didn't have a pocket watch, but estimated that his turn on guard duty was winding down. Say thirty minutes more, by rough accounting, and he'd roust Dawkins out of his blanket for the next shift. Save the chitchat for another time and not risk starting anything tonight. Better to sleep on it and see how things looked to him in the morning.

There was little doubt in Kilgore's mind that he'd be standing watch again tomorrow night, and every night until they got to Gilead. This wouldn't be his final opportunity to move against the Mayfields, if he thought that was the way to go.

A little patience, sometimes, was its own reward.

Judge Isaac Dennison had come from home to meet Floyd Larson at the courthouse, spent a quarter of an hour listening and questioning, then sent the farmer on his way with thanks. His offer of a room at one of Enid's two hotels had been declined, Larson explaining that he'd left his family alone and meant to get back home before sunrise. Dennison wished him well and put him out of mind.

Guy Hampton dead. Jack Slade wounded, but in pursuit of four escaped convicts and two or more associates. He'd understood that coming back to Enid and reporting the escape himself would only give the fugitives more time at large and doing God alone knew what.

Instead of rushing out to raise a general alarm, the judge sat down behind his desk and made a mental list of things he must do. First, obviously, send more men to follow Slade and the escapees, though it wasn't something he could do immediately. Only one of his six marshals was in town at present, and recalling others from the field would take too long, assuming he could even reach them in the badlands they patrolled. Any civilians he could find immediately would be patronizing one of Enid's several saloons, in no state to go manhunting. Besides, a posse couldn't set out in the middle of the night with any realistic prospect of success.

He *would* reach out to Deputy Mike Bowers, get him started knocking on the doors of sober citizens who might agree to ride at first light and remain afield until the job was done. Shopkeepers wouldn't want to leave their stores or families for days on end, but there were men in town who owed him favors and could be reminded of that fact.

His second task was waking up the undertaker, making sure that he was ready for a long ride in the morning, to retrieve Guy Hampton's body. Dennison couldn't remember anything about the young man's family, where he should look for next of kin, but that was something he could work on when the urgent jobs were done.

He thought about the fugitives and tried to rank them on the basis of the risk they posed to anyone who crossed their path. He rated Fergus Mayfield as the worst and Orville Washington least likely to begin a murder spree, but in the present circumstances Dennison acknowledged that his best guess still came down to only that: a guess.

Mayfield.

Something about the sneering outlaw troubled him, beyond the obvious concern that he might rob—and likely murder—anyone he met, if it would help him make good his escape. Something the man had said when Dennison pronounced his sentence.

Tell 'em I'll be back, Your Highness. It don't matter how long I'm locked up.

Tell who? The jury that convicted Mayfield had been present at his sentencing, but Mayfield hadn't even glanced at them. He had addressed his words to Dennison, telling the judge to pass his message on to "them." The judge had taken it as empty bluster at the time, but now . . .

Who would the outlaw hold a special grudge against? Not one person, but *them*?

It clicked, then, and he knew the answer. Mayfield had been captured, and his two accomplices gunned down, by citizens of Gilead. A small town on the prairie with no telegraph to link them with the outside world. They'd borne the brunt of Mayfield's hatred on the day he'd drawn his sentence—but would Mayfield risk his newfound freedom riding back to seek revenge? It sounded like a long shot, but he just might try to make good on his threat.

Another problem, then. Aside from trackers ready at the break of dawn, Dennison had to find a messenger who'd make the ride to Gilead and warn the people there to be on guard. If there was someone he could trust to do it properly.

If they were not too late.

"The hell?" Reese Dawkins cracked an eyelid, recognized Dan Kilgore crouching next to him, and muttered, "Damn. Midnight already?"

"Close enough," Kilgore replied.

Dawkins took care to keep it quiet as he crawled out of his bedroll and retrieved the shotgun he had picked up at the homestead where they'd stopped for lunch and the surprise dessert. He knew the gun was loaded, didn't need to double-check it, only making sure he'd left both hammers down to keep from firing accidentally. He didn't want to wake up Fergus, knowing that he'd catch hell for it.

"Somethin' wrong with you?" he asked Kilgore, noting the sour expression on his face.

A silent shrug in answer to his question.

Glancing at the three Mayfields, still seemingly asleep, Reese beckoned Kilgore farther from the heart of camp, leading him toward the tethered horses. There, his voice pitched in a whisper, Dawkins said, "There ain't been time for us to talk about this little trip we're takin'."

"No."

"An' I been wond'rin' what you think about it," he pressed on.

He saw suspicion flicker back at him from Kilgore's eyes. "Did Fergus put you up to askin' me?"

"Hell, no! I'm askin' for myself."

"So, whadda *you* think?"

"Ain't made up my mind yet," Dawkins said. "I don't mind tryin' somethin' new, if we can pull it off. Don't feel like gettin' kilt for someone else's grudge, though, either."

"That's about how I feel," Kilgore said.

"Way I look at it," Reese continued, "we can stick with 'em a while, an' still cut out if somethin' don't smell right along the way."

"An' if they say we gotta stay, then what?"

"Do what we gotta do," said Dawkins. "Three on two, that ain't so bad. We take 'em by surprise . . ."

"Or when they's sleepin'."

"Now you're talkin'. I was thinkin' that, myself."

"An' if it looks like we could take this town okay . . ."

"Just go along with it. Why not?"

"We got a deal, then?"

"Deal."

Another glance at the three sleepers, then they shook on it. Dawkins felt better right away, knowing he had an ally in the camp, against the three Mayfields, if it came down to that. And if it all worked out the way that Fergus seemed to think it would . . . well, what the hell.

He'd run wild in a town or two when he was punching cattle, and had served ten days jail for it one time, when things got out of hand. But *taking over* was another story altogether, and he liked the sound of it, in principle. The thought of everybody being under his command excited Dawkins, even though he figured Fergus would be claiming all the best things for himself.

A town of any size at all, there should be plenty left to go around.

And if there wasn't, he still had his deal with Kilgore.

Take 'em by surprise and show 'em who was *really* boss.

Despite his wish, Slade dreamed. It started on a windswept prairie, no surprise, except he didn't recognize the landmarks that surrounded him, and he was going somewhere, traveling by means he couldn't quite identify, at speeds beyond what any horse could manage at a gallop. More like flying, and he knew that made no sense—but, then again, it didn't have to, in a dream.

At one point in his flight, a bloom of smoke appeared on the horizon, all shot through with circling specks that Slade soon recognized as vultures wheeling on a thermal draft. An instant later he was wrapped inside the smoke cloud, peering down at the inferno of a burning town, with people running helter-skelter through the streets. He didn't recognize the buildings, couldn't tell if it was Enid or some town he'd fabricated out of bits and pieces from disjointed memories, then he was gone and sweeping off across a range of hills, dipping again to hone in on a ranch.

The spread he recognized as Faith's, no question there. A spike of pain lanced through him as he saw the wedding party in the dooryard, knowing what was bound to happen next, riders advancing hell-for-leather from the north—and wrenched himself awake, thrashing his blanket free, the

Springfield carbine's barrel smacking painfully against his kneecap.

"Damn it!"

It was cold, but Slade was clammy with the sweat his dream flight had evoked. He rose and walked a circuit of his campsite, carrying the Springfield, checking on the dapple gray and scouting the perimeter.

All clear.

Slade was prone to nightmares lately, a development he didn't care for, but he couldn't seem to shake them. There was no one he felt comfortable sharing with, but he was getting better when it came to interrupting dreams that troubled him. The downside of it was that, once he broke out of a nightmare, getting back to sleep was difficult. He'd spend an hour, sometimes two, lying awake and second-guessing things he'd said or done, no hope of going back to change them now. And when he fell asleep once more, there was no guarantee he wouldn't find another nightmare waiting for him, primed to spring from ambush.

Whiskey helped a little, but he'd seen enough sad drunks to know it was a palliative, not a cure. No man could truly drown his sorrows in a bottle, only muffle their infernal grumbling for a while.

If he could talk to Faith . . . but, no. That door was closed to him.

And he had something else to think about, more pressing at the moment. He was hunting killers, with a score to settle for Guy Hampton and a job to finish for Judge Dennison.

Maybe his last job as a marshal?

Slade had thought of that before and found himself unable to decide. One thing he absolutely *couldn't* do was quit before he'd fixed the problem that confronted him.

An owl swept past him, twenty feet away, a ghostly image

with the pallid moonlight on its wings. The swooping hunter startled Slade, got his heart thumping double time, until he recognized it and relaxed. Nothing to fear, unless he was a field mouse or a prairie dog.

Not yet.

Tomorrow, though, he would return to hunting men, outnumbered and outgunned.

That moment, underneath a midnight sky, Jack Slade would not have had it any other way.

8

Slade was already up and moving, a cold break-fast in his stomach, when the eastern sky turned gray, then slowly kindled into daylight. He felt antsy, waiting for the sun to creep an inch or two above the far rim of the world and give him light enough to find his quarry's tracks again, a part of him imagining they might have disappeared during the night. They hadn't, though, and by the time dew started steaming off the prairie, he was on his way, still riding steadily northwestward.

It was getting on toward half past seven when he saw the barn and farmhouse, still at least a mile in front of him, the tracks he followed leading him directly toward the isolated homestead. As he closed the gap, the buildings grew in size, and so did Slade's conviction that he wouldn't like whatever he found waiting for him up ahead.

Mayfield and his companions wouldn't be there. Slade was sure of that, knew it would be too much to hope for.

But they definitely would have stopped to visit, hungry, horny, perfectly incapable of thinking any other humans had the right to live, or just be left alone. They'd stop, all right, and Slade's gut told him that they wouldn't want to leave a witness breathing afterward.

Slade didn't need to check the Springfield, knew he had a cartridge in the chamber and a pocketful of spares ready at hand. On the approach, he spent some extra time to circle wide around the place and come in from the southwest, so the barn prevented anyone inside the house from seeing him, if they were still alive.

An effort wasted.

From a hundred yards, Slade recognized the two dray horses that had pulled the prison wagon, grazing on a scruffy patch of grass beside the barn. They paused to watch him for a moment, then went back to feeding, having judged Slade and dismissed him as a possible threat. As he drew even with them, Slade surveyed the animals for injuries, saw none, then noted a corral nearby, empty, its gate wide open.

Mayfield's crew had swapped for other horses and moved on.

Slade rode on toward the house, its front door gaping onto darkness where the sun's rays didn't reach. His ears picked up a kind of scuffling sound, with snarling mingled in to raise the short hairs on his nape. He hoped it was an animal, but wasn't taking any chances. He dismounted, tied his dapple gray to the corral fence, than walked toward the house, cocking the Springfield as he went.

At thirty feet, and angled off to one side of the open door, Slade stopped and called out to the house. "Inside the house! Come out with empty hands!"

No answer, just more snuffle-snarling, and a noise like something being dragged across floorboards.

Slade gave whoever, whatever it was a final warning. "I'm a U.S. marshal, and I'm coming in! Somebody pulls on me, I'm shooting anything that moves!"

Just give me time to fumble with my carbine here, he thought, but kept it to himself, advancing toward a shaded porch that ran the full width of the house. His first step onto it, Slade heard a louder scrambling noise inside, and edged back farther from the door, the carbine rising to his shoulder, index finger on the trigger.

And he nearly pulled it, when a knee-high shape burst from the doorway, racing off across the yard. He'd barely recognized the mangy gray coyote when another and another fled the house, snapping and snarling at the interruption of their feast. The last one out, Slade saw, trailed tattered fabric from its maw.

He let them go and peered around the door jamb, making sure the last of them was gone before he stepped across the threshold and inhaled the stench of death. He hadn't noticed it before, since he was focused on the eerie sounds, but it was on him now, full force. Nothing Slade hadn't smelled before, but there was still no getting used to it.

Five dead, and Slade supposed the only man among them had been lucky with the clean shot to his forehead. Then again, Slade couldn't say *when* he'd been shot. For all he knew, the farmer had been forced to watch what happened to his wife and daughters, maybe carried that sight with him when the bullet came as sweet relief.

No doubt about it now. Mayfield and every other bastard riding with him had a rope waiting, if they were caught alive.

Or maybe Slade could save Judge Dennison the bother of a trial.

The posse had a hard time getting started out of Enid. It was midnight, more or less, before Mike Bowers managed to persuade six able-bodied men that they should take time off from work and help him track the fugitives. Those who agreed, reluctantly, included a bank clerk, a hostler from the livery, a barber, two shopkeepers, and a bouncer from the Lucky Strike saloon. By sunrise, when the group was scheduled to be deputized and hit the road, two members of the party had been urged to reconsider by their wives, and nothing Isaac Dennison could say would get them back on board.

Those two defections nearly made the others quit, until the judge lit into them with everything he had. He'd started out appealing to their sense of civic duty, saw that he was losing them, and wound up asking how they planned to face their families and customers with everyone in Enid knowing they were cowards who'd allowed a gang of savages to roam at will across the countryside, preying on helpless victims as they pleased. They'd knuckled under, then, but Dennison still wasn't certain he could count on any one of them to pull a trigger if the fugitives were cornered and preferred to make a fight of it.

Which Dennison had every confidence they would.

Going to Leavenworth was one thing, with its walls and bars and rules, hard labor for the convicts who could manage it, and isolation for the malcontents that had been known to drive offenders crazy. Still, there was the prospect of parole, time off for good behavior, even possible escape. But once they'd killed Guy Hampton and had left Jack Slade for dead, their fate was sealed. Dennison meant to try and execute the lot of them, however many were involved, and every one of them would know that.

When it came down a choice of deaths, a noose or bullet, which of them was likely to surrender?

It was going to get bloody, and the judge hoped that he wasn't sending four incompetents to slaughter. Hoped, as well, that their mistakes would not cost him another deputy. Mike Bowers was a married man himself, no children yet, but he was hopeful. Tracking criminals kept him away from home a lot, but guaranteed a steady salary—as long as he survived.

It had been pushing nine o'clock when Bowers and his four uneasy deputies rode out of town, trailed half an hour later by the undertaker's wagon heading off to fetch Guy Hampton's body. In the meantime, Dennison had wired two of his other deputies—Tom McAvoy at Medford, Billy James out in Taloga—telling them to hurry back as soon as possible. His other men were out of reach until they finished the assignments they were working on and came home with reports of prisoners in tow.

It had been easier to find a messenger for Gilead. He didn't need to deputize an errand boy or coach him on the law concerning apprehension of a fugitive. It was a simple job that anyone with half a brain could manage, if he had the skill to navigate across the open prairie without getting lost and winding up in Texas by mistake. His chosen volunteer, Lem Wilkins, was a carpenter and handyman, late twenties, who had actually passed through Gilead the year before, while on his way to Enid, down from Kansas for a visit with his brother. Lem had liked the city well enough to stick around, but twenty dollars had convinced him he could spare the time to warn potential victims of their peril.

Dennison still hoped the errand was a waste of time, but he could not afford to skip it. If he failed to warn the townsfolk and disaster struck, he'd have a hard time living with himself.

And God knew it was difficult enough already, on the best of days.

It hadn't been the best night's sleep of Fergus Mayfield's life, but after weeks of sitting in a dank hole underneath the Enid courthouse, camping on the ground was close to heaven. Or, as close as he'd be getting to it, anyway.

No matter how you sliced it, if there was a Man Upstairs who kept a ledger on the deeds of men, He had to be displeased with what he saw in Fergus. On the other hand, Mayfield had never seen a lick of evidence suggesting that He gave a damn.

Breakfast was smoked ham and some biscuits from the homestead, cold and lacking coffee, but a fairly decent meal. Dawkins and Kilgore had their sour faces on but kept their carping to themselves. His cousins, typically, didn't seem much concerned about whatever happened next or where they wound up at day's end.

They had another full day's ride, plus some, before they got to Gilead. He knew that Reese and Dan were skeptical about his mission, but it didn't matter. They could tag along or go their own way, live or die, whatever they decided. Fergus didn't know the word *complusion*, but he understood the feeling, when you had to press ahead with something, even knowing it was bad for you.

Even when it might get you killed.

"We're done," he said to no one in particular, mouth full of ham. He stood and dusted off his stolen clothes, picked up his stolen gear, and went to put the stolen saddle on his stolen horse.

Who needed cash when everything a man might need was right there for the taking?

Dan and Reese muttered a little bit while they were saddling up their animals, but that was normal. They were lazy, shiftless characters who'd sit around all day if someone didn't order them to get up on their feet and do a job. Stupid and surly, Fergus rated them, but neither one had sand enough to call him out, nor speed enough to take him if they tried it.

Now, the two of them together, maybe . . .

No. He didn't see that happening. They'd likely fuss around and wind up talking one another out of it, remembering how Orville Washington had dropped dead from his saddle, right in front of them. That memory would stick with them as far as Gilead, at least.

And after that, he didn't need them anyway.

Even with Fergus glaring at them, telling them to hurry up, it still took most of twenty minutes for the others to get mounted up. "Northwest again?" asked Kilgore.

"All day long," Mayfield confirmed.

"Mebbe we'll find someplace to get some more home cookin'," Reese suggested, leering.

"Rest assured, we won't let any opportunities slip by us," Fergus said. "Now, if you boys are ready? Finally?"

Mayfield didn't care if they met anybody else along the way or not. He would accept whatever Fate dropped in his path, and if the road was barren, he could focus on his plans for Gilead, its mayor and lawman, all of the self-righteous folk who'd done their best to kill him and, failing at that, to see him caged for life.

In his mind, he had laid waste to Gilead a thousand times, with subtle variations in his method. Should he hang the mayor and constable, as they'd have done to him if given half a chance? If he could find a bullwhip, should he go that route, instead? It didn't seem that shooting was enough, but maybe if he took his time about it—starting at the knees, say, and proceeding on from there.

A brand-new image came to mind: the fat mayor roasting on a spit, with everyone in town corralled to watch, then lining up to get some barbecue. If they ran short, hell, he could always cook the preacher who'd come by the little jail to lecture him on sin before the marshals hauled him off to Enid.

Tough old bird, that one had been. But with a little salt . . .

Judge Dennison was in his chambers, frowning at a brief submitted by a lawyer who maintained his client had been crazy when he raped a neighbor's daughter on two separate occasions, nineteen days apart. The girl had been ashamed to tell her parents following the first assault, but couldn't hide the second after part of it was witnessed by her little brother. Dennison was grateful to be holding court over the rapist, rather than a father charged with murder, but he'd have someone to hang, regardless.

Halfway through the convoluted written argument, his clerk rapped on the door and stuck his head in. "Sorry to disturb, Your Honor, but a lady's come to speak with you."

"What lady?" Dennison inquired.

"A Miss Faith Connover, Your Honor."

On his feet at once, Dennison ordered, "Show her in, Claude, by all means."

He nearly had his coat on when Faith entered, seeming hesitant. She wore a dress of cobalt blue and had her long black hair pinned up under a little lace-trimmed hat for town.

"I'm sorry to intrude, Judge."

"Not a bit of it. Please, have a seat."

She sat and spent a moment staring at her hands, their fingers tangled in her lap, before she met his eyes and said, "I understand there was some trouble with the transport up to Leavenworth."

The grapevine was a fact of life in Enid, as in every other town. Dennison guessed that one of Faith's hands must have been in town last night, but didn't ask.

"There was, indeed," he said. "I lost one of my marshals, young Guy Hampton. And the prisoners, of course."

"Hampton? I never met him, I'm afraid."

"Just starting out," said Dennison. "And now . . ." He shrugged and let it go.

Faith hesitated at her sticking point, then said, "I also heard that Marshal Slade was injured?" Making it a question, with a pinched look on her face, as if embarrassed for inquiring and afraid of what he'd say.

"That's true," said Dennison, "but from the information I've received, a farmer's wife has treated him—some stitches for a bullet graze—and he's gone hunting for the fugitives."

"Alone?" Her tan complexion seemed to lose a bit of color.

"On his own to start, but I've dispatched a posse to assist him."

"Can they find him, much less get to him in time?"

"That is my hope and their intention," Dennison replied.

"I understand, but honestly . . ." She stopped herself, then said, "I'm sorry. This is really none of my affair."

"Oh, no?"

And now she blushed. "Not anymore, at least," Faith said. "Perhaps the gossip here's a bit behind the times."

"No," Dennison acknowledged. "I did hear rumors that the two of you had parted ways, after the setbacks you've endured."

"Jack hasn't told you anything, himself?"

Dennison shook his head. "Nor would I ask."

"You are a gentleman."

"No matter what they say?" he teased her, in a vain attempt to lift her spirits.

"I don't listen to such prattle."

"Ah."

"If you should hear from Jack . . ." She stopped, frowning, uncertain how to finish it.

"Should I tell him that you asked after him?"

"No! I mean . . . I wouldn't want to make him think . . ." She winced as if the words were painful to her. "There's been no communication since, well, for a while."

"That seems a shame, if you don't mind my saying so."

"It's for the best, I think," she said.

"And not my business to contest it, certainly," the judge replied. "I'll make no mention of your visit, then."

"Thank you. As long as he's all right, that's fine."

"I can't say when he'll be returning, with this pack of jackals running wild."

"It doesn't matter, really."

Meaning the opposite, he thought. And pressing on, he said, "I've heard some talk that you were selling off your place and heading east."

"It's possible. I still haven't decided, finally."

"Well, no point rushing into something that you can't undo, unless you're sure."

She rose, saying, "I've wasted too much of your time already, Judge. Thank you for seeing me."

"My pleasure, ma'am, at any time."

"Good-bye, then."

And she left him with a nagging riddle in his head, unsolved. Frowning, he turned back to the brief that had been penned in vain, to save a rapist's life.

Jack Slade felt like a ghoul, prowling around the farmhouse with its former occupants sprawled out in the front room. He felt time slipping through his fingers, didn't even know for sure what he was looking for, but felt obliged to search the place for any clues that might give him an edge over the so-called men he was pursuing.

Mayfield's crew had left two horses in the yard outside, but precious little in the house. The shambles of a kitchen told Slade they had taken any food that wouldn't rot too quickly on the trail, before they got around to eating it. He noted wall pegs, where a rifle or a shotgun might have hung, but it was long gone now.

He found a butcher's knife someone had dropped and kicked aside, its edge still razor-keen, and wondered about carrying it bare until he had a minor brainstorm, wrapped the long blade in a kitchen towel, and stuffed it in his boot. A knife was always useful, and particularly if there was some quiet work required, too delicate for squeezing off a Springfield thunderclap.

Not that he *planned* on stabbing anybody, but you never knew.

Prowling their bedrooms was the worst, made him ashamed, but it paid off. In a nightstand by the parents' bed, under a Bible, he found a Colt Model 1877 double-action revolver, chambered in .32-20 Winchester, with a box of extra cartridges. Instead of whooping, Slade checked out the pistol's cylinder and found five of its chambers loaded, with an empty underneath the hammer. After loading that to make it six, he stuck the Colt under his belt and took the box of ammo with him as he left the house.

Looting?

He wouldn't venture to deny it, but his need for weapons at the moment superceded any common gesture toward propriety. He muttered, "Sorry" to the huddled corpses, as he left their dying room and stepped back into sunlight, knowing the smell of death would cling to him unless he found someplace to bathe and wash his clothes.

No time for that.

If Mayfield and the others smelled him coming, it could be a foretaste of their fate.

The Colt, although a smaller caliber than Slade was used to, made him feel a little better about going up against five men—or more, for all he knew. That, with the Springfield, gave him seven shots before he had to start reloading either gun. It was his job to take the fugitives alive, if possible, but he would leave that up to them and trust Judge Dennison to understand, if they preferred a fight over another trial.

It might have seemed presumptuous, thinking that he could bag them all without some kind of reinforcements to assist him, and he wasn't counting on it. Couldn't count on *anything,* in fact. Slade only knew it was his job to try and keep on trying, till the issue was decided.

Jail or death, for one side or the other. That was, if he found them, and they didn't just evaporate like some mirage. That was a possibility he didn't want to think about, although he couldn't rule it out.

Some manhunts never ended. Sometimes fugitives escaped and disappeared.

Sometimes the bad men won.

"But not this time," Slade told his gelding. "Not if I have anything to say about it."

He allowed the dapple gray to drink its fill and have some oats, while Slade went back to scout his quarry's trail on foot. As far as he could tell, the raiders had departed on the same course they'd been following since their escape, riding northwestward, more or less.

Slade didn't have a compass with him, or a map of Oklahoma Territory, but he wouldn't need them if the cons kept leaving tracks for him to follow. In addition to the outlaws, now his enemies were rain and wind, or ground so dried and hardened that it wouldn't let him see where they had gone. If nature turned against him now, his cause was lost.

Which didn't mean he'd give it up.

Not even close.

9

 "Why do I have to be a boy out here, where we see no one?"

"I have told you why," Milos Costello answered. "We *might* meet someone. Away from settlements and the police, it's better no one knows that you're a girl."

"Young woman," Esmerelda contradicted him, over a rustling sound of clothing from the rear compartment of their wagon.

"Young woman, then." *And that's the problem,* Milos thought, but kept it to himself. "All the more reason to be careful, eh?"

"I'm tired of traveling. Why can't we find someplace to stay?"

She knew the answer to that question, too, but still harangued him with it. Traveling was in their blood. They were Romanies—"Gypsies" to the settlers they encountered—with their roots in eastern Europe, one foot in the old world and another in the new.

Or, as it often seemed, with both feet on thin ice.

Their reputation went before them, into towns and territories Milos and his daughter might be visiting for the first time. At some point in the past, it seemed, a band of Gypsies had passed by or, possibly, had been imagined in the neighborhood. When chickens and small articles of property went missing, they were easy scapegoats, even if no theft was ever proved. The next group coming through—even a family as small and humble as Costello's—bore the stigma of whatever had been done or fabricated in the past. They were permitted, sometimes, to perform small services or offer certain wares for sale, with the injunction that they move on soon and not return.

So, settle where?

"What is the next town, Papa?"

"Enid."

"That's a funny name."

"A woman's name," he answered, broadening her education one piece at a time. "In Celtic, it means *soul* or *life*."

"How do you know these things?"

"When you're as old as I am," Milos said, "you'll know things, too."

"I know things now."

"But not enough to keep you out of trouble."

"Papa!"

"Take that boy in Wichita, for instance."

"He was handsome," Esmerelda said. "Didn't you think so?"

"Handsome as the Devil," Milos granted. "And about as trustworthy."

"He only kissed me, Papa."

"Thanks to me. Another moment, and I might have been a *puri daj*."

"You'd be a fine grandfather," Esmerelda told him, almost giggling.

"Certainly. But you're not fit to be a mother yet, at your age. Your own mama, rest her soul, would say the same."

"How old was she?"

"When you were born? Just turned eighteen."

"Much younger than yourself, then."

"Much. Five years from now, you find yourself an old Romani gentleman, we'll talk about it."

"Ugh! The old part's bad enough," she said, "but where would I go looking for a gentleman?"

"The gentleman finds *you*," Milos replied. "He makes his pure intentions known to me, your papa."

Esmerelda snorted over that. "Were your intentions pure, when you met Mama?"

"Of course! What else?"

That set them both to laughing, and he hoped that the interrogation was completed for today.

"Papa?"

"Hush, now."

"But—"

"I said *hush*!"

Leaning forward on the driver's seat of their unique and ornate home on wheels, Milos Costello peered into the southern distance.

"What is it, Papa?" She had recognized his worried tone from long experience.

"Riders approaching. I can't count them yet," said Milos. "Are you dressed?"

"I am."

"Hair underneath your hat, none hanging out."

"Yes, Papa."

"And your binding?"

"Papa!"

"Answer me!"

"All done. I told you that I'm dressed."

"And remember not to talk, even if someone speaks to you directly. You're a *mute* boy, yes? Called Luca."

"If I'm a mute, why is my name important?" Acting childish, now.

"Because I say so! Keep your mouth shut, starting now. There are five riders, and I do not like the look of them."

His pistol, a Smith & Wesson Model 3 revolver—often called the Russian Model—lay beside him, underneath a rag that he kept close to wipe the perspiration from his face on long drives in the sun. It was a .44-caliber weapon, a man stopper if he could line up his target.

But what about five?

Milos doubted that he could protect Esmerelda in that case, and he grimaced as a leaden weight of apprehension settled in his stomach.

"Easy, now," he muttered to himself. "Be easy. Wait and see what happens next."

Jack Slade was tired and hurting. Tired of riding, peering at the ground in front of him and making sure he didn't lose the tracks of those he hunted, still proceeding more or less northwestward. Hurting from his head wound and the stitches that had closed it, and his backside from a saddle broken in by someone else, to fit their own. Between those hurts, his stomach grumbled and his lower back was starting to protest the lazy, slouching posture he'd adopted to accommodate his rump.

The dapple gray, by contrast, seemed as if it could go on forever at their present pace.

Which, Slade supposed, might just turn out to be their future.

Another man, he thought, might have surrendered when he woke to find his partner dead, himself afoot and wounded, stripped of his supplies. Or when he stumbled on the homestead massacre that made it six dead now, instead of one—or seven, if he counted Orville Washington, a fugitive-turned-victim. Would a wise man have retreated then, instead of stealing weapons from the dead and pressing on?

Maybe.

"I make no claim to being wise," he told the gelding, trusting it to keep his confidence. "Just stubborn."

One quality he absolutely *did* possess.

"This could be a long haul," he advised the dapple gray, not feeling foolish in the least. "I hope you're ready for it."

When the horse responded with a chuffing sound, Slade took it for a *yes*.

A little bit of wishful thinking never hurt, unless it got confused with stark reality.

He let the conversation lag, sweeping the skyline with his eyes and wishing that he'd brought his spyglass. Trouble was, they hadn't set off hunting anyone at the beginning, and whoever shot him would have swiped it from his saddlebag, regardless. He'd be squinting with the same tired eyes right now, in any case, and wishing that he had *another* telescope.

Nothing stood out on the horizon for as far as he could see, except more prairie broiling underneath the sun. Some clouds had gathered to the west, but Slade couldn't have said if they were blowing his direction or away from him. They didn't look like full-on storm clouds, but he wouldn't mind a sprinkling, just to break the day's fierce heat. He knew the grass was thirsty, and he wouldn't mind if they could happen on a stream before much longer.

Slade preferred a long shot at the fugitives to start, if he could get one, but he'd have to make damn sure who he was shooting at. Judge Dennison would swallow some of them returning draped across their saddles, since they'd killed once of his deputies, but nailing innocent civilians by mistake was something else entirely.

How much farther? If he rode on after dark tonight, what were the odds they'd light a campfire, thinking they were safe? He made it slim to none, against the chance his dapple gray would step into a hole and break its leg, or walk over a prowling rattler in the dark. Not worth it, even though the thought of camping cold a second night, with even less to eat, increased Slade's sense of weariness.

"Long haul," he said again and didn't like the sound of it.

He'd never minded drifting in the past, as long as he was *going somewhere*, but he had no destination this time. Whether Mayfield and the others had one fixed in mind, Slade couldn't say. If so, he only hoped they'd reach it soon and let him overtake them.

Let him pick his time and place. Start settling the score.

Of course, he didn't plan to shoot them all on sight. The law dictated that he had to call them out, identify himself, give them a chance to hoist their hands and take their medicine in court. That was the theory, and he couldn't absolutely rule out some miraculous event—like shock at seeing him alive causing the fugitives to faint dead in their tracks.

One in a million chance of that, Slade thought.

But he'd be ready, come what may.

To haul them back, alive or dead.

"Well, now. What's this I see?"

"Looks like a wagon, Cousin Fergus," Earl suggested.

Jesus wept. "You think so, Earl?" asked Fergus. "Not an elly-fant or gy-raff from the circus, then?"

"I'm purty sure," said Earl, heedless of Reese and Dan both snickering behind him.

"Awright, then," said Fergus. "If you're purty sure, let's us go say hello."

He led the way, taking it easy, unsure what was waiting for them in the covered wagon up ahead. It might just be the driver slouching on his high seat, or there could be half a dozen brawny workmen in the back, all packing pistols, on their way to some new job. He doubted that, from the appearance of the wagon and the man who held the reins, but taking things for granted was the quickest way he knew of getting killed.

"Mornin'," he called out to the wagon's driver, right hand raised and empty to suggest a peaceable intent. The driver nodded back at him but didn't answer, which was just a trifle rude in Mayfield's view.

The lie came to him as they closed the gap to normal talking distance. "Friend, we're lookin' for some convicts what escaped a day or so ago, goin' from Enid up to Leavenworth. You hear about it?"

"Have heard nothing," said the wagon's driver, with some kind of funny accent and a slow shake of his head. "They come this way?"

"We think so," Mayfield strung it out. "Headin' for someplace up the road a piece, called Gilead. You ever been there?"

Just the head shake, this time; no reply.

"You ain't real talkative," said Mayfield, struck by sudden inspiration. "Are you sure you didn't meet them fellas?"

"No, sir."

"'Cause, I'm thinkin' that the reason *why* you ain't too talkative is maybe someone sittin' in the back, there, with a pistol pointed at your melon. Any chance of that?"

"No."

"Then, you won't mind if we have a little look-see for ourselves, eh? Just to satisfy my curiosity?"

"Is only things I sell in one town or another."

"Nothin' to be scairt of, then, is there?"

Mayfield told Tad and Earl to keep the driver covered, then rode forward and along the left side of the wagon, looking at the advertisements painted there for pots, pans, lamps, and such. Some kind of tinker, maybe palming off some snake oil on the side if he could get away with it. Coming to the tailgate of the wagon, Mayfield reached down, opened one of two doors—and recoiled to see a slim kid staring back at him, wide-eyed.

"Say, now," he called out to the driver. "Di'n't you just tell me there's nothin' back here but the stuff you sell? You ain't a slaver, are you? That's illegal, last I heard."

"He is my nephew," said the driver. "When his mother dies, I take him in."

"Right nice of you." Mayfield turned to the youth whose eyes were fastened on his face. "That true, sonny?"

"He cannot hear or speak," the driver said.

"Jesus, a dummy, huh? That's rough." Mayfield rode back up front, leaving the wagon's rear door open. "Now, my friend, we've been out on the road a while, chasin' them cons, and I'm afeared we're runnin' short of cash. In fact, we're just flat broke."

"The sheriff does not pay your salary?" the driver asked.

"He'll pinch a penny till it screams," Mayfield replied. "So, I was thinkin' that you might contribute to our travelin' account. Call it a public service."

"We have very little money, also."

"Still better than none. Why'n't you hand it over."

"It is what we live on," said the driver.

"Problem solved," said Mayfield, as he drew his stolen Peacemaker and shot the driver once, pitching him off the wagon seat. "Somebody get the kid," he told the rest of them. "And find that money."

His cousins got right to it, while Kilgore and Dawkins sat back in their saddles, watching. In another minute, Mayfield heard a girlish voice say, "Take your hands off me!"

"Kid ain't no dummy, Fergus," Tad called out.

He heard a sound of ripping cloth, then Earl piped up. "And somethin' else. He ain't no boy!"

The way Lem Wilkins saw it, no one said he had to kill his horse getting to Gilead. He had to rest the buckskin stallion every couple miles or so, slowed to a walking pace, and let it drink out of his hat, pouring the water from a spare canteen he'd brought along. And he would have to camp that night, of course, since riding in the dark would get him lost—or thrown and laid out with a broken neck.

No, thank you.

The twenty dollars from Judge Dennison was unexpected bounty, but he couldn't blink his eyes and land on Gilead's main street by magic. It was still a two-day ride from Enid, and he'd reach his destination sometime after dark, tomorrow, if his luck held all the way.

The messenger's full name was *Lemuel*. His parents were religious types. They told him it meant *devoted to God*, which wasn't a feeling Lem normally had, even sitting in church on a Sunday. Still, you might say he was doing something on the godlike side, riding to warn the folk of Gilead about the danger that was maybe headed their way.

Maybe.

Wilkins wasn't sure about the story he'd been hired to tell.

It didn't make much sense to him that three tough convicts, freshly broken out of custody, would join a fourth to ride *away* from Mexico and safety to hurrah a town they'd likely never seen. Risk getting caught or shot, just for the hell of it?

Maybe.

But what he *knew* was that he had four days away from normal work, just riding—which he loved to do—and twenty dollars in his pocket, adding up to nearly two weeks' pay from carpentry.

Not bad.

To keep it on the safe side, just in case the cons *were* on their way to Gilead, he'd brought along a pistol he'd been carrying since he had started traveling in search of odd jobs, town to town. It had been made in France, and Wilkins had never learned to pronounce its name correctly, though he could spell it out: Chamelot-Delvigne MAS 1873. He knew the MAS stood for *Manufacture d'armes de Saint-Étienne*, the French maker, since that was engraved on the revolver's barrel. He'd won it in a card game, up in New Madrid, Missouri, with a box of funny cartridges to feed it, and he'd only fired it once, to make sure that it worked. Since then, he'd kept it clean and oiled and out of sight, so nobody would think that he was trying to act tough.

Wilkins wasn't any kind of big-time shooter, but he'd had enough fights on the road to understand that getting in the first lick often made the difference between a beating and a victory. Same principle with gunfighting, presumably, although he wasn't anxious for a chance to try it out, especially against five outlaws all together. If he spotted any bunch like that along his way to Gilead, Lem had decided, he would lie low and avoid them if he could.

They had a head start on him as it was, assuming that

they planned on visiting the little prairie town, but Lem had promised to relay the judge's message. If he got to Gilead too late, well, that was pure bad luck and not his fault, starting so far behind the pack and all. One thing he absolutely *didn't* feel was any obligation to involve himself, if he arrived to find the convicts raising hell in town. There was a constable in Gilead, and others who had caught one of the outlaws in the first place, as he understood it. If they couldn't do the job, how was a simple carpenter supposed to save the day?

"C'mon, Bill," Wilkins told his stallion, giving it a little nudge. "Let's trot another mile or two and gain some time."

He'd never shorted anyone who paid him twenty dollars in the past—not that there'd been a lot of them—and Wilkins wasn't starting now.

"People are funny," Dawkins said.

"You think?" Fergus replied.

"Take this old fart, for instance. Ridin' all over the place, pretendin' that his little filly was a dummy boy."

"Keepin' her to hisself," Kilgore suggested.

"And she just goes along with it? That's what I mean," Reese said. "People are funny."

Already bored and itching to move on, Fergus inquired, "You all find anything of use to us, inside the wagon?"

"Not unless you wanna haul a bunch of pots and shit along behind us," Kilgore said.

"Money?"

"The old man had five dollars and some change," said Dawkins.

"Give it over," Fergus said.

"How come?"

"We gonna have this talk *again*? Because I run this bunch and anyone who's stickin' with it. Are we clear?"

Reese shot a sidelong glance at Kilgore, who was trying to ignore him, then said, "Mebbe I won't stick, then."

"That's no problem," Fergus told him. "But the money stays with me."

For just a second there, he thought that Reese might try his hand. Was ready for him with the lawman's Colt, to make it two kills for the day, but Dawkins shrugged after a second and came over with the greenbacks and some coins in hand.

"Why not?" he said, and passed them off to Fergus with a smile you couldn't trust.

Mayfield accepted it without comment, then asked the others, "Ever'body set?"

"All ready," Tad replied.

"And what about the girl?"

"Uh, well . . ."

"Well, what?"

"I mighta choked her just a little," Earl admitted, "when she started squealin'. It was gettin' on my nerves. And she ain't breathin' now, I guess."

"You guess."

Earl shrugged at him and gave a nervous little smile. "I guess."

"Get back up in that wagon, now, and make damn sure, before we leave."

"Okay!"

Earl pulled his knife, an Arkansas toothpick, and went in through the tailgate, coming back a moment later with some kind of rag in hand, wiping the twelve-inch blade. "All set," he said.

"Mount up, then," Fergus said. "We're wastin' time."

They left the wagon, with its wares and bodies, for some other passerby to find. Maybe the next ones who discovered it would loot the stock, or do the Christian thing and plant the stiffs, whatever might be left of them. No witnesses meant nobody could tie the kills to Mayfield, even if it was suspected.

Not that it mattered, since they'd hang him for the lawmen if he ever let himself go back to jail. Fergus had done what was required to get away, and now it meant a life of running, hiding out, however short or long that was. He'd known what he was getting into when he shot the deputy, and that was fine.

As long as he could settle things in Gilead before manhunters gunned him down or put a noose around his neck.

The way he saw it, dead was *dead*, and how you got there didn't matter much. Given a choice, he'd pick the quickest way available and take a couple of the bastards with him. Leave them knowing they'd been in the worst fight of their lives.

Mayfield was hoping that their latest bit of recreation kept the others quiet till they saw the lights of Gilead, tomorrow night. If not, and Dawkins started in on him again, he was resolved to shut the little weasel up for good. He wouldn't have his new campaign—maybe his *last*— ruined by idjits. Better just to leave them in his dust and press on with his cousins than to haul the excess baggage.

Was the law behind them yet? They still weren't overdue at Leavenworth, but now he almost wished they'd taken time to hide the prison wagon. Too late now, of course, and there could be no turning back.

Full speed ahead, he thought. And wasn't that the only way to go?

10

Slade's headache had returned, rolling around inside his skull like storm clouds trapped inside a cave, with no way to escape. The sun's glare in his eyes made matters worse, and he was squinting with his eyelids narrowed down to slits when he saw something up ahead.

What was it?

Boxy-looking but familiar, even from a distance. Restless movement on the near end, which he took to be the front. A wagon, he decided, sitting in the middle of the prairie with some kind of animals in harness. Likely horses, Slade decided, though it could be oxen. Some of them were still around and used for haulage on outlying farms.

Slowing down the dapple gray, he took his time on the approach. It didn't smell like Mayfield's bunch—there should have been more horses, and you couldn't hide them all behind a wagon—but he wasn't taking any chances. Closing in, Slade had his right hand on the round butt of his Colt, finger inside its trigger guard, prepared to draw and fire immediately if it proved to be some kind of trap.

From fifty yards, Slade knew that wasn't right. There was a man's boot sticking up out of the foot well, underneath the driver's seat, no place that anyone in his right mind would choose for napping in. The horses watched Slade dolefully as he approached, not shying, as if they had given up on any thought of rescue and resigned themselves to standing there until they dropped from thirst.

Passing the wagon, Colt in hand now, Slade glanced down into the driver's foot well, where a man of middle age lay huddled, blood already drying rusty brown against the denim background of his shirt. A few steps further took Slade to the wagon's tailgate, where a set of double doors stood open on a nightmare.

The odd thing was that seeing her—what Mayfield's pigs had left of her—immediately cured Slade's headache. Some kind of shock, perhaps, though he'd seen worse. Maybe the killing rage that blurred his vision for a heartbeat then edged back to leave it crystal clear, racing through Slade's body like the caffeine kick from strong black coffee.

He couldn't guess her age, exactly. She'd been caught somewhere between the awkwardness of childhood and the flowering that likely would have made her beautiful, if she'd survived. Now she was broken, with her spark snuffed out, and the expression on her pale face told Slade that she'd had a glimpse of Hell.

Slade didn't want to touch her, but he couldn't leave her as she was, exposed to any passerby or scavenger that caught a whiff of death. Dismounting, he reluctantly climbed up into the wagon, eyes averted from the corpse, and found some bolts of cloth shelved to his left, presumably for sale in towns the wagon visited. Slade chose a plain dark blue, pulled down enough to cover her, and cut it with the butcher knife he carried in his boot.

He'd barely finished tucking in the dead girl when he heard a moaning mutter from the general direction of the driver's seat. Advancing past the wares that lay and hung around him, Slade edged forward, peered over the driver's seat, and found the man he'd given up for dead regarding him with narrowed, almost glassy eyes. They seemed to focus on Slade's badge. His lips moved, made another sound that Slade couldn't identify.

He moved in closer, clambering over the wooden seat and kneeling on it, bending closer to the nearly dead man. "What was that?" Slade asked.

"Daugh-ter."

Slade glanced back toward the covered form behind him, judging that a lie could do no harm.

"I think she'll be all right," he said.

"I heard . . ."

"Don't think about that now. How many men were in on this?"

"Fi-five."

The outfit still together, then, and that meant there had only been one sniper in the shadows when they hit Slade's camp. What else to ask, while time remained?

"Did they say anything about where they were headed?"

"After something." Barely the suggestion of a whisper now. "At Guh . . . Guh . . ."

Goldsby? That was in the wrong direction, for a long ride south. *Goodwell?* Way out in the western panhandle. Or maybe—

"Gilead." A fading gasp.

And he was gone.

At noon, Judge Dennison walked down to Slawson's Funeral Parlor, to identify Guy Hampton's body. The wounds he'd suffered last year, in a shooting at the courthouse, pained him some and made him thankful that he'd brought his walking stick along. He had postponed his midday meal, thinking an empty stomach might be beneficial on this errand, and the smell that stung his nostrils as he entered, still detectable in spite of scented candles, proved he'd made the right decision.

Milo Slawson bore a vague resemblance to a giant praying mantis: he was tall, thin, balding, with a sharp face and a way of standing with his pale, long-fingered hands clasped at his midsection, as if praying or preparing to applaud. He always had the proper solemn air, and never dressed in anything but black, making himself a living advertisement for his trade.

"Good afternoon, Judge. Please accept my most sincere condolences. You've come to view your deputy?"

"I have."

The bald head bobbed. "This way, please."

Dennison had tried to brace himself for anything. He'd been around and seen corpses on a battlefield during the War Between the States, and he had viewed the aftermath of murder as a jurist. This was different, somehow, seeing a young man he'd known personally, after nature had attempted to reclaim him.

"This is all from vultures?" Dennison inquired, masking a grimace as he studied Hampton's ravaged face.

"Primarily," Slawson replied. "I can't rule out predation

by some other scavengers, before his body was secured inside the wagon. Even then, of course, the insects—"

"Yes. I see."

"We'll clean him thoroughly, of course, but I'm afraid an open casket would be ill-advised."

The judge's legal mind took over. "He was shot, I take it?"

"Yes, sir. In the head, here," Slawson told him, pointing. "And the chest, approximately . . . here."

"Approximately?"

"With the scavengers, you understand . . ."

"All right. It's definitely murder, then."

"Oh, yes. I'd say so, absolutely, in the given circumstances."

"There's no way that a lawyer could pretend it was an accident, or suicide?" asked Dennison, already looking down the long road toward a trial.

"I never heard of anyone shot twice by accident," Slawson replied. "Perhaps in hunting season, thick woods, if he walked into a cross fire. Not in this case."

"And the other?"

"Suicide? I had a man once who *did* shoot himself, apparently because he couldn't stand the pain of a preceding wound. With Mr. Hampton, I can say the chest shot should have been debilitating, ultimately fatal. I would rate the chances of him having strength enough to make the head shot somewhere close to zero."

"Fair enough. The court will cover all your costs."

Another quick head bob, as Dennison retreated from the undertaker's operating room, out through the front room of his shop, and back onto the street. He didn't feel like eating now, thought for an instant that he'd never want another meal again, but that was foolish. People get through anything, he knew from long experience. The pain might never go away entirely, but for most, it faded over time until remembering took effort and the images that haunted you were largely relegated to the world of dreams.

Or nightmares.

Dennison wished he would hear from Slade, if nothing else to let him know his other deputy was still alive and hadn't fallen off his borrowed horse somewhere, after he left the Larson spread. The posse was en route to help him—that, assuming they could *find* Slade in the first place, or pick up the convicts' trail.

And in the meantime, Slade was on his own, wounded, hurting, no doubt mad as hell about Guy Hampton, maybe suffering additional distraction from whatever he had going on with Faith. Dennison's pledge was to uphold the laws of the United States, meaning that criminal defendants had a list of basic rights they had been guaranteed as citizens, at birth. The right to trial before a jury of their peers, and to be hanged like sides of beef once they had been convicted in a lawman's death.

But, damn it, if they came back dead, he might not feel like splitting hairs.

"Remind me what we're s'pose to do with these men if we find them," Jubal Leach requested.

"That depends on them," Mike Bowers said, over his shoulder, from the posse's point position. "If they give up, we arrest them. If they don't . . . do what you have to do."

"I never shot a man before," Leach said.

"None of us have, 'cept maybe Ed," Floyd Dooley said.

"That's just a rumor," Ed Schultz answered back.

"I should have listened to my wife." A mutter from Vance Underwood.

Bowers stopped short, half turned his sabino mare, and faced the others. "Listen up, now. You can turn back any time. Just ride on back to town and tell Judge Dennison you were mistaken, thinking you had balls enough to follow through."

"Hey, *I'm* not quittin'," Schultz declared. "It beats throwin' a bunch a sloppy drunks outta the Lucky Strike."

"I'm sticking," Dooley said. "Nice break from shovelin' that horse shit at the livery."

"Jubal?" Bowers prodded, focused on one of the town's anomalies: a barber as bald as an egg.

"I never mentioned quittin', did I?" Leach replied.

"Just you, then, Vance," said Bowers. "If it's *adios*, you'd better start back now, while there's still light."

"And be the only one gets tagged a yellow belly? How'd that be for business?" asked the shopkeeper.

"I guess you'd have to wait and see," Bowers replied.

"No, no. I'm with you," Underwood acknowledged. "To the bitter end."

Deputy Bowers couldn't blame the four civilians for their qualms. They'd had a good look at Guy Hampton, what was left of him, before Bowers had found the outlaws' tracks and got them pointed in the right direction, traveling northwestward. They were making decent time now, but without a clue as to their final destination.

Prior to leaving Enid, Bowers and Judge Dennison had talked about the possibility of riding straight to Gilead, trying to head the convicts off, but Dennison still wasn't sure about the one con, Mayfield, making good on what he'd said in court. The truth be told, it sounded like a long shot, and they'd look like fools for camping out in one place while the fugitives ran riot somewhere else or gave them all the slip for good.

His posse wasn't much to look at, Bowers realized, and

he could understand why they were worried about facing off with hardened criminals. He would have much preferred four other marshals, even two or three, but none had been available. That was the consequence of being spread so thin over a territory larger than some foreign countries.

At least the men he had were armed, all but Dooley with rifles, and he had a .45-caliber Colt Model 1878 double-action revolver with a seven-inch barrel. Any one of them could drop a man if they held steady and remembered not to jerk their triggers. Then again, he'd never seen a neat and tidy showdown, so the odds were stacked toward something going wrong.

Bowers had killed two men himself, in stand-up fights, and winged another from a distance, trying to escape. It wasn't something that excited him, but he'd been lucky and had lost no sleep over the shootings. Part of manhunting was bringing down your quarry when the time came, by whatever means you had available. On this hunt, Bowers didn't think pulling a trigger would be any problem.

None at all.

"See that?" Schultz called to Bowers, from the middle of the pack.

"Got it."

A wheel of buzzards circled in the sky, a mile or so ahead of them. Bowers picked up his pace, the others following his lead. He'd heard Jack Slade was wounded when the cons killed Hampton, and his stomach tightened at the prospect of another half-devoured marshal's corpse.

It wasn't Slade, though, as he realized from thirty yards. One of the convicts, and unless he missed his guess, it was the colored one. A little hard to tell, between the damage done by scavengers and blackening from natural decomposition underneath the prairie sun, but Bowers would have bet a week's pay that they'd stumbled onto Orville Washington.

"That one of 'em?" asked Dooley.

"Washington, I'm pretty sure," Bowers replied.

"You plan to bury him?" asked Schwartz.

"Hell, no." Bowers began to steer his mare around the corpse. "We need to find the ones who left him here."

Faith Connover saw Judge Dennison emerge from Slawson's Funeral Parlor, pausing on the sidewalk for a squint into the midday sun, then watched him walk back toward the courthouse in the heart of town. He hadn't seen her coming out of Arnie Sundberg's dry-goods store, and that was fine. She'd been uncomfortable speaking to him in his chambers, wished in retrospect that she had never gone to see him, but she couldn't take it back. The word that Jack Slade had been wounded, maybe seriously, had evoked a host of feelings that she'd tried to put away, bringing them back full force.

After talking to the judge, she knew that Jack was injured, but still strong enough to keep on hunting for the fugitives who'd killed their other escort on the trip to Kansas. Faith had no idea how Slade had managed to survive, but he was good at that. It seemed to be his specialty.

He had survived hunting the men who killed his brother—Faith's fiancé at the time, before she'd known that Jim Slade was a twin—and Jack had helped *her* to survive a run-in with the same men, when they'd kidnapped her for ransom. After that, it seemed to Faith that every time she turned around there was another scrape, some life-or-death decision Jack was forced to make within the time it took to blink.

Or draw a gun.

Slade wasn't just a born survivor. Those who tried to put him down had learned the hard way that he took some extra killing. She and Jack had both come close to dying on their almost-wedding day, and even gravely wounded, he had come back strong enough to track the shooters down to Mexico, eliminating most of them along the way, bringing the main ringleader back to hang in Enid.

That had been the last straw. Faith had broken off with Jack, told him that she was selling out and heading east, no destination named. She wouldn't talk to him beyond delivering the news that they were finished, and another job had called him out of town before Faith realized that she was pregnant. She had told Jack, when he made it back to town, believing that he had the right to know, but she wanted nothing further from him. Made it clear—or so she thought—that she neither required nor wanted any help.

And now?

"It's good to see you, Faith. How are you?"

Nancy Sizemore, passing with a wicker shopping basket on one arm, her smile stuck somewhere in between concern and curiosity.

"Fine, Nancy. And yourself?"

A litany of minor woes ensued, Faith nodding through it, making little sounds when Nancy paused for breath, as if she was absorbing every word. The other woman was a lawyer's wife, with two fine healthy children, but she never failed to register complaints about the weather, crowding on the streets, or clients who were slow to pay their bills, the gossips at her church, the hours Aaron spent in court or at his office—everything, in fact, that was the part and parcel of her life. The fact that she seemed happy while complaining made it stranger, still.

"So, what's been happening with you?"

"Oh," Faith replied, "nothing worth mentioning."

"You're all recovered from . . . your injuries?"

"I'm fine," Faith said, although she still felt twinges from the bullet scars at times: mounting a horse, lifting some heavy object at the ranch.

Thinking of Jack.

Sleeping alone.

"I can't imagine how you . . . Well, I mean, it must have just been *terrifying*."

"Nancy, it's been good to see you. I have some appointments, and—"

"Of course! Don't let me keep you. We can talk another time."

"I'm looking forward to it," Faith lied, with a smile.

"And tell your handsome man hello, from me."

"I will," Faith said and passed along Main Street, trying to remember where she'd meant to go.

Slade freed the horses from their harness, set the wagon's water barrel down for them to drink from as they pleased, and left them to their own devices otherwise. The prairie would supply them all the grass they needed, and he guessed they had a fairly decent chance of being found by someone passing by. Better than starving in their traces, anyway, and Slade had no intention of destroying them himself.

His bullets all were spoken for.

He had no sense of how long Mayfield's gang had spent with the young woman in the wagon. Hating to believe she'd been alive to feel a minute of it, on the other hand, he thought she might have bought some time for him—and hated thinking that, as well. Not for the first time, Slade wondered if he was turning into something like the animals he hunted, human in his aspect, although less than civilized in fact.

It might be best for all concerned, Slade thought, if Faith went east and kept their baby from him. What could he contribute to the raising of a normal child? Suspicion? Cynicism? Skill at reading faces in a poker game? The tricks of drawing fast and shooting straight enough to stay alive?

It could be providential if his son or daughter never knew a thing about him. Faith could spin a story out of gossamer and daydreams, build him up into the man he should have been, and fabricate some fine, heroic reason for his absence from their lives. Perhaps he'd been a sea captain and went down with his ship, saving the passengers and crew. Or what about a doctor dedicated to his patients, carried off by some disease he'd caught from one of them, while healing dozens more?

"A bunch of bullshit," he informed the dapple gray, who didn't seem to care.

Slade cleared his mind of Faith and thought ahead to Gilead. He'd never been there, but he knew approximately where it was. Northwest, the same direction Mayfield and his thugs had been proceeding since their getaway. Slade had not attended Fergus Mayfield's trial, knew nothing of his parting threat against the town where he'd been captured, and he wouldn't have expected Mayfield to make good on it, in any case.

No matter.

If the cons were heading up to Gilead, it gave Slade's search a focus. Still compelled to follow them, in case they changed their minds, at least he had a sort of terminus in mind for his pursuit. A chance to catch up with the riders when they stopped, instead of chasing them forever, always half a day behind.

Better than nothing, anyway.

And help was coming. Slade believed that, even if he couldn't peg the time or day when reinforcements would arrive. If they were late, and he found Mayfield's bunch in Gilead while he was still alone, so be it. He would tackle them himself, rather than sit and wait, risk watching them escape a second time.

A town meant cover, maybe even people who would help him, if they weren't somehow allied with Mayfield. *That* would be a problem, but he couldn't picture it, a whole community in league with killer convicts on the run. Maybe a friend or two, but when had outlaws ever had a town to call their own?

He'd have to watch his step, tread softly, maybe mask his badge until he got a feeling for the place and found out what was going on. See if the convicts planned to hide a while and then move on, or maybe settle in. If that turned out to be the case, he'd try to catch them all together, penned up somehow. Offer them an ultimatum, standing ready when they came out fighting.

With some townsfolk helping?

Wait and see.

The one thing that he absolutely *didn't* want to do was spark some kind of Main Street massacre with innocent civilians in the cross fire. He'd be better off to creep in close and use the butcher knife, rather than turning Gilead into a bloody free-for-all.

One thing Slade knew for sure.

If he found Mayfield and the rest in Gilead, he meant for it to be their last stop on the road.

11

"Can't rightly say I like the look of this," Floyd Dooley said.

"Seems awful quiet," Jubal Leach observed.

"Be careful going in," Mike Bowers cautioned all of them. "But don't get trigger-happy. You don't want to kill some farm kid coming out to feed the chickens."

"I don't see no chickens, Marshal," Dooley answered.

"Just the same."

They rode in five abreast, strung out across the plain, so anybody watching from the farmhouse could observe and count them, but without making an easy, clumped-up target. Every one of them was ready with the guns they'd brought, and Bowers desperately hoped that none would suffer an attack of nerves, start shooting at livestock—or worse, at innocent homesteaders.

Where *was* the livestock?

Bowers scanned the spread again, and saw a horse emerging from behind the barn. Another followed, grazing lazily.

He couldn't swear to it, but Bowers thought they looked a lot like the dray animals that had been harnessed to the prison wagon when it first rolled out of Enid, bound for Leavenworth. Which meant the fugitives had been there, and had traded mounts for any horses that the farmer had on hand.

And what else had they done?

From sixty yards, he shouted out, "Hello, the house! Is anybody home?"

No answer, and he saw the front door to the farmhouse standing open now. That had to be a bad sign, in the circumstances, and he drew his Winchester out of its saddle boot, preparing for whatever happened next. A part of him already knowing they were too damned late to do the farmer and his family any good.

They reined up in the dooryard, everyone uneasy, none adept at hiding it. No one would move, Bowers supposed, unless he set them to it.

"Floyd," he said, "take Vance and check the barn."

"What're we lookin' for?" asked Dooley.

"Anything that don't seem right."

"What *does* seem right about this place?" Ed Schultz inquired.

Bowers ignored the question. "I'll check the house. Rest of you cover me, and make damn sure that you don't shoot me coming out."

A couple of them cocked their rifles, *click-clack* in the quiet yard. Bowers dismounted, taking his Winchester with him on his slow walk to the open farmhouse door. He paused, before stepping into the porch's shade, and once again addressed the silent house.

"If anybody's in there, I'm a U.S. marshal. These men are my deputies. We're here to help you if there's been some trouble."

Bowers caught the smell of death before he reached the threshold, nearly turned around, but it was his job to observe, remember, and report. Whatever had been done here, by the fleeing fugitives, it must be tabulated, added to their butcher's bill.

Inside, with daylight bright and hot behind him, Bowers had to stop and let his eyes adjust. The only sounds he heard were horses shifting nervously outside, and creaking from his own weight on the floorboards. His nose led him to turn and face a portion of the family room that had been turned into a slaughterhouse.

"Jesus!"

His own voice startled Bowers, nearly made him jump. Instead, he stood rock-still and took in everything, each detail, so he could describe it later to Judge Dennison, and to a jury if it came to that. Five dead, and he could understand the killing, if you didn't want to leave a witness. But for God's sake, who would do the rest of it to children? To a little girl?

He pictured Fergus Mayfield and the others, kicking at the end of slow ropes, no clean drop to make it easy for them. Let it take a quarter of an hour, strangling slowly— or, would he be able to resist the clean shot when he had them in his sights? Did animals like that deserve another trial, at taxpayers' expense?

Bowers knew what Judge Dennison would say, but at the moment, wasn't sure he cared.

When every detail of the massacre was burned into his memory, he warned the men outside, "I'm coming out." Daylight was painful in a way it hadn't been before, making him squint and grimace.

"Well?" asked Schultz, the bouncer.

"Five dead in there," Bowers replied. "We've come too late."

"We gonna bury 'em?"

"No time," said Bowers, mounting his sabino mare. "They've killed seven people that we know of, in a day, and something tells me they're just warming up."

The trick was making decent time, without running his horse into the ground. Slade wasn't sure about the dapple gray's endurance, though it hadn't gotten winded yet from galloping a mile or so in spurts, trying to shave his quarry's lead.

To kill time, Slade considered what he knew of Gilead. A small town in the Oklahoma panhandle, not known for much of anything. Good grazing land, and maybe they were hoping for a railroad spur to make it worth their while with cattle, but it hadn't happened yet and maybe never would. Building a life out on the prairie was a gamble at the best of times. Towns had been known to wither up and blow away, leaving a sour memory and little else.

Slade knew that Fergus Mayfield had been caught in Gilead, trying to rob the small bank there, and lost a couple of his cronies in the process when the town rose up against them. Other marshals had escorted him to Enid for his trial, while Slade was on another job, but Mayfield's reputation had preceded him. Now that he thought about it, Slade remembered talk of Mayfield threatening revenge against the townies who had bagged him, but how many convicts followed through on big talk in a courtroom?

Maybe one was all it took.

Nine dead so far, within a day of Mayfield and the others busting loose. How many homesteads lay between the gang and Gilead, if that turned out to be their destination?

Would they stop and plunder each one that they found along the way?

That kind of thing would slow them down, might help Slade overtake them, but at what cost in the blood of innocents? And if the fugitives reached Gilead—what, then? The odds would be against them, forty-some to one, but Slade had seen the kind of damage that determined, ruthless men could do amidst the population of a civilized community. The town's inhabitants had proved their mettle once, but had that been a fluke, or could they pull it off again?

Slade didn't know, and hoped they wouldn't have to try. If he could overtake the gang before they got that far . . .

He would be running short of food soon, hadn't pressed the Larsons for enough to keep him more than two days on the trail. Slade wasn't worried about starving, but he'd have to keep his eye out for a stream along the way, replenish his canteen with water for the gelding and himself. As for the men he hunted, Slade had no idea how much they'd taken from the homestead they had plundered, or the wagon he'd found earlier that day. For all he knew, they might be carrying enough food for a week or more.

Or were they riding light, counting on a reward in Gilead?

"By God," he told the dapple gray, "I wish you had a pair of wings."

There'd been a flying horse in certain stories that his mother used to read, when Slade and brother Jim were small. In ancient Greece, he thought that might have been, but couldn't recollect the horse's name or much about its various adventures. Something with a dragon and a golden fleece, if you could feature that. All fantasy, of course, and no damn good to Slade at all in Oklahoma Territory, tracking mad-dog killers on the run.

No, scratch that. Mad dogs couldn't help themselves. They had no choice but to run wild, snapping at anyone who crossed their path. A human being made decisions during every waking moment, chose to work and build a life or tear things down and make each day a misery for others. Either way, people were held accountable and had to settle up for what they'd done, before they shuffled off the planet to oblivion.

And when they broke the law within his jurisdiction, it was Slade's job to collect the tab.

Lem Wilkins wasn't sure if he should be relieved or apprehensive as the town of Gilead came into view ahead. Relief came from the thought of finishing his long ride and delivering his message, then relaxing for a while before he started back to Enid. Apprehension sprang from wondering if he'd arrived too late and was about to ride into a hornet's nest.

"Only one way to find out," he told himself.

Before proceeding into town, Lem checked his pistol, making sure that all six chambers of its cylinder were loaded, then returned it to the spot under his belt that he'd selected for a cross-hand draw if any kind of shooting was required. That done, he urged his buckskin stallion forward, watching as dusk lowered and the lamps in town were lit.

Not much to look at, Lem remembered, from his last visit to Gilead, and nothing much had changed as far as he could see. Maybe some new paint on the hardware store, but nothing else stood out. Of course, he hadn't paid that much attention, stopping for a meal and a cold beer before he kept on going southward. There'd been nothing in the small town that appealed to him, particularly. Nothing that had beckoned him to stick around.

He found the marshal's office, but the door was locked up tight, no light or other sign of life inside. That stymied Lem, whose next thought was to ask at the saloon, but Gilead didn't appear to have one. Beer was offered at the town's lone restaurant, and he considered barging in there, interrupting people in the midst of eating supper, but a merchant saved him the embarrassment, emerging at that very moment from his shop next door.

Lem approached him with a twinge of trepidation, never easy when he had to break the ice with strangers. "'Scuse me, sir," he said. "There any chance that you could tell me where'd I find your law this time of day?"

"I would imagine Coop's gone home."

"Coop?"

"Marshal Declan Cooper."

"And when you say home . . ."

"North end of Main Street. Yellow house."

"Appreciate it. Thank you kindly."

Lem decided he was tired of riding, so he walked his buckskin two blocks to the marshal's house and the picket fence serving as a hitching post. His nervous agitation spiked as he approached the yellow house and rapped on its white door.

The man who answered wasn't stout, exactly, but he wasn't missing any meals. He had a florid face—whether from temper, sun, or liquor, Wilkins didn't know and wasn't keen to learn. He wore no badge or gun, but Lem supposed he wasn't likely to, in his own home.

"Beggin' your pardon. Are you Marshal Cooper?"

"Yes. And you are . . . ?"

"Wilkins. Lem. Just in from Enid, with a message from Judge Dennison."

Frowning, the marshal asked, "And what's your message, Mr. Lem?"

Not wanting to correct him, maybe get off on the wrong foot at the start, Lem answered, "Fergus Mayfield's busted out of custody, together with some others. They was on their way to Leavenworth, from what I understand, and someone helped 'em jump the deputies. Kilt one of 'em and lit out, goin' who knows where. Judge Dennison remembered somethin' Mayfield said in court, that sounded like a threat against your town, and here I am."

"You think they're coming here?"

Lem had to shrug at that. "Don't know, sir. And I got the feelin' that the judge wasn't entirely sure, hisself. Figured you oughta have a warnin', just in case."

"And when did they escape?"

"The night before last, that would be. Judge sent me straight away, next mornin'."

"You say four of them broke out?"

"Yes, sir. Plus one or two, at least, to help 'em. Judge was fuzzy on the numbers."

"Six or seven, anyway," the marshal said, and Lem got the impression he was talking to himself. "You think that they'd risk coming here? With posses hunting for them?"

"That I couldn't say. Guess it depends on how bad Mayfield hates your town."

"Who are the others?"

Flustered, Lem said, "Sorry. No one filled me in on that. I know one was a colored boy."

That didn't seem to ring a bell with Cooper. "Right," he said at last and fished a silver dollar from his trouser pocket, handing it to Lem. "Go on and get yourself a hot meal. If you're staying over, tell them at the hotel and the livery, the town will cover it."

"Yes, sir! I thank you kindly!"

Lem got out of there before the lawman started asking any further questions. He could hear his stomach grumbling as he headed for the livery, already focused on a fat, rare steak.

Another night, another camp, and Fergus felt the others getting restless. Not his cousins, who would follow anywhere he led without complaint, but Reese and Danny Boy. Their sporting with the old man's daughter had worn off by now, and they were thinking with their brains again, what there was of them. Neither of them fancied taking orders, though it chafed less when they wound up getting paid or having access to a woman. What he had to do, right now, was either keep them focused or get rid of them entirely, so his mind and hands were free to do their work in Gilead.

"Tomorrow, early," he announced.

"Tomorrow, early *what*?" asked Kilgore.

"Gilead," Fergus replied. "We ought to be there."

"Finally," said Dawkins. "Then, what?"

"Then, you find out how it feels to own a town, with ever'body at your beck and call."

"Or how it feels to get our asses shot to hell," Kilgore suggested.

"Don't you fret. We'll catch 'em with their trousers down," said Fergus. "By the time they know what's happening, we'll have it all sewed up."

"You said they got a bank. What else?" Dawkins inquired.

"Some stores. They'll all have money in the till."

"How 'bout saloons?" asked Kilgore.

"Nope. They got a restaurant serves beer, though."

"Jesus, what's a town without saloons?"

"No whorehouse, then, I guess," said Dawkins, sounding glum.

"Just wives and daughters," Fergus said. "Yours for the taking, once we've got the men in hand."

That set the pair of them to whispering and gave him time to think. Looking ahead, the fantasy unfolding in Mayfield's mind. This time, he took it further, though, because he planned on living after he was done in Gilead. Maybe out west, where no one knew his face or name. Maybe in Canada, although he'd never been that fond of snow. His last resort was Mexico, where he would have to learn the lingo if he meant to stay for long, but how hard could it be?

Choices. Exactly what you *didn't* have in prison.

The self-righteous folks in Gilead had tried to steal his choices from him, and they were about to learn how that felt when the shoe was on the other foot. And if he made their little town a legend in the process . . . well, too bad they wouldn't be around to celebrate. Maybe their ghosts could have a party in the ruins, after he'd moved on.

A *real* ghost town. The prospect made him smile.

"What's funny, Cousin Fergus?" Earl inquired.

"Funny?"

"You're laughin'."

"Was I?" Fergus guessed he must have been. "Just thinkin' about all the fun we'll have tomorrow, puttin' stodgy little bastards in their place."

"I hope their wives ain't stodgy," Dawkins said, getting a laugh from Kilgore.

"Or their daughters," Kilgore said, still snickering.

"May have to stick around a day or two, we wanna get to all of them," said Dawkins.

Fergus let them ramble on. When he was finished with
the work he planned to do in Gilead, the rest of them could
stay or go, as they saw fit. If Reese and Danny Boy wanted
to hang around until a posse overtook them, that was fine.
His cousins, too, for all that Fergus cared. They'd served
their purpose, helping him escape, and family had never
meant that much to him, for starters.

Blood *was* thicker than water for some, he supposed.
But ever since he'd learned to spill it, as a youngster, Fergus hadn't cared much for the ties that bind. After tomorrow, or the next day, he'd be fancy-free and off to find
himself a brand-new life.

As soon as he had settled up old scores.

Slade wondered if he ought to risk a fire tonight, but then
decided not to bother, since he had nothing to cook. He'd
found a campsite with a spring, some grass, no snakes in evidence, and made a frugal meal of what remained from Katherine Larson's generosity, leaving enough to get him started
in the morning. Still not sure exactly how far he remained
from Gilead, Slade hoped to reach it before midday.

If the convicts he was tracking didn't pass it by.

In that case, Slade supposed that he could stop in for
supplies, spend what he had to get enough food for another
day or two, and get back on their trail. It would mean losing
time, but that couldn't be helped. Slade had to keep up
strength enough to face the men he hunted, if and when he
found them, and he couldn't do that if his ride turned into
a starvation trek.

And if the gang was bound for Gilead, so much the
better.

Slade had no plan in his mind for dealing with the five of

them. It wasn't something he could think through in advance, without knowing the layout of the town, what time he'd get there, or how members of the gang might be preoccupied. Surprise was key, of course, whenever one man had to deal with five. Beyond that basic understanding, though, he drew a blank.

Give them a chance, or come in shooting? That depended on the circumstances: whether they were all together when he found them, wide-awake or drunk and dozing, with their weapons handy or beyond an easy reach. There had to be a jail in Gilead, since Mayfield had been locked up there before his trial in Enid, but it wouldn't be a picnic, getting five men in a cell when they all knew a rope was waiting for them.

So, shoot first and make it count. Take no unnecessary chances with the men who'd killed Guy Hampton and the others he'd found scattered on their trail. Slade wouldn't let his anger over what they'd done, the lives they'd ruined, rush his hand or spoil his aim. And maybe he'd keep Faith in mind, to help him through the worst bits, since he couldn't seem to help it anyway.

Slade wasn't sure that he could sleep, but managed anyway. By moonrise he was dreaming of a life he'd never had, and as it seemed now, that he never would. And if he woke to sadness on a killing day, it was unlikely he'd remember why.

12

"My point is that we don't *know* if he's coming back or not," Clint Hilker said. "Why send the town into an uproar till we're sure?"

"I'd say that's pretty obvious," Mayor Hardy Lowman answered. "By the time we're sure, the whole damn bunch of them will be here, and it's too late to prepare."

"We only have this stranger's word that anybody's coming," said Lloyd Mortimer, proprietor of Gilead's Rosecrest Hotel.

"Judge Dennison wouldn't have sent him if he didn't think there was a danger," Marshal Cooper said.

Hilker was unconvinced. "I don't like getting everybody up in arms."

"You do know what *prepare* means, don't you?" Lowman asked him. "It's defined as getting ready in advance, not after trouble comes along and blows your house down."

"Do not speak to me like I'm some kind of half-wit child," Hilker replied. "You want me handing guns and ammunition out like party favors to a bunch of nervous people who could turn this town into a shooting gallery."

A flush of color rose in Lowman's cheeks. "I'm simply trying to explain that—"

Simon Woodley's baritone cut through the argument. "You know I've got more reason to be worried about Fergus Mayfield than the rest of you," he said. "It was my bank he tried to rob. His friends died on the sidewalk, right outside, with bags of money in their grimy hands. I testified against him, just like Cooper, here. I hate to think about him coming back, but does it seem that likely?"

"He made threats against the town," said Lowman.

"True enough," the banker granted. "But he's broken out of prison now—or, anyway, a prison wagon—and he's killed a U.S. marshal in the bargain. Do you think he'd risk a hanging, coming back to mess with us, when he could run for Mexico instead? And what about these others, running with him?"

"What about 'em?" Cooper asked him.

"Think about it," Woodley said. "Four men break out, and only one of them has ever been to Gilead, as far as we know. Let's say Mayfield *was* bent on revenge, when running makes more sense. Why would the others play along and risk their lives to help him?"

"All I know," Mayor Lowman said, "is that I have a duty to the people of this town. When they elected me—"

"It's not the time for campaign speeches, Hardy."

"Will you let me finish, Lloyd?"

Mortimer rolled his eyes, but answered, "Go ahead, then. Make your point."

"I have a duty to perform, the same as Declan. The protection of this town is our concern. If you all don't believe there's any threat—"

"No *proven* threat," said Hilker.

"—then you're free to wait and see what happens next. But when that gang rides into town—"

"*If* they ride into town," Mortimer said.

"—you'll find it's too damned late to run around alerting people to the danger. If you think it's wrong to take precautions, then do nothing. That's the easy way."

"I never said *do nothing*," Hilker said. "I just don't think that passing rifles out to all and sundry is a wise idea."

"So, what would *you* do?" Lowman asked the hardware merchant.

"Deputize a couple men and have them watch the roads. Sound the alarm if Mayfield shows his face."

"And *then* what?" Cooper interjected.

"Then, we deal with him," said Woodley. "Like the last time. No one had to raise an army when those three were in my bank. The town just rallied on its own."

"I say we vote on it," the mayor replied. "A show of hands. Who wants to arm the town and be prepared?"

He raised his own hand, and the marshal followed suit. The other three sat still, Hilker shaking his head.

"All right, you win," said Lowman. "And God help us if you're wrong."

"So, today's the day," Reese Dawkins said.

"It better be," Kilgore replied. "We coulda been damn near to Mexico by now."

"And Mexico'll still be there next week."

"The question is, will we?"

"I didn't take you for the nervous sort."

"I ain't," said Kilgore. "And I ain't the stupid sort, neither."

"You takin' off, then?"

"I been thinkin' back to what we talked about."

Meaning the breakaway. Dawkins finished cinching up the flank strap on his stolen palomino's saddle, straightened with a creaking from his spine, and turned to watch the Mayfields breaking camp. He wasn't sure that Earl and Tad could claim a single brain between them, but the thought of bracing Fergus, with the pair of them behind him, set his teeth on edge.

"This likely ain't the best time," he told Kilgore.

"Nope. But do you think we'll have a better time, today?"

"Maybe in Gilead. Things go like Fergus says, there's bound to be confusion. If it looks like it's goin' sour on us, we could likely slip away and no one be the wiser."

"Well . . ."

"Or try our luck against 'em now," he said, keeping his voice low-pitched. "You wanna do that, we should just start shootin'. No point sayin' anything to tip 'em off."

"Just shoot 'em in the back."

"Keep them from shootin' us in front," said Dawkins.

Kilgore thought about it for a moment, frowning, then decided. "Naw. I reckon not."

"We ride on with 'em, then?"

"I guess."

Relieved, Dawkins told Kilgore, "If you change your mind, just give a wink or whistle, and I'm with you."

"Good to know."

"You two 'bout ready?" Fergus called across the campsite, as he swung into his saddle. "Well, hustle up. We've got a couple hours' ride to Gilead, from what I calculate. Quicker we get to town, the sooner we can start to have some fun."

Dawkins mounted his palomino, watched as Kilgore

climbed aboard his tobiano gelding, hoping that he hadn't talked them both out of their last chance to escape. A part of him was itching to find out what Fergus had in mind for Gilead, but on the other hand, he wasn't suicidal. If it looked like going bad, once they got into town, Dawkins was still committed to abandoning the Mayfield cousins to protect himself. If Kilgore made it out, okay. If not . . . well, that was all right, too.

Whatever happened, once the shooting started, he was looking out for Number One.

Slade woke up stiff and cold before true sunrise, just a hint of gray on the horizon telling him which way was east. He ate the final biscuit from his cache and saddled up the Larsons' dapple gray, mounted and moving by the time gray eastern light shifted to subtle rosy pink.

Maybe today, he thought but wasn't banking on an early wind-up to his hunt. He only had a dead man's word that Mayfield and the rest had set their sights on Gilead. It could be a mistake, something the old man thought he heard as he lay dying—or he could have been delirious, remembering the last town he had stopped in.

Not that any of it mattered. He was headed in the right direction, following the same tracks he'd been after from the start. Wherever Mayfield and the rest were headed, whatever they had in mind, Slade had a fix on them. Unless a rainstorm came along and washed their tracks away, he would eventually overtake them.

And today, so far, the sky was clear.

Most of the time, Slade had no problem traveling alone. He'd grown accustomed to it over time, before he took the marshal's job in Enid, and since then most of his hunting had been solitary. The open prairie didn't bother him, by day or night, and he preferred a thoughtful silence to the jibber-jabber of some hanger-on with nothing sensible to say.

Today, though, he was missing company. It was a feeling that he'd only grown acquainted with since meeting Faith, but what he felt this morning wasn't the familiar craving for her arms around him, or her soft voice telling him that everything would be all right. Slade knew damn well *that* wasn't true, and likely never would be. His fault, her fault, no one's fault—what difference did it make?

This morning, Slade wished he had someone who would simply listen to him, while he spewed his anger, self-doubt, and his sense of failure. On the other hand, that smacked of weakness, which could be a fatal attribute for any man. It could come back to haunt him when he least expected it, used in the wrong hands as a tool to break him down.

No pitiful confessions, then, unless he shared them with the dapple gray—who clearly wasn't interested and could not repeat them, even if it wanted to. The best confessor Slade could think of, and he didn't even have to put a buck in the collection plate on Sunday for the privilege.

Slade thought about the odds against him, and they weren't the worst he'd ever faced. After the shooting on his wedding day, he'd gone in search of ten men, injured worse than he was now and starting later in the game. Of course, he'd been accompanied by a Comanche who had helped him with the tracking, and the fighting, too. But Little Wolf was dead now, murdered by a gang of thugs whom Slade had brought to book as recompense.

Same thing this time. Hang on and do the job.

Give everything he had, if that was what it took, to make things right.

"Jesus, not another one." Vance Underwood sounded as if he was praying for relief.

Mike Bowers focused on the wagon standing there in front of them, a man's boot visible, propped on the driver's seat. "Looks like it," he replied and goaded his sabino to a trot, advancing.

Peering down into the foot well of the wagon seat, a moment later, Bowers saw the man was dead. No doubt on that score. He proceeded toward the open tailgate, looked inside, and felt his breakfast threatening to come back up.

"Son of a bitch!"

"What is it?" Jubal Leach inquired, then got his own look and recoiled, then leaned off to the right side of his brindle gelding as he vomited.

The others took their turns, as if to prove themselves, some cursing bitterly, Floyd Dooley wiping teary eyes and scowling at his own embarrassment.

"What kind of animals are these?" asked Underwood.

"The worst you'll ever meet," Bowers replied. "The human kind, with nothing much to lose."

Nobody asked him about digging graves, this time. The sickness they all felt was turning into anger—which was good and bad. The good side: it would keep them going, motivated to pursue and overtake the fugitives. The bad: Bowers supposed that he could have a lynching party on his hands, unless he kept the members of his posse reined in when they found the bastards they were hunting.

When, or *if*.

Manhunting was a tricky business. Sometimes, trails evaporated and were lost for good. Some fugitives were lost and never seen again. Bowers had come back empty-handed twice—one runner made it down to Mexico; another simply vanished, as if into God's thin air—and he had never liked explaining failure to Judge Dennison. Worse yet, he had to live with knowing that the men he'd missed were out there somewhere, riding roughshod over decent folk who simply wanted to survive. His fault, the way that Bowers saw it, even if he'd done his very best.

Sometimes, that wasn't good enough.

He found the trail and told the others, "You can see they kept on north, from here."

"What's north, besides the border?" Underwood inquired.

"Must be a town, sooner or later," Leach advised.

"We gonna chase 'em into Kansas?" Ed Schultz asked him.

"I am, if I have to," Bowers answered. "Anybody feels like quitting, you can turn back now, and no hard feelings on my part."

"Nobody's quittin'," Dooley said, the youngest of them speaking for the group.

When no one disagreed with him, Bowers said, "All right, then. Let's ride."

He wasn't sure how far the heat of rage would carry them. Another day and night, perhaps, but when the sun came up tomorrow, would it weaken their resolve? If Mayfield and the others made it into Kansas, they were someone else's problem. You could argue that the smart thing was to go back home, alert the Jayhawk law by telegraph and let them finish it.

Why not?

Because the fugitives had killed *his* friend, and made *him* view the aftermath of their atrocities. Mike Bowers owed them something now, for all of that, and he'd be damned before he let a stranger pay that debt.

Lem Wilkins ate his breakfast at the Sunshine Inn—fried eggs and taters, ham, and coffee strong enough to pour itself—considering what his next move should be. He'd done his job, delivering the warning for Judge Dennison, but overnight he'd started wondering: *What happens now?*

The obvious would be returning to the work he knew was waiting for him back in Enid. Check in with the judge, and then go on about his normal life. It wasn't what you'd call exciting, but it kept a roof over his head and put food on his table, ample work for able hands with the expansion going on in town.

But, on the other hand, the jobs he had lined up could wait a few more days. If Mayfield and the other cons were on their way to Gilead, he calculated that they should arrive today, tomorrow at the latest. With the judge's twenty dollars in his pocket, he could spend another night or two at the hotel. See if the outlaws showed up, after all.

And then . . . what?

Lem still hadn't worked that part out, in his mind. He got a creepy feeling when he thought of standing back and watching wild men raze the town, but the alternative was pitching in to fight them, and he didn't see himself as any kind of hero, either. Maybe, when the town was wide-awake this morning, he would see some evidence that people took his warning seriously. Setting up defenses, doing *something*. He could help with that—build barricades, whatever—but avoid the gunplay, if and when it came to that.

He had a window seat for breakfast, watched the merchants opening their shops for business, but for all of their activity, no one had made a move to fortify the town. Lem wondered if the marshal, Cooper, had decided there was no real threat at all. He would have talked to others in the town—the mayor, whoever—and decided what was best for them to do. If they'd selected *nothing* as the answer, then it wasn't Lem's place to persuade them otherwise.

What did he know about it, anyhow?

But what if they were wrong?

Nothing that he could do about it, on his own, but if the gang *did* come and find the townsfolk unprepared, a helping hand might be appreciated, even from a stranger. On the other hand, if nothing happened, Lem could get another night or two of hotel sleep, some more good food under his belt, before he started back to Enid and reported that his trip had been for naught.

Which would be good news, meaning that no one had gotten killed.

A winning proposition, all around.

So, why did he feel disappointed at the thought of Mayfield's mongrels going somewhere else?

Damn foolishness, Lem thought and gestured to the waitress for another mug of coffee, just to wash the sudden sour taste out of his mouth.

"That's it?" Dan Kilgore asked.

"Don't look like much," Reese Dawkins said.

"You think that now," Fergus Mayfield replied, "wait and see what it looks like tomorra."

Kilgore and Dawkins traded glances. "Awright," Dawkins grumbled. "Le's get to it."

"Not so fast," said Fergus.

"What the hell? We're here, aint we?"

"Yes, Danny Boy, we're *here*, not *there*. We can't just waltz down Main Street like we're farmers comin' in to market."

"So, what, then?" asked Dawkins.

"First, they know my face," said Fergus. "From the other time. Soon as they spot me, they'll be raisin' the alarm."

"Why don'tcha pull your hat down?"

"Reese," Fergus replied, "you need ta try'n hold the line against stupidity. When you feel somethin' slippin' out that makes you sound a fool, it's best to shut your trap."

"Hey, now!"

Ignoring him, Fergus pressed on. "I need a coupla men to get things started. Tad 'n' Earl, you ready?"

"Ready," both of them responded, almost simultaneously.

"What'cher gonna do is ride in there and find the marshal. Tell 'im that you're cattle buyers, name of Johnson. Ridin' in, you seen some bad men headed this way, and you thought it was your duty to report it. Once you got 'im listenin', get the drop on 'im and lock 'im up in jail. But do it subtle-like, okay? Don't wave your guns around the street or make a damn commotion."

"We can do that," Earl said, speaking for them both.

"Meantime, Reese and Danny Boy, y'all ride around and come at Main Street from the north. Nobody knows you here, and if they was expectin' trouble, it'd be from Enid, to the south."

"We cattle buyers, too?" asked Dawkins, not quite mocking him.

"Don't matter what you are," Fergus replied. "Head for the hardware store. Be on your left, the way you're goin' in. Front's painted red, with white trim. I don't recollect the name, but it's got farm tools in the windows."

"Then what?" Kilgore asked him.

"Then, *go in* the store," said Fergus, "and secure it."

"Meanin' what?"

"It's *hardware*, Danny Boy. They carry guns and ammunition, axes, hammers, knives—you name it. I don't want the yokels runnin' in to arm theirselves against us. Can you follow that?"

"Makes sense."

"When that's all done, say noon, I'll slip in through a side way and announce myself," said Fergus, smiling. "Once the town's sewed up, we take our due."

"You're tellin' us the only guns in town is at the marshal's office and the hardware store?" asked Dawkins.

"Nope. There's bound to be some others," Fergus said.

"Most likely with the folks who shot you up the last time," Kilgore said.

"I'd say."

"So, what's to stop the same thing happenin' again?"

"Four things," Fergus replied. "First is, there's five of us this time, instead of three. Second, we got a plan for the whole town, not just the bank. Third thing, before they know what's happenin', we'll have the marshal and the hardware merchant's family for hostages."

"And fourth?" asked Kilgore.

"Most important," Fergus said. "I've seen 'em do their worst. They ain't about to take me by surprise a second time."

"Sounds like you got it all worked out," said Dawkins.

"Bet your ass. Now, for the last time, are you in or out?"

"We're in," Reese answered for them both.

"You best get movin' then. Remember, come in from the north."

13

 "We're s'pose to act like cattle buyers, right?" asked Tad.

"You heard him, di'n't you?" Earl replied.

"Okay. So, what's a cattle buyer do?

"Buys cattle, dummy. What'cha think he does? Sell Watkins products door to door?"

"Who's Watkins?"

"Never mind."

"My point is; if we're after cattle, don't it strike you odd that we'd be runnin' to the marshal, tellin' him we seen some bad men on the trail? And how we s'pose to know they're bad?"

"Don't matter how it *seems*, Tad. By the time that law man has a chance to think about it, we's already got the drop on 'im."

"I guess." Not sounding sure at all.

"Just back my play, awright? That's all you gotta do."

"Okay."

Now it was time to do this, Tad Mayfield was nervous, but he couldn't come right out and say it. Cousin Fergus did the thinking for them, Earl next after him, and Tad was just the tail that wagged along behind them. There was nothing wrong with that, most times, but after hearing Fergus talk about the way these folks in Gilead had shot his friends to hell and gone, it gave Tad pause. He wasn't an idea man, granted, but the feeling that he got, town drawing closer by the minute, was a sense of something crawling underneath his skin.

Somebody's walkin' on my grave, he thought.

"Wha's that?" Earl asked him.

"What's what?"

"Whatever you just said."

"I di'n't say nothin'," Tad replied, alarmed that he'd been talking to himself out loud.

"Christ all Friday, you're an odd'n."

Tad had no reply to that, since talking to himself *was* odd. He wasn't sure it made him crazy, necessarily, but it was something that he ought to keep a lid on, anyhow. Especially right now, with Earl and Cousin Fergus trusting him to do his part without a hitch.

Riding into Gilead, Tad felt like Lady What's-her-name, the one from olden times who had to ride through town buck naked for some reason that he couldn't recollect. He felt like every pair of eyes in town was watching him, although there weren't that many people on the street, no curtains twitching as he rode past with his brother, looking for the marshal's office now.

And there it was, ahead and on their left. Earl steered his horse in that direction, trusting Tad to follow him. There was a hitching post outside the office, made it easy, both of them dismounting, tying off their reins. Tad wished he could be calm and confident like Earl, but felt a tic beginning at the outside corner of his left eye, hoping that the marshal wouldn't take it for a winking fit.

"Just lemme do the talkin'," Earl instructed, as they crossed the wooden sidewalk. "Don't say nothin', 'less he asks you somethin' straight out."

"What's our name, again?"

"Johnson, for Christ's sake! Hush up, now!"

Of course, they couldn't go by *Mayfield*, since the law was bound to recognize it. Simple.

Earl opened the office door, not knocking first. Tad followed him inside and saw a stocky, red-faced man coming around a desk, tin star pinned on his shirt. "I help you fellows?" he inquired.

"It might be *we* can help *you*, Marshal," Earl replied.

"How's that?"

"We's cattle buyers, passin' through. Name's Johnson, Earl and Tad. We's brothers."

"I suspected," said the marshal.

Tad was wondering, *Suspected what?* when Earl said, "Yeah, most people say we look alike."

"And what's this help you're gonna do for me?"

"It may be nothin'," Earl replied, "but ridin' in, we saw a passel of bad-lookin' hombres headed this way. Not our bidness, but it seemed the Christian thing to let you know."

The lawman had a worried look now, frowning fit to bust a gut. "How many of these hombres was there?"

Tad thought that one was aimed at him and answered, "Six," the same time Earl said, "Five."

Earl blinked it off and told the marshal, "Five or six. We didn't wanna look like we was starin' at 'em, bein' just the two of us."

"Uh-huh. You gentlemen mind comin' with me for a minute, while we go and see the mayor?"

Tad saw his brother trying not to smile as he replied, "I reckon we could do that, Marshal. Sure, why not?"

Today for sure, Slade thought. *It can't be that much farther in to Gilead.*

He hoped not, anyway, since he was out of food and running low on water for the dapple gray. They hadn't come across a spring since breaking camp, and Slade could only stretch the contents of his one canteen so far. The bare necessities aside, he also had to worry about Mayfield's gang and what they might be up to, who they might be robbing, raping, killing, every hour that they managed to elude him.

Slade hoped there was a posse coming, wished it would catch up to him, but that meant standing still and waiting for it, gambling that whoever came along behind him wouldn't lose the trail that he'd been following. A cloud bank in the west was headed his way, shadowed with the threat of rain, and that could hurt him two ways, wiping out the gang's tracks at the same time it erased his own.

"It's you and me," he told the dapple gray and got no answer, as expected.

Slade had tried to picture Gilead and came up with a bland, generic portrait of a prairie town: a dusty main street lined with shops and offices, a church and a saloon vying for customers, maybe a school and a hotel. He couldn't get a feel for it, the people who had built it out of dreams or desperation, but he knew the kind of havoc that a band of renegades could wreak if no one drew a dead line and enforced it. Scaring lots of people was, sometimes, a simpler thing than frightening a single man, since one man might have nothing much to lose. A town, though, by its very definition was composed of things men valued—wives and children, money, and possessions they had worked a lifetime, in some cases, to accumulate.

And you could threaten all of that with one lit match.

If Mayfield *did* have plans for Gilead, there was a chance—Slade called it slim—that townspeople would take him down again and make it stick, this time. Slade wouldn't mind if they went on and shot the whole gang down, but that was wishful thinking, nothing he could count on coming true. And if it did, would he feel cheated out of getting even for Guy Hampton?

Probably.

How far to go? Slade didn't have a fix on Gilead, or any maps to work from, but he guessed a few more hours ought to see him there. Say noon, if he was lucky, and he didn't have to deal with any unexpected obstacles—or victims—strewn along the outlaws' trail.

No more of that, he thought, but didn't have the faith to make a prayer of it. If there was anybody sitting on a cloud and keeping score, he guessed that men like Mayfield would be stricken down before their faces started decorating wanted posters.

No, Slade realized. Whatever needed doing, he would likely have to do it on his own.

Lem Wilkins saw the marshal, Declan Cooper, leave his office with a couple of guys he didn't recognize. No reason why he should, of course, but from their look and how they stopped to get their horses, walking them along Main Street, he figured they were new in town.

So what?

Nothing to do with him, was it? The gang that he'd been warned about had five or six men in it, and these two weren't threatening the marshal any way that he could see. Why should he have the sudden urge to follow them and see where they were going?

Then again, why not?

It wasn't like eavesdropping, was it? They were walking down the street in broad daylight, and if Lem started heading in the same direction, walking off his breakfast, that was no one's business but his own. Seeing the sights and trying to decide if he should leave today or wait until tomorrow, living out the judge's twenty bucks in Gilead.

One way to look at it was being on vacation, paid to waste his time. The other side, if truth be told, was that he'd started getting bored. A day and night of nothing much but eating, sitting in his hotel room, or idling on the street and feeling out of place was getting underneath his skin. He had the long ride back to Enid, yet, and camping someplace overnight along the way, but he could spare another hour or so. Maybe have lunch before he fetched his buckskin stallion from the livery and started out of town, his business for Judge Dennison completed.

He drifted north, along the eastern side of Main Street, trailing Marshal Cooper and his two companions on the west. None of them noticed him or even glanced around to see if anyone was watching them. Wilkins was half a block behind them, dawdling in a lazy way, when they turned off the sidewalk and approached a gray two-story house with blue trim on the door and window shutters. Marshal Cooper knocked and waited till a man with ginger hair and sideburns opened up.

While Wilkins watched, the marshal introduced his two companions to the fellow on the threshold, then the ginger man invited them inside. He was about to close the door behind them, when the last man through it drew a pistol from his belt and shoved it in his ribs, then shut the door himself.

Lem Wilkins felt as if someone had dashed a bucket of cold water in his face. He stood and listened for the sound of shots, heard none, then turned his thoughts to how he should react. It wasn't every day he saw a crime in progress—truth be told, he'd *never* seen one, if you disregarded barroom fights—and if he *had,* his first impulse would be to tell the nearest lawman. Just his luck, the marshal was inside the gray house, likely with a six-gun pointed at him, and in no position to do anyone a bit of good.

Crazy.

So, what should he do now? Who do you turn to, when the only law in town is either taken hostage or—Jesus, he hadn't thought about it that way—maybe wrapped up in the crime, himself? Cooper had brought the gunmen to their destination, after all, and Wilkins couldn't swear that he'd been duped.

Who's next in line for coping with emergencies?

The mayor, Lem thought. But where in hell was he?

Find someone who can tell you. Do it now!

"You ready to *secure* the hardware store?" Reese Dawkins asked.

"Think I can handle it," Kilgore replied.

"O' course he lets his cousins take the lawman."

"So?"

"So, I ain't sure they's smart enough to do it right."

"How smart you haveta be? Jus' tie 'im up or kill 'im. What's the difference?"

"I don't like trustin' somebody I hardly know," Dawkins replied.

"Like me, you mean?"

"I come to know you purty well, since bein' locked up with you."

Kilgore said, "You wanna turn around an' call this off, we's got another chance right now. Nobody knows us here. Nobody gonna try'n stop us."

Dawkins thought about it for a minute, then said, "No, I reckon not. We're here now. May as well see how it plays out, to a point."

"You gonna know when that point comes?"

"Believe I will."

They'd ridden east of town, a wide half circle to come back at Gilead from due north, as instructed. Entering the town, Dawkins felt out of place—not just a stranger, but a secret enemy of everything the small town stood for: peace and quiet, cleanliness, community. He'd never felt at home in any place where people put their work and church and children first, ahead of whiskey, whores, and games of chance. Give him a mining camp or rowdy trailhead any day, over a sleepy burg like Gilead.

But when it came to raising hell, sometimes a quiet spot was best.

It took the townsfolk by surprise.

"I see the hardware store," Kilgore announced.

"Got it."

The place was red and white, like Fergus said, no change there from the day he'd been arrested and his two friends killed. The sign out front said HILKER'S HARDWARE and a small one in the window told him they were OPEN.

"Ready?" he asked Kilgore.

"Damn straight."

"Awright, then."

Tying up outside the barbershop next door to Hilker's,

Dawkins freed his six-gun in its holster, peering up and down Main Street for any indication of an ambush in the making.

"What'cha lookin' for?"

"Surprises, Danny Boy. I hate 'em."

"Just a buncha yokels shoppin'," Kilgore said.

"Yeah, I guess."

They went into the hardware store, Dawkins on point, a small bell jingling overhead when he pushed through the door. A tall, lean man stood watching from behind a glass-topped counter, long guns racked behind him. Putting on a smile, he asked, "How may I help you gentlemen?"

"This your place?" Dawkins queried.

"Yes, sir. That it is. Clint Hilker at your service."

"Good to meet'cha, Clint," said Dawkins, going to a first-name basis right away. Keeping it cordial. "Me'n Danny here are thinkin' we might throw a party an' we're lookin' for supplies. Know what I mean?"

"Well, not exactly. If it's food you're after," Hilker told him, "Slawson's grocery across the street can likely fix you up. I've got hard candy, but aside from that—"

"I tell you what we really need," said Dawkins.

"Yes, sir?"

Smiling as he drew and cocked his pistol, saying, "Ever' goddamn gun an' cartridge in the place. Along with ever' ax an' hatchet, hammer, knife—hell, anything a man could use to kill somebody, if he had a mind to."

Hilker blinked at him and asked, "Is this a robbery?"

Dawkins grinned back and told him, "Nope. Your shop just got *secured*."

"I'm sorry, but I still don't understand."

Mayor Lowman hated sniveling and sweating in his own

front room, apologizing to a pair of strangers pointing guns
at him. They had disarmed Dec Cooper once the door was
shut behind them, so they held three pistols now, two aimed
at Lowman, one to keep the marshal covered. Lowman's
wife, Elaine, wedged in beside him on the sofa, softly weeping, didn't seem to count.

"How stupid is you?" asked the one who'd introduced
himself as Tad.

"I don't believe—"

"Shut up!" Tad snapped and giggled at his own odd wit.

"Not stupid," said the one called Earl. "Just damned forgetful. How's that sound, Your Lordship?"

Lowman was about to tell him that there were no lords
in Oklahoma territory, but he kept it to himself, afraid of
making matters worse by sassing back. Instead, he asked,
"What do you mean, forgetful? Have we met before?"

Earl shook his head, as if bemused. "I kinda thought
you'd see the family resemblance. Most folks do. I shoulda
tol' ya that our family name ain't 'Johnson.' We was only
funnin' with ya, there. It's Mayfield."

Lowman felt his stomach churn, his throat tighten, restrict-
ing speech. It took him two attempts to say, "That sounds
familiar."

"Damn well oughta," Tad injected, "since you nearly
kilt our cousin in the street out there, a few months back."

"I had no part in that," said Lowman, truthfully. He'd
never fired a shot in anger, not at Fergus Mayfield, nor at
any other man.

Earl scowled at him. "You run this shithole town, or not?"

"I am the mayor," Lowman agreed, "but I am not in
charge of law enforcement or the bank your cousin tried
to . . . well, um . . . rob."

"So, you do nothin'?"

"On the contrary. I—" Lowman nearly jumped out of his seat as Elaine pinched him, warning him to put his pride away before it got them killed. "Um, now I think of it, I really don't do much."

"An' you get paid for that?"

"A nominal amount."

"Speak English, damn it!"

"Very little," Lowman translated.

"So, how'd you get a house like this?" asked Tad.

"I own the livery," Lowman explained. "And I'm a partner in a restaurant."

"Reckon we'll haveta try your cookin'," Earl said. "Mebbe get a few fresh horses from ya when we go."

"Of course," said Lowman, feeling like an utter coward. "Only fair."

"I like the way you crawl," Earl said.

"I like his missus," Tad chimed in. "Might try her on for size, my own self."

"Keep your britches on. We don't jump nobody till Fergus gives the word."

"He's coming?" Cooper asked the brothers, sounding dry-mouthed.

"Bet'cher life," said Tad.

"It wasn't just a rumor, then."

"What rumor?" Earl demanded. "Someone tol' you we was comin'?"

Damn it! Lowman spoke before Cooper could make it any worse. "Just talk," he said. "After we heard about the jailbreak. Someone passing through mentioned your cousin's name."

"An' none a y'all believed he'd do it?" Earl was laughing now. "That's rich."

"It's true," Lowman admitted. "Some of us did not."

Tad grinned. "Guess you was wrong, then, weren'tcha?"

"It appears we were."

"Mmm, 'It appears we were,'" the weasel echoed, mocking Lowman to his face.

"T'hell with that," said Earl Mayfield. "The ones I wanna hear about are them that thought we *would* come. Odds are, they been getting' ready for us right along. It's them we want."

"I don't know what you mean," said Lowman, bluffing.

"Well, let me spell it out for ya, Your Royal Hind-ass. I want a list, with names and where they live in town. Right now, afore I set Tad on your missus, there."

The pocket watch he'd taken from the head-shot deputy told Fergus it was straight-up noon o'clock. He got up off the ground and stretched, then climbed aboard his stolen claybank mare. Sat easy in the saddle while he stared at Gilead a little while, then started off to ride around the far west side of town.

There'd been no shooting so far, that he'd heard, which was encouraging. With any luck, the others had achieved their goals, had Marshal Cooper and the hardware store locked down, at least. It wasn't feasible for them to spread out, searching door to door for weapons. That would only agitate the townsfolk in advance of his arrival on the scene, maybe provoke resistance when he wasn't there to help suppress it.

Fergus counted on surprise to bring the town under his thumb. The merchants and their women would feel different about fighting when they saw the marshal with a pistol at his head and realized they couldn't raise an arsenal by running over to the hardware store. Some still might fight, and that was fine with Fergus. He preferred some measure of resistance to immediate submission, giving him the chance to draw first blood.

And once the party started, Devil take the hindmost.

Coming into Gilead from westward, Fergus took his time and watched the windows facing his way, till he realized he couldn't tell if anyone was peering out at him or not. He hurried up, then, heading for a shaded alleyway between a couple of the shops, dismounting when he got that far and walking in, leading his claybank by the reins, left-handed. Right hand free to draw his pistol if he needed it, but hoping that he wouldn't.

Not just yet.

He reached the far end of the alley, fronting Main Street, and hung back a second there before he stuck his head out, glancing left and right along the storefronts. There were people moving on the sidewalk opposite, but none of them appeared to notice him—or if they did, none of them recognized him from the last time he had blown through town.

That riled him more than anything, the thought that they could damn near end his life and then forget about it, like they'd shrug off stepping on a bug. That reinforced Mayfield's conviction that the whole town ought to learn a lesson, not just those who'd pumped lead into Deke and Lennie on the day they hit the bank, or those who'd caged him for the deputies to haul away.

Plenty of pain to go around, by God, and Fergus couldn't wait to start dishing it out.

But first, he had to catch up with the others, making sure they'd done their part. If something had gone wrong—say someone got the drop on Reese and Danny and his cousins, somehow—he could still ride off and save himself while they kept lawmen occupied. Too bad, but which of them was dumb enough to think Fergus would risk his life to save the four of them, against long odds?

Well, maybe Tad.

Time to move, he thought and pulled his hat low down, hiding the top part of his face, chin tucked against his neck to keep the rest in shadow. Walking with his claybank down the west side of the street, he kept the mare between him and the shops on that side, so that only people on the far side of Main Street would glimpse his profile. Tilt the head a little to the right, like he was listening for something in the distance, and it made him that much harder for a hasty glance to recognize.

He'd check the marshal's office first, then hit the hardware store. See who he found, and whether they were in control as planned.

If so, then they could start to have some fun.

14

Lem Wilkins craved a drink to calm his nerves, but all they seemed to have in Gilead was beer—and even that, as he'd found out, wasn't available until they started serving lunch at noon. Too long to wait. He'd have to get along without Dutch courage from a bottle, and he didn't like it one damned bit.

His mission: find someone who could direct him to the mayor of Gilead without a lot of questions that he didn't want to answer, needless conversation that would only slow him down. The mayor, he reasoned, would have some idea of what to do with Marshal Cooper stuck under the gun. But where in hell *was* he?

Lem chose the barber, finally, because in every town he'd ever visited or lived in, barbershops were staffed by know-it-alls. They'd talk your ears off while they lowered them, giving opinions that you hadn't asked for, rambling on with gossip they'd collected from their other customers, adding refinements of their own. Most times, Lem wouldn't bet a nickel on the accuracy of their stories, but he didn't need a local history or editorial today. Only directions to the man in charge of Gilead.

He crossed Main Street, watching the townsfolk as they went about their normal business, unaware of how much danger they were facing. Part of him wanted to shout a warning in the middle of the street, alert them all, but what would that accomplish other than creating panic? What he needed was a cool head, someone whom the people trusted and who knew the town, knew which locals could be counted on to lend a hand—or gun—in an emergency.

Lem spent a moment on the threshold of the barbershop, swallowed a lump of fear, and stepped inside. The barber had a fat man in his chair, face lathered up for shaving, razor poised as he glanced up at Lem.

"I'll be another five, ten minutes here," the barber said.

"Don't need a shave," Lem told him.

"We might disagree on that, friend."

He was right. Lem's fingertips scraped bristles on his chin and jaw line. "Have to wait on that," he said. "I'm lookin' for the mayor."

"Not here," the barber said. "Although, I'd have to say he's overdue. It's been almost a month since—"

"Do you know where I might find him?" Rude to interrupt, but now Lem's nerves were twanging like a banjo's strings.

"Likely at home, or at the livery," the barber said.

"And where's home, if you don't mind saying?"

"North on Main." The barber nodded in that general direction. "It's a gray house."

Lem could feel his stomach twist. "Two-story? Blue trim on the door and windows?"

"That's the one."

"Thank you." The words tasted like ashes on his tongue.

Outside, he felt like screaming, *Wake up, people! Bad men have your marshal and your mayor! Do something!* He could vent the tension building up inside him, maybe get his horse out of the livery and ride through town like Paul Revere, then keep on going while they solved the problem for themselves.

Or didn't, either way.

It wasn't Lem's fight. He'd been paid to take a ride and pass a message. It was done, and that was all he had agreed to do. Judge Dennison hadn't inquired if he would like to face a gang of killers single-handed, fighting—likely dying—for a bunch of people that he didn't even know.

But he was here now, damn it. Something wouldn't let him ride away and leave the strangers to their fate.

He moved into a nearby alley, out of sight of people passing by, and double-checked his Chamelot-Delvigne revolver. It was ready for a showdown—but was he?

Still undecided on that point, Lem Wilkins stepped back onto Main Street and began to make his slow way north.

Another hour, Slade decided, maybe less, until he saw the first dark smudge of Gilead on the horizon. He was looking forward to it now, whether the gang had stopped in town or not. There would be water and supplies, although he wasn't sure exactly how much he could buy with pocket change. Enough to keep him going, maybe, until he could spot some game along the trail.

What if you lose it? asked a small and wicked voice inside his head.

A town meant traffic—horses, wagons, buggies—that could easily obscure the tracks he had been following.

If that turned out to be the case, what would he do? Keep heading north by northwest and assume that his quarry hadn't changed directions?

Or, another problem: what if they swung wide around the town, to east or west? Could he afford to follow them without stopping for water and supplies? And if he stopped, would he be able to regain the trail when he was finished with his meager shopping?

The best that he could hope for, Slade decided, was for Mayfield and the rest to pass through Gilead, be noticed by the residents, and keep on going without raising hell in town. He'd have a fix on them that way, confirm their line of travel, without adding any further crimes or corpses to their tab. It was a lot to hope for, but it didn't hurt to wish that just this once, something might work out for the best.

And if the gang *had* passed through Gilead en route to someplace else, what were the odds that he could raise a posse to pursue them? The odds on that, he thought, would pretty well depend on how the fugitives behaved in town. If they were quiet, passed on by without a fuss, Slade guessed the townspeople would not be eager to go after them. Conversely, if they'd left a bloody mess behind, it could go either way, depending whether fear or rage had taken root in Gilead.

He'd keep it on the safe side, Slade decided, not expecting anything.

He wished that it was finished, one way or the other. Make it through alive, and he could head on back to Enid, maybe try one absolutely final time to speak with Faith and see what she'd decided about leaving. There was likely nothing he could say or do to change her mind, if she was set on going, and he damn sure couldn't follow her back East. To what? A clerk's job in some shop, assuming anyone thought he was suited for it, living underneath a sky turned murky gray by smoke from factories?

She'd have their child alone, Slade never knowing if it was a boy or girl unless she deigned to write and tell him. Faith would never ask for anything, would likely send the money back if he tried helping her, in fact. The plain truth was that, once she sold her spread, she could afford to buy and sell Jack Slade, with change enough left over for a new life anywhere she settled.

Leaving him the life he had right now.

The dapple gray snorted and brought him out of his reverie, drawing his notice to the sight that he'd been waiting for. From where he was, it might have been a line of trees or stubby hills, but Slade could spot a prairie town by now, and no mistake.

Grim-faced, he made his way toward Gilead.

Fergus Mayfield stopped outside the marshal's office, made believe that he was checking on the left-hand stirrup leather while a pair of ladies passed, then moved up to the half-glass door and peered inside. No one was visible, but there were cells in back, as he had learned from personal experience. The lawman could be back there with his cousins, out of sight, and Fergus wouldn't see them from the street.

He tried the doorknob, found it wasn't locked, and went inside, hand resting on the curved butt of his six-gun. "Anybody home?" he called out toward the back room, nerves strung out so tightly that he almost giggled like a little girl.

No answer.

Fergus went ahead to check and found the two cells

empty. Frowning now, he doubled back into the office, staring through its windows at the street outside, more people passing without giving him a second glance.

Damned fools.

The gun rack to his left, behind the marshal's desk, held two Winchester rifles and a double-barreled shotgun. Fergus liked the look of them, but quickly found they were secured by a chain drawn through their trigger guards and padlocked on one side. He checked the marshal's desk for keys, found nothing, and decided that the lawman must be carrying the key ring on his person. Lacking any kind of tool that he could use to free the guns without a racket audible outside, Fergus decided it was best to leave them where they were. Come back and get them later, when they started the festivities, or maybe leave them racked and burn the whole damn place.

Why not?

He had to find the others now, and quickly, before someone recognized him, raised a hue and cry. The cousins should have been where he was standing, with the marshal in their custody, but since they weren't locked up, he guessed there might be two solutions to the riddle. One, they'd had to track the marshal down and found him somewhere else. Or two, they'd started thinking for themselves—never the best idea—and taken him along to someplace they believed was more secure.

And where might that be?

Fergus couldn't work that out, right now, so he decided it was best for him to check on Reese and Danny Boy, across the street and down a block, at Hilker's Hardware. He'd forgotten what they called it till he saw it, took the whole of Main Street in, and then it all came back to him. The bank, the gunfire, Lennie Stovall and Deke Hagenmaier all bloody, twitching as the slugs ripped into them, and Fergus throwing up his hands, surrendering to save himself.

That was the worst part, breaking down and giving in. The shame of his humiliation, something he would never let himself forget, much less forgive.

Back on the street, his horse untied, he angled toward the hardware store. He'd almost mounted up, ready to run for it if someone called his name or showed a weapon, but instead he forced himself to take it slow and easy, just like any other normal person on a hot and lazy afternoon. No rushing to attract attention as he crossed the street.

And saw Reese's face pressed up against the window of the hardware store as he approached, grinning ear to ear at sight of him like some fool kid on Christmas morning. Fergus took his time, tying his horse outside and entering the shop. The owner and a woman Fergus took to be his wife were standing statue-stiff behind the counter, hands on top of it where they were clearly visible.

"We all right here?" asked Fergus.

"Fine as frog's hair," Dawkins said.

"You seen my cousins anywhere around?"

"Ain't they at the marshal's office?"

"If they were, would I be askin' you?"

"Well, we ain't seen 'em," Dawkins said, a beat before Dan Kilgore blurted out, "The hell we ain't. Look here. They's comin' now."

Fergus turned toward the window facing Main Street, frowning as he saw five people headed for the hardware store. He recognized the marshal and the mayor, together with a woman that he'd never seen before. His cousins were behind them, bringing up the rear, hands on their holstered pistols.

"Well, now," he said. "Looks like they brung a little some-thin' extra to the party."

"We'll be in Kansas pretty soon," Vance Underwood com-plained.

"Not even close," Mike Bowers said. "We've got another day, at least, before we hit the border."

"So, you plan to chase them clean out of the territory?" Ed Schultz asked him.

"If I have to," Bowers answered.

"Marshal," Jubal Leach chimed in, "we feel bad for your friends, and all them other folks, but we've got work to do in Enid, and it won't get done with us out here."

"You reckon someone's hair is growin' faster than it would without you?" Bowers asked the barber.

"You've got no call to—"

"Listen!" Bowers reined around to face the other mem-bers of his posse. "We've already had this conversation, and I don't plan on rehashing it each time we ride another five, ten miles. You want to turn around, go on. Nobody's beggin' you to stay. But if you stick, for God's sake stop your whining."

Leaving them to chew on that, he turned and started north again, still following the tracks that Mayfield's gang—and possibly Jack Slade—had left behind. A quiet moment, then he heard them coming after him, couldn't have said if there were four or not, and didn't care enough to turn and check. He'd keep on with the hunt alone, if that was what it came to, and be glad to see them go if that was what it took to get some peace and quiet.

When the shopkeeper had started in on him, Bowers was thinking down the road, imagining a map and trying to remember what was waiting for them up ahead. There was a town, he thought, not one he'd visited himself, and couldn't name it for the life of him. How far? Another half day, more or less, if he was thinking straight and hadn't mixed it up with someplace else.

"Who knows this stretch of territory? Any of you?" Bowers asked, not turning in his saddle as he spoke.

"I been through here before," Floyd Dooley said. "A couple years ago."

"We should be comin' to a town," said Bowers. "Am I right?"

"There *was* a town," Dooley replied. "Still is, I guess. We've got a ways to go, yet."

"You remember what they call it?"

"Somethin' from the Bible," said the hostler. "I don't rightly recollect."

"It's Gilead," Schultz said, surprising Bowers.

"Have you been there, Ed?"

"Just passin' through. There weren't much to it. Didn't even have a real saloon, if you can feature that."

"I shoulda figured that," said Bowers, talking to himself more than the others.

"Figgered what?" asked Dooley.

"Gilead. Judge Dennison already sent a warning up there, thinkin' Mayfield might be comin' back to where he was arrested in the first place."

"Lookin' to get even," Schultz suggested.

"That's the general idea."

"So, are we gonna head straight there," asked Jubal Leach, "or keep doggin' these tracks?"

"Looks like they're headin' that way," Bowers said. "The thing we need to watch is that they don't change course."

"If Mayfield's looking for revenge," said Underwood, "we're riding straight into a fight."

"Something to tell your kids about," said Bowers. Thinking to himself, *That's if you make it back.*

Too late, Lem Wilkins thought and cursed himself as he saw the marshal and the man who must be mayor of Gilead leaving the gray house, walking with a woman, and the two who'd grabbed the lawman following along behind. Their guns were holstered now, but they looked ready for a fight, eyes twitching every which way as they moved along Main Street and started crossing.

Going where?

Lem turned and focused on the shop window behind him. Women's dresses, just his luck, but he thought shifting to another store would make the gunmen even more suspicious. He could be a farmer, looking for a present that his wife might like, and with the awning shade just right, the window made a fairly decent mirror. He could see the mayor, the marshal, and the rest making their way across Main Street toward Hilker's Hardware.

Now what?

If they were looking for a place to rob, he would have thought the bank a better prospect. On the other hand, if these were some of Mayfield's men—and he'd seen nothing yet to make him doubt it—then a simple holdup likely wouldn't be their final goal.

A couple passing by the hardware store said something to the marshal or the mayor, maybe to both of them. Lem couldn't hear it, but he saw them smiling, faces just a bit distorted by the windowpane, and they passed on with no sign of alarm, like it was just another normal day in Gilead. Lem's mind was racing, working overtime to hatch a plan. Some way to help the hostages without getting them killed.

But how?

The best he could come up with, as the marshal's party disappeared inside the hardware store, was to go looking for another entrance at the rear. Try sneaking in, if he could manage it, and maybe get the drop on Mayfield's men somehow. It would be risky, sure, but what else could he do?

Once they were out of sight, he ambled north on Main for half a block, taking it slow, then crossed the street and ducked into an alley on the other side. Lem ran the last few yards from there and came out into nothing, flat land trailing off to the horizon from the backside of the Main Street shops and offices.

He turned right, counting doors, but didn't need to, since the hardware store was painted red in back, as well as out in front. There was a back door, sure enough, its brass knob turning smoothly as he gripped it in his sweaty palm—then froze. What if they had one of those bells hanging above the door, like many stores had on their entrances, to herald the arrival of a customer? One jangle, and the pair of Mayfield's boys would be on top of him with guns in hand.

Be ready for 'em, then, he thought, and drew his Chamelot-Delvigne revolver, cocked it as the back door started swinging inward, inch by inch.

"The hell you been?" Fergus demanded, as his cousins trailed their three companions through the door to Hilker's Hardware. "I was lookin' for you at the jail."

"We got to thinkin', Cousin Fergus," Earl replied.

"Oh, didja now?"

"Yes, sir. Seemed like a good idea to grab the mayor, while we was at it. An' we got a list of them he's talked to since the message come an' warned 'em that we might be comin' here."

"Message?"

"Yep." Earl poked the marshal in his ribs and ordered, "Tell 'im!"

"Well," the lawman said, "they sent a messenger from Enid, like he says."

"Who's *they*?" Fergus demanded.

"That would be Judge Dennison."

"So, he remembered what I said in court, eh? Good for him. An' where's this messenger right now?"

"I couldn't tell you," said the marshal. "Could be half-way back to Enid by this time, for all I know."

"Was he a marshal?"

"Just some errand boy."

"He talk to anybody else?" asked Fergus.

"I didn't follow him around," the marshal said.

"But *you* did, din'tcha?"

That was where the mayor spoke up. "We talked about it, naturally."

"With who else?" Fergus asked him.

"Just town council members."

"Who would be . . . ?"

"We got their names," said Tad.

"I wanna hear 'em from the man in charge," Fergus replied.

The mayor looked worried. Probably the first time since he was elected that he didn't relish being Number One in town. "Well, there was Clint, here," he told Fergus, nodding toward the lanky guy behind the counter, standing with his woman. "Simon Woodley from the bank. Lloyd Mortimer from the hotel."

"That's all?"

"The five of us," the mayor confirmed.

"Nobody else?"

"I can't speak for the others, but on my part, no."

"Well, now, I gotta say it don't look like you took the warnin' very serious," said Fergus.

"*We* did," said the mayor, nodding to indicate the marshal standing next to him. "The others voted just to wait and see what happened."

Fergus turned to face the hardware man, allowed himself a smile, and asked him, "How's that goin' for ya?"

No response.

"Cat got'cher tongue, I guess." Back to the marshal, he said, "What we're gonna do is walk back to the jailhouse, nice'n easy like. I want'cha under lock'n key while we round up the others from your high-and-mighty council. An' I'll have the key that fits that padlock on your gun rack."

"Please," the mayor injected, red-faced. "If it's an apology you want—"

A barking laugh from Fergus cut him off. "Apology! That's rich. You kill my two best friends on earth, you lock me up, and now you wanna make it right with an *apology*? I need a big shot of whatever you been drinkin'."

"Pour me some, while you're about it," Dawkins said.

"I'm trying to be reasonable," said the mayor.

"Yeah? The time for that was *last* time, Mr. Mayor. You run outta second chances."

"So have you," a strange voice said, somewhere behind Fergus and to his right. "Put up your hands, an' I mean empty!"

Fergus turned slowly toward the sound and saw a young man standing in the doorway to the store's back room, hands trembling slightly from a case of nerves and from the weight of the revolver he held aimed at Mayfield's chest.

"I guess nobody checked the back door," Fergus said, to no one in particular.

"Second mistake," the stranger said.

"What was the first?" asked Fergus.

"Comin' back to Gilead," the young man said.

15

Now that he had the town in sight, Slade wasn't sure exactly how to handle it. The tracks that he'd been following split up when he was still a mile or so outside of Gilead, two riders swinging to the east, two others toward the west, while one—his money was on Fergus Mayfield—took a more direct route toward the settlement.

For what?

If they were trying to avoid the town, why separate? Slade figured they were flanking Gilead, running some kind of pincers movement to surround the town, Mayfield sending his flunkies in ahead of him. That way, if anything went wrong, he'd hear the shooting and could leave them to it if he came up chicken-hearted, without running any risk himself.

Which left Slade in a quandary. If he rode into town as bold as brass, showing himself to Mayfield and the other fugitives, he might touch off a shooting match that wouldn't start as quickly, otherwise. Conversely, sneaking in would take more time, potentially allowing Mayfield's bunch to do more damage on a smaller scale—to women, property, whatever.

"Damned, regardless," he informed the dapple gray, who didn't seem to care much either way.

Slade spent a moment taking inventory of his weapon. For the Springfield carbine, he had twenty-seven rounds. For the Colt, a full cylinder and nineteen spare cartridges. When those were gone, if he still had an adversary breathing and he hadn't picked up someone else's gun along the way, Slade would have to work with the butcher knife in his boot.

It wasn't much against five killers, in a town full of guns and potential hostages. Slade knew he'd have to watch his step, avoiding any move that might spill innocent blood. By the same token, however, he could not stand by and watch the outlaws run amok in Gilead without attempting to corral them.

"Slow and easy, then," he told the dapple gray and reined it off to westward, following the double line of tracks that led in that direction, veering out another half mile from the town before they started turning back to reach it. Part of Slade's mind told him he was wasting precious time, that Mayfield's bandits could be robbing, raping, killing, while he tiptoed into Gilead behind them, but he wasn't willing to provoke an all-out battle if he could avoid it.

More particularly, one that he might lose and leave the town worse off than if he'd never come at all.

When Slade had closed his range to half a mile from Gilead, he started feeling itchy, conscious of the possibility that someone would observe him on the open plain, approaching town. He would be coming in behind the shops and offices on Main Street's western side, but most of them had windows at the rear, and anyone could spot him if they glanced his way. Slade couldn't picture Fergus Mayfield thinning out his meager troop by posting guards to watch the prairie, but a resident of Gilead—even a child—could spread the word of an approaching rider, rob him of the opportunity to take his quarry by surprise.

Nothing to do about it, he decided and pressed on.

At least they wouldn't know he was a lawman till he got close enough for them to spot his badge. And if somebody saw it prematurely, how would that affect whatever might be happening in town? Would it provoke the fugitives into a killing spree?

Frowning, Slade took the tin star off the outside of his vest and pinned it inside, on the left over his heart, concealed. He could display it if the need arose, or keep it to himself, depending on what he discovered once he entered Gilead.

A slow half mile to go, imagining a bull's-eye painted on his chest and waiting for a rifle shot to take him down.

"The hell are you?" Fergus demanded, staring at the shaky kid who held a pistol pointed at him.

"Reckon I'm the fella's got the drop on you," the kid replied.

"No arguin' with that," Fergus agreed. "But can you see there's five of us?"

"Don't matter," said the kid. "Your pals start shootin', you go down, no matter what."

"You'd better hope so, boy." Risking his life, maybe, to put a brave face on. "'Cause if you miss, you won't much like what happens next."

"Five guns or not," the kid said, "you can only kill me once."

"Thing is, they may *not* kill ya," Fergus said. "In fact, boys, what'cha wanna do is wing this little turd, cripple him up some, so he drops his smoke wagon, then get your bowies out an' carve 'im up like Sunday mornin' bacon."

"That suppose to worry me?" the kid asked Fergus. "They don't kill me, I keep shootin' till they do, or till they're down."

"With these fine ladies and their handsome gents all in the line o' fire?" Fergus inquired. "Some kinda hero you are, boy."

The kid considered that and swallowed hard, then answered back, "I guess a lady'd rather be shot down than left for scum to toy with. If it's preyin' on your mind, why don't you turn 'em loose?"

Fergus felt angry heat rising into his face. "You got a bad mouth on you, son," he said.

"I ain't your son. Reckon I'd die from shame if that was so."

"You'll die from somethin' soon enough," Reese Dawkins cautioned him.

"Go on and pull it," said the kid. "Before I drop, I give your boss another belly button. How'd that suit ya?"

"Smart-mouth bastard!"

"Watch your language here, around the ladies, Mr. Dawkins," Fergus chided. "Set a good example for the boy."

"The hell you mean?" Reese answered back.

"This kid don't wanna kill nobody," Fergus said. "Just thinks he's helpin', when the truth is that he's makin' matters worse for ever'one."

"Don't feel like jawin' with you anymore," the kid told Fergus. "Drop your gunbelt, nice an' easy, then them others do the same, one at a time. First move that makes me nervous, you get ventilated."

"I guess he means it," Fergus told the others.

"Hell with what he means," said Kilgore. "I ain't givin' up my gun."

"Me, neither," Dawkins said.

The cousins kept their traps shut, leaving it to Fergus. "I believe we got ourselves a standoff," he advised the kid.

"Your problem. What I said still goes, about you droppin' first."

"You ever kilt a man before?" Fergus inquired.

"First time for ever'thing."

"Tha's true. My first time, I puked. Can ya believe it? I was only up against one man, o'course, so that was fine. I didn't have four others drawin' down on me."

"I'll manage," said the kid.

"You might, at that." Fergus was shifting slightly as he spoke, trying to show the kid a profile, cutting down the target area he'd have to work with. "Then again—"

He drew and fired while speaking, saw the kid's revolver flash before the echo of the shot hammered his ears, and felt the bullet rip across his chest like a hot poker searing flesh.

Slade heard the shots when he was still a hundred yards or so from Gilead, distant and muffled, but he knew the sound of pistols firing when he heard it. His first impulse told Slade to gallop in and find out what was happening, but then he paused to think about it, recognizing his mistake. The shots—a flurry of them, maybe half a dozen altogether—weren't repeated. That, in turn, told Slade two things.

First, whoever was shooting had already finished—for the moment, anyway. There wasn't one damned thing that he could do for anyone on the receiving end of that brief, concentrated fire.

And second, if he blundered in without a look-see, unprepared, he could be making matters worse.

Six shots in rapid-fire could mean some kind of showdown, or an execution. Worst case, it could mean five or six dead townsfolk. Which left—what? Two hundred, more or less, still facing danger if he charged in and provoked the outlaws into firing willy-nilly, maybe executing hostages. To act without at least some basic knowledge of the situation would be irresponsible at best, catastrophic at worst.

From the sounds he'd heard, Slade gathered that the shooting had occurred indoors, somewhere along Main Street. That didn't help him much, but it suggested that he might be able to sneak in and have a look around before Mayfield or any of his hangers-on knew he'd arrived. As far as Slade knew, they believed him to be dead, and while he didn't plan on posing as a ghost, at least his first appearance should induce a certain measure of surprise.

Which meant he had to time it perfectly, to get the most from it. If he could catch them all together, gaping at him, startled, maybe he could take down two or three before they started shooting back.

Or not.

Whoever laid out Gilead had placed a narrow street or alley running east-west every hundred feet, approximately, separating buildings into blocks of three together, sharing common walls. Five alleys on the side Slade was approaching, meaning eighteen shops and offices on one side, and the alley he was nearing stretched on to the other side of Main Street, telling him the east-side layout was the same. So call it thirty-six specific businesses, with several other structures standing at the northern end of town: a church, a school, a blacksmith's shop and livery.

Your basic normal prairie town—until today.

Slade reached the west end of the alley he'd selected, satisfied that no one had observed him—or, that if they *had*, they weren't concerned with sounding an alarm. Dismounting, he stepped into shade, leading the borrowed dapple gray, and found a wooden ladder fastened to the gray wall on his left. He left the horse there, reins tied loosely to one of the ladder's rungs, where it could tug free in the case of an emergency. Before he left it, Slade sipped out of his canteen, then poured the rest into his hat and let the gelding drink its fill. That done, he dumped the rest and put the wet hat back atop his head.

Holding the Springfield carbine cocked and ready, pistol in his belt, the towel-wrapped butcher's knife still snug inside his boot, rubbing his shin each time he took a step, he moved along the alley toward Main Street. Another thirty feet to daylight, more or less, with buildings shading him on either side, but it was hot shade, stuffy, not the least refreshing.

Coming to the alley's mouth at last, Slade stopped and listened, and blinked at Main Street sunshine, nearly blinding him.

"God*damn*, that hurts!"

"It's just a graze," Earl told him. "Lucky that you turned just when you did."

"It don't *feel* lucky," Fergus muttered, through clenched teeth. "Feels like he shot my nubs off."

"Didn't even touch 'em," Earl assured him.

"Not that you got any use for 'em," Dawkins chipped in.

"Where is he?" Fergus asked, half turning on the spot where he had slumped, during the gunfight.

"'Zactly where we dropped 'im," Kilgore said.

And Fergus saw the kid now, stretched out by the doorway to the hardware store's back room, all shot to hell. He hoped his own bullet had done that damage to the youngster's face, but he supposed it didn't matter much. The little turd was dead and he was still alive, if you want to call this living.

"What's happenin' outside?" he asked, of no one in particular.

"A couple people lookin' this way," Dawkins said. "Ain't stoppin', though."

Funny, like they were used to shooting in the middle of the day—or maybe just afraid to come and see what happened.

"This'll likely sting some," Earl advised, then swabbed the graze across his chest with a rag doused in liquor they'd found underneath the shop's showcase.

Fergus cursed a blue streak, mixing blasphemy, scatology, and plain old filth without a thought to either of the ladies standing by and listening. Both married women, anyhow. He guessed they would've heard it all before, and done a good deal of it with their husbands.

"Lemme up, damn you!" he growled at last and shoved Earl back away from him. It hurt some, standing, and he knew the blood would soon soak through his shirt, might even stick it to his wound, but Fergus wasn't in a patient mood. The kid had almost spoiled his party—put a painful damper on it, at the very least—and he was tired of wasting precious time.

When he was on his feet and reasonably steady, Fergus glowered at the dead boy on the floor and said, "That little bastard made me jump the gun, but that's all right. We'll make it work, regardless."

"Some of 'em could be gettin' ready for us, Cousin Fergus," Earl observed.

"Screw 'em," he growled. "Take Tad and Marshal Fat-ass, here. Go fetch them guns outta his office. Bring 'em right back here, you unnerstan' me?"

"Sure."

"Reese, you an' Danny go'n find the preacher. He was all concerned as hell about my soul, when I was locked up in their little jail. I wanna thank 'im for his kindness."

"This ain't Sunday," Kilgore answered. "Where we s'poseta find a preacher if he ain't in church?"

Fergus turned to the mayor. "How 'bout it?" he inquired.

"The Reverend Hawthorn lives behind the church," Mayor Lowman said. "He's got a little parsonage back there."

"Well, there ya go."

"He might not wanna come," said Dawkins.

"So, persuade him," Fergus said. "Tell 'im he's got a soul in danger of perdition. You don't haveta let him know it's his."

"If we run into trouble on the street—"

"You'll thinka somethin'," Fergus finished for him "Git, now."

Left alone with Lowman, Hilker, and their women, Fergus found a chair and dropped into it, covering the four of them from where he sat. The sharp pain in his chest had faded slightly, more a dull ache now, but it had taken something out of him. Maybe the letdown that he felt after a shooting, sometimes, when the fact that he'd survived another close call settled on his shoulders like a pall of weariness.

"What do you have in mind for Gilead?" the mayor asked him, a moment later.

"Funny you should say it that way," Fergus answered. "No concern about yourself? Your lady, there?"

"I was elected to protect the town," Lowman replied.

"Well, then, I guess you're gonna disappoint 'em," Fergus said. And smiled.

"Preacher, he says. The hell is up with that?" Kilgore inquired.

"My guess'd be their sin buster insulted him," Dawkins replied.

"They'll do that."

"Prob'ly told him he should mend his ways."

"Reckon it's bad luck if you kill a gospel sharp?"

"Why would it be?"

"Well . . . you know. God an' all."

"Don't tell me you just got religion," Dawkins jeered.

"I went to church when I was little."

"Somethin' tells me that it didn't take."

"Not so you'd notice. Still . . ."

"Still, what?"

"You ever think about what happens when we die?"

"I'd say you fall down, 'less you're hangin'."

"No, I mean your soul."

"For Christ's sake, Danny!"

"Never mind."

The whole way over, Dawkins swept Main Street with anxious eyes, watching for anyone who'd heard the shots and looked like they were organizing some kind of defense. One man had stepped out of the lawyer's office, next door to the jail, and had a short talk with the marshal as he got there, with the Mayfield cousins trailing him. Whatever explanation he received appeared to satisfy him, since he went on back inside. Farther along the street, the barber had come out to have a look around, then made believe he had to sweep the sidewalk when he noticed nothing to alarm him.

Stupid people, Dawkins thought and shrugged it off.

They reached the church, white paint from ground to steeple, all except the double doors in front, which had been painted yellow for some reason Dawkins couldn't figure out. No sign out front to tell him the denomination, and he wondered if it mattered, in a town with only one church to attend. Putting a name on it might keep some folks away, and cut back on donations to support the preacher. Anyway, it made no difference to him, since they weren't staying for the sermon.

Dawkins tried the yellow doors, just testing them, but they were barred from the inside. That done, he walked around behind the church with Kilgore, to a little bungalow in back. He knocked, and they stood waiting till a shortish, square-built man opened the door.

His first impression of the parson was that he had built a house to fit him, small and blocky. Second thought: Dawkins imagined that he'd need a wooden crate to stand on, of a Sunday, so that he could see over the pulpit while he preached hellfire and brimstone. He was stern of face, clean-shaven, bushy eyebrows almost meeting in the dent above his stubby nose, with dark hair rising like a wall above his forehead.

"May I help you gentlemen?" he asked, deep-voiced. Dawkins could almost hear him bellowing damnation in the chapel, scaring money out of sinners who were scared of roasting over red-hot coals.

"You needta come along with us," said Dawkins, "to the hardware store."

"And why is that, pray tell?"

"Exac'ly right," said Kilgore. "Prayin's what we had in mind."

"Explain yourself," the preacher said.

"We got a soul in need of savin'," Dawkins said.

"Whose soul?"

Reese drew his six-gun, cocked it, held it leveled at the stubby parson's chest. "Yours, if you don't start walkin' purty goddamn quick."

"There is no need for blasphemy, my son."

"This is your last chance, Daddy. Do you walk, or should we drag your holy ass across the street?"

"I vote for draggin'," Kilgore said.

The preacher saw they meant it, glared at each of them in turn, then passed between them, moving out with short but steady strides in the direction of the hardware store.

"Remember me, preacher?"

"I do, indeed," the minister replied.

"Surprised to see me, are ya?" Fergus prodded him.

"I thought you'd be locked up and doing penance for your sins."

"Tha's what the judge thought, too. Guess both of you was wrong."

The pastor wasn't showing any fear. Not yet. "All right," he said. "What is it that you want from me? From us?"

"I wanna pay you back for all the kindness that you showed me an' my friends, last time I come through town."

"To rob the bank, you mean."

"We mighta tried to make a small withdrawal," Fergus granted, smiling.

"Theft, I call it. And a violation of the sacred Eighth Commandment."

"Here we go," said Dawkins. "Hallelujah!"

"You ain't here to preach," said Fergus, with his smile long gone. "You're here to listen. What you're gonna do is get the townsfolk all together and—"

Before he finished, Tad and Earl returned with Marshal Cooper, carrying the long guns from his office, with their extra ammunition. Earl saw that they'd interrupted Fergus in the middle of a speech and muttered, "Sorry, Cousin."

Fergus stared at him a second, then pressed on. "Get your people all together and—"

"I will not," said the preacher.

"Come again?"

"I serve the Lord. I don't take orders from a thief and murderer."

"Is that a fact?"

"It is."

"Awrighty, then." Fergus approached him, two long strides, drawing his Colt. He cocked it, pressed its muzzle to the parson's forehead, and inquired, "You sure about that, now?"

The pastor closed his eyes and said, "The Lord is my shepherd, I shall not want. He maketh me to lie down in green pastures. He leadeth me beside the still waters."

"What'n hell is this?" asked Kilgore.

"Sin buster's prayin'," said Dawkins.

"He restoreth my soul. He leadeth me in the paths of righteousness for His name's sake."

Fergus slapped the preacher with his free hand, focused his attention. Asked him, "How's He feel about you lettin' women die while you do nothin'?"

With his last words, Fergus turned the Colt toward Mayor Lowman's wife, already weeping where she stood beside her husband.

"Wait!" the parson blurted out.

"Wait, *what*?"

"Wait . . . please?"

"Tha's good enough. Now, as I tried to say before I was so rudely interrupted, what you're gonna do is get your people all together, in the street."

"And how am I supposed to do that?" asked the preacher.

"I already seen you got a bell up in your steeple," Fergus said. "You're gonna ring it till they gather. Till your arms drop off, if need be. Since it ain't a Sunday, that should bring 'em out."

"And if it doesn't?"

Fergus thought about it for a moment, then replied, "You raise a cry of 'Fire.' "

"What fire?"

"The one I'm gonna light inside your chapel, if the bell don't work."

The pastor blanched. "You'd burn God's holy sanctuary?"

"I've done worse'n that," said Fergus. "You can bank on it."

"And when you have your audience? What then?"

"We're gonna have a hoedown nobody in this burg will forget, long as they live."

Which won't be very goddamned long, he thought.

"It seems I have no choice," the preacher said.

"You're catchin' on. We're gonna walk across now, for some bell-ringin'. Earl, you an' Tad stay here and keep an eye on all these guns."

"Yes, sir," the cousins said, together.

"Awright," said Fergus to the rest. "Let's go. And bear in mind, the first one tries to run'll be the next one meetin' Jesus."

16

Slade was about to leave the alley when he saw two of his convicts crossing Main Street, with a third man walking out in front of them. Dawkins and Kilgore were dressed up in clothes that they'd stolen somewhere, both wearing pistols on their hips. The third man, from his outfit, looked to be a preacher—which made sense, since they were coming from a church. The parson's face was grim, unhappy with whatever errand he was running, while the fugitives looked shifty, peering up and down the street as if expecting somebody to call them out.

Not yet.

Slade could have dropped one of them with the Springfield, easily, but then he'd have to duel the other with an unfamiliar six-gun and the minister to think about. Besides which, he still had to locate Mayfield and the shooters who had sprung him, make sure everyone was present and accounted for, before he turned Main Street into battleground.

The preacher and his escort crossed Main Street diago-
nally, stepping lively, till they reached the sidewalk on the
east side of the street and entered Hilker's Hardware. Slade
immediately thought of guns and ammunition, probably at
least one hostage in the shop, as well.

But why a preacher?

He'd have bet his yearly salary that neither Mayfield nor
is friends were praying men. Fetching the minister particularly must mean something, but he couldn't work it through
without more information, so he let it go. Slade was considering a shift, hoping to find a better vantage point without
one of the convicts stopping him, when people started
trooping from the hardware store.

First came the preacher he'd just seen, followed immediately by a well-dressed couple in their early forties, and a
stocky man who wore a tin star on his shirt, but no gunbelt.
Behind those four came Fergus Mayfield in the flesh,
Kilgore and Dawkins flanking him. The fugitives looked
wary, careful not to let their hands stray far from holstered
guns.

Now, what the hell? Slade asked himself.

The group of seven crossed Main Street, the preacher
leading once again, until they reached his church and passed
inside. Slade let them go, holding his fire. He still had two
men unaccounted for—the one who'd come into his camp
before the shooting started and another who'd been firing
from the dark during the break. He guessed that they were
likely in the hardware store, but couldn't count on it unless
he saw them there.

And seeing them was critical, since one of them had
done his dirty work long-range, unseen. Slade could have
passed him on the street and never known it, since he
hadn't seen the shooter's face.

Something he planned to remedy, and soon.

But first, he had to have a plan.

With three men in the church, no windows facing toward the street that he could see, Slade had a certain freedom of mobility. From where he stood, he should be able to cross Main Street without being recognized from Hilker's Hardware. Keep his head down, tilt his hat a little to the left and shade his face that way, his badge already out of sight. The shooters who'd left him for dead on the trail weren't expecting to see Slade again, so a glimpse of a man crossing Main Street should raise no alarm.

His problem: with two shooters unaccounted for, he had to locate both, before he started anything. It wouldn't do to have the fifth man popping out from somewhere unexpected, once the fat was in the fire.

So, nice and easy. Should he risk a stroll past Hilker's, glancing through the broad front window? Slade decided that would be too much, pushing his luck too far. Better, perhaps, to find the shop's back door and try to slip inside— although attempting that might jeopardize another set of hostages he hadn't seen, so far.

Damn it! There must be something he could do, some kind of a preliminary move that wouldn't put himself or anybody else directly on the firing line before he was prepared to strike. Now, all he had to do was think of it and press ahead.

Slade hadn't found the answer when the church bell started tolling, as if summoning the parson's flock to Sunday services.

"You reckon Cousin Fergus means to leave us stuck in here?" Tad asked.

"We're stickin' with the guns, is all, jus' like he said," Earl answered.

"Mebbe so."

"What other reason would there be?" Earl tried to keep from sounding too exasperated with his brother, bearing in mind that his brain didn't work quite like most men's his age.

"Dunno," Tad said. "Mebbe he wants to keep us from the fun."

"The fun ain't started yet," Earl said, eyeing the hardware salesman's wife. "He'll tip us when it's time."

"He better."

Earl frowned at his brother's sullen tone. He moved in closer, lowering his voice, and said, "We kep' him outa prison, didn't we? Why'd you think he'd wanna gyp us?"

"He leaves us here with *them*," Tad answered, nodding toward their nervous-looking hostages. "What happens when he rings the bell and people start to flock around the church? We's separated from the others, on our own. Somethin' goes wrong, we's penned up like them fellas at the Alamo."

"The hell you know about the Alamo?" Earl challenged. "Did you see a single Mexican out there?"

"I didn't mean—"

"You're worryin' for nothin'," Earl said, interrupting him. "First thing we oughta do is get that stiff moved in the back."

"I dunno, Earl."

"You dunno *what*?"

"I don't like touchin' dead folks."

"Oh? I don't recall you havin' any trouble with that little girly, at the homestead."

"You shut up about that, now!"

"Or, what?"

No answer. Tad was glaring at his own feet, while his cheeks flushed crimson. Earl had learned to recognize the signs of an explosion coming on and dropped it. Turning to the shop's proprietors, he said, "You two, come on and shift the dead meat outya sight, in case a customer comes in."

The man looked sour about it, and his missus made a little gaspy noise, but both of them hopped to it when they saw Earl pull his shooting iron. He watched them move the corpse, him lifting underneath the dead boy's arms, her tugging at his pants cuffs, sort of dragging him into the back room, leaving him beside a rolltop desk, beyond the line of sight of someone entering the store.

Returning to the main room, Earl found Tad loading one of a half-dozen Winchester rifles displayed in a wall rack for sale. "The hell you doin' that for?" he demanded.

"Getting' ready, jus' in case," Tad said.

"In case of what?"

"In case the folks don't like whatever Cousin Fergus tells 'em, once he gets 'em all together."

And he had to give the kid credit for that. Earl hadn't thought of it, himself. It was the five of them against a *town*, for Christ's sake. Even with the main stockpile of guns corralled, it stood to reason there'd be others floating around Gilead. Most men, in Earl's experience, liked having guns nearby, for an emergency, or just to make them feel more manly. There was bound to be some shooting, even if his people did it all. So why waste time reloading, when they'd seized a good-sized arsenal.

"You ain't as dumb as people say," he told Tad, coming closer to a compliment than usual.

"Told ya," his brother said, smiling.

Earl grabbed another of the Winchesters and started

loading from the box of cartridges that Tad had opened on the glass-topped showcase. Having loaded guns around their hostages was risky, but he didn't think the pair of them had nerve enough to make a play. The man wasn't a fighter, and he had his shit-scared wife to think about. He might try something later, when they got around to her, but in the meantime . . .

The tolling of the church bell startled Earl, although he'd been expecting it. Somehow, he had expected it to be a smaller sound, like come and get it from a chuck wagon, instead of rolling tones that echoed up and down Main Street, from one end to the other. Truth be told, its ringing made the short hairs on his nape stand up, as if it were foretelling doom.

"We better hurry up," he told his brother. "Case we need these rifles sooner'n I thought."

"We ever gonna see this town?" asked Jubal Leach.

"If you can last another five, six miles," Mike Bowers said, "we should be comin' up on it."

"And no saloon, you said." Floyd Dooley speaking up.

"*I* said," Ed Schultz corrected him. "The beer was all right, at the restaurant."

"I'm getting hungry, anyway," Vance Underwood allowed.

"First thing we have to do," Bowers reminded them, "is have a look around and see that everything's shipshape. If there's no trouble, you can go'n eat or drink your fill. I'll find the constable and have a word."

"And if there *is* trouble?" asked Leach. "What, then?"

"Depends," said Bowers. "If it's obvious the gang's in town and raisin' hell, we ride in strong and put a stop to it."

"You don't suppose they might be quiet, like, about it?" Dooley asked.

"You can't be quiet while you're hazing round a town," Bowers replied. "But how's this: if it all looks normal, I'll ride in alone. The rest of you wait close enough to hear if anyone starts shootin' at me. Give it fifteen minutes, more or less, and follow me if nothin' happens."

"But suppose they *do* start shooting at you?" Underwood inquired.

"Then let your conscience be your guide. Either help or cut and run. Whatever you can live with best."

He left it there, on them, and concentrated on the bare suggestion of a road in front of him. That was the trouble with civilian posses, thrown together from a bunch of guys who meant well when they started, then got bored or saddle sore and started thinking about all that they were missing, back at home. Their women, home-cooked meals, a roof over their heads, and money in the till if they were businessmen. Before it ever came to shooting, they were half worn down, and some of them were bound to soil their britches when the bullets started flying.

Amateurs.

They liked the thought of riding after bad men, bringing them to justice, but reality was something else. Most didn't care for sleeping on the ground or eating campfire beans, much less for burning powder in a showdown to the death.

But here they were, his motley band of moaning, groaning volunteers.

Five miles to go, based on the estimate Ed Schultz had made, some hours back. Bowers had hoped they might meet Jack Slade on the trail, but there had been no sign of him. Slade either had a solid lead on them, or he had gone some other way and wasn't bound for Gilead. Too bad, since he was known to be a steady hand in killing situations, but that wouldn't matter if the gang was headed somewhere else, and they found Gilead at peace.

He'd lose his posse then, Bowers was fairly sure—or most of them, at least. Dooley might stick. He had a kid's enthusiasm for the chase, but Underwood and Leach would definitely turn for home, since going on meant riding into Kansas and beyond their vision of the world. Schultz might go either way, after a good night's sleep in Gilead, but three men hunting five wasn't the best deal Bowers ever heard of.

Then again, it beat hell out of pressing on alone.

Which he was bound to do, unless something they found in Gilead convinced him that the fugitives had gone another way. He couldn't think what that might be, off hand, but he would try to keep an open mind.

And try to think up some excuse Judge Dennison would swallow, if he came back empty-handed.

Lost my posse wouldn't cut it. Neither would *They didn't go to Gilead*. The badge he'd volunteered to wear was heavy on a day like this, when there were grave decisions to be made. It sometimes made him wish he'd picked another line of work, but when he thought of the alternatives, that flipped him back the other way.

Five miles or less now. Say an hour and a quarter at their present walking pace. They should be spotting Gilead on the horizon in another thirty minutes, maybe sooner.

Soon enough to worry, Bowers thought and did his best to make his mind go blank.

The church was more or less what Fergus Mayfield had expected. Straight-backed wooden pews that looked as if they were designed to make your back and butt ache, all at once. A podium up front, on risers, so the runty preacher could look down on his parishioners while he lambasted them with threats of hellfire. Up behind the dais, where a more affluent church might have a stained-glass window, hung the biggest cross he'd ever seen, made out of rough-hewn logs.

"You call this place God's house?" Mayfield inquired.

"I do," the preacher said.

"So, where's he at?"

"Our Lord is everywhere."

"Spread purty thin, I take it."

"I can tell you that He's watching every move you make and judging you."

"He wouldn't be the first," Mayfield replied, treating his little audience to one of his unsettling smiles. "Guess he can stop me anytime he wants to, then?"

"If that's His pleasure," said the minister.

"Well, while we're waitin' for the lightning bolts to hit me, grab that bell rope and start ringin' like your life depended on it. 'Cause it does."

The preacher had his glare down to a science, doubtless honed through years of scaring children, but he did as he was told. At first, Mayfield was worried that the bell might be defective, then he realized it took a second for the preacher's tugging on the stout rope to elicit a response up in the belfry. When the bell started to clang, it echoed through the nearly empty church, and he could hear its tones rolling along Main Street, down through the heart of Gilead.

"Tha's good. Keep at it," he commanded, moving past Dawkins and Kilgore, past their hostages, to peer out through the door that they'd left standing open. From the north end of the street, he had a clear view straight through town, where people had begun to poke their heads from doors and windows.

"Now they're gettin' it," he called back to the pastor. "Keep it comin'!"

The preacher had removed his hat on entering the church, and Mayfield saw him sweating now, either from his exertion or the knowledge that he might be ringing out his last moments on earth. He wondered if the gospel sharp was sorry he'd come by the jail to rant at Mayfield on his first visit to Gilead, or if he simply saw himself as one more righteous martyr for the Lord.

Whichever, he was bound to bleed the same.

People were stepping out of shops and offices along the street, now, looking toward the church, a couple of the men drifting in that direction. Mayfield hung back in the shadowed doorway, out of sight, noting that none of those he saw so far were armed.

Why should they be? Who would expect a church bell's summons to announce their end of days?

Mayfield knew people, and he figured some among the couple hundred souls in Gilead would hang back, even with the bell demanding their attention. They'd see others answering the call and leave it to their neighbors. Lazy ones, the housebound, maybe those with just a bit more natural suspicion in their hearts. When they saw Mayfield and his partners rounding up the rest, there could be trouble, but he'd planned for that, rehearsed it in his mind.

Last time around, with Hagenmaier and Stovall, he'd been careless. Mayfield's first mistake had been expecting everyone in town to stand around and gawk while they cleaned out the bank and rode off with their loot. He hadn't counted on the spirit of community, but this time it would work against the good people of Gilead. They'd rally to their pastor's call, and by the time they found themselves under the gun it would be too late for them to fight back.

Most of them, anyhow.

If any tried, they'd have to shoot through friends and neighbors, or sit by and watch while Mayfield executed hostages at random. He'd have been surprised if any let it go that far, but since he planned to wipe out Gilead in any case, he didn't give a fig who was the first to die.

There were enough to go around, and then some.

Slade watched the folk of Gilead respond to the insistent chiming of their church bell. He'd considered stepping out and warning them, but then thought better of it. Mayfield and his two gun hands already had three prisoners inside the church, and probably at least one more inside the hardware store. If Slade raised the alarm, he'd put those hostages at risk.

And what would he achieve by waiting?

Maybe nothing, but he figured Mayfield wasn't summoning the town en masse just for the pleasure of observing them. He'd want to dress them down for starters, going back to when they'd captured him and killed his two accomplices. While he was doing that, before he got around to anything more serious, Slade hoped to find an opening, an opportunity to make his move and interrupt what likely had been planned out as a slaughter.

Knowing, at the same time, that a false move on his part could set it off.

Slade judged the distance to the church, from where he stood, at right about two hundred yards. That was the nearest calibration on his borrowed carbine's graduated sight, well within killing range for the Springfield's .45-70 Gov-

ernment rounds, but he'd have to be careful about slinging
lead down Main Street, with a crowd in the way.

If he could find a better vantage point . . .

The church was Gilead's tallest building, with its steeple, but the hotel came close. To reach it, Slade would have
to cross the street, then hope that he could find a way up to
its flat roof from ground level. If he couldn't manage that,
maybe another building on the east side of Main Street
would do as well. If nothing else, he might be able to
reduce the distance to his target, find a way to fire over the
heads of townspeople who were already trooping toward
the church, and cover Hilker's Hardware, too, while he was
at it.

Maybe.

But not likely.

Mayfield had been smart in splitting up the gang. The
way it stood, the folks who were advancing toward the
church were in a cross fire, once they passed the hardware
store. Nowhere to turn when shooting started, and no cover
in the middle of the street. Five gunmen likely couldn't
drop them all, before some scattered into shops along the
way, but they could still wreak bloody havoc. After that, it
would come down to hunting those who lived, hunting them
from door to door.

Or, they could always torch the town.

Fire was the dread of every prairie settlement—a wild,
ferocious thing that could devour a town the size of Gilead
within an hour's time, if there was wind behind it. Slade
had seen a mining town burn once, in Colorado, after
someone dropped a lamp in the saloon and couldn't beat
the flames out quick enough to stop them spreading. It was
something that he never hoped to see again.

That choice, however, wasn't his.

He'd found the fugitives that he was looking for, all ripe for hanging now, whatever they had done before the prison break. Bringing them in, alive or dead, was his responsibility— but so, in turn, was the defense of their prospective future victims.

Time to move.

At least three dozen people were proceeding toward the church, by now. Slade took advantage of the crowd to cross Main Street, making a beeline for the alleyway directly opposite his starting point. The tolling bell provided a distraction, no one on the street paying attention to the stranger in their midst. He reached the other side and ducked back into shade, circling around the east-side buildings. Slade had counted doorways heading northward, so he'd know when he had reached the rear of the hotel. From there, he would rely on luck to get him topside, with a clear shot at the church.

His luck was holding. With an eye toward safety, the hotel provided fire escapes for tenants occupying bedrooms on the second floor. Just wooden ladders, but they granted access to the roof, as well as to the ground, for workmen who might have to make repairs.

Slade chose the nearest ladder, clutched the Springfield carbine awkwardly beneath one armpit, and began to climb.

17

"A couple more tugs oughta do it," Mayfield told the preacher. "Put your back into it now, and give it ever'thing you got."

The Bible thumper had begun to sag from his exertion, clinging to the bell rope now as if it was the only thing preventing him from dropping to the floor. For all of that, the expression on his sweaty face remained a mixture of contempt and rage toward Mayfield.

"Penny for your thoughts," he told the minister. "I bet they ain't real Christian."

The preacher gave his rope one final yank, tolling the bell above, then let it go and took a backward step. "You'd be correct," he said. "I'll ask forgiveness of our Savior when your soul's burning in Hell."

"Mebbe I'll se ya there," Mayfield replied. "I never knew a preacher in my life who wasn't sinnin' on the sly."

"I've fallen short, no doubt. But—"

"Save it for your sheep, pastor. They're linin' up outside to see what made you call 'em."

With a motion of his six-gun, Mayfield brought the preacher forward, prodding him in the direction of the open door. "You, too," he told the others. "Marshal. Mayor. Let's make it ladies first, why don't we? Danny, grab them lanterns in the corner, there, and get 'em lit. I want 'em front 'n' center in the aisle, here."

With the hostages in front of him, Mayfield stepped back into the daylight, squinting at the townsfolk gathering in answer to the bell. He guessed that there were forty standing in the street already, and another couple dozen straggling in behind them. Not the full turnout he'd hoped for, but he had a good idea of what would fetch the rest.

Angling his Colt skyward, he fired a single shot and chuckled as the preacher flinched, ducking his head. "Don't worry, parson," Mayfield said. "I'm told you never hear the shot that kills you."

"Not unless they shoot ya in the gut," Dawkins chimed in, behind him.

Mayfield raised his voice now, to address the milling crowd. "Stand easy, now," he said, taking control. "You prob'ly wonder why your preacher called you like this, but it was my idea. Y'all remember me?"

He pushed out, past the hostages, to stand in front of them for all to see. Some of the good folk had begun to mutter, recognizing him from when they'd all come traipsing past his cell, like they were looking at a monkey in a zoo.

"That's right, I'm back," he told them, beaming. "You most likely heard that I was on my way to Leavenworth, to get my just desserts. Thing is, I didn't feel like spendin' twenty-five years in a cage, so here we are. One happy family. And this time, *I* decide who takes the medicine."

More muttering, but none of them were armed, as far as he could tell. He didn't think the men would rush three guns, with women in the crowd, but just in case—

"Before some of you start to feelin' brave," he said, "get set to lose your preacher, mayor, and marshal when the shootin' starts. Since none of you are packin' guns, it's gonna be a bit one-sided. And did I mention that we ain't alone? I got more boys across the street there, in the hardware shop, who don't mind back shootin' a bit."

That turned some of their heads around and got a couple of the women looking weepy-eyed. One of the quickest ways to soften up a man. Mayfield kept smiling, gaining confidence with every passing moment.

"What I got in mind," he told them, "is a little taste of justice. Not the kind you're used to, mebbe, but I'd say it's overdue."

Dead silence now, and more folks coming down Main Street to join the gathering. He called to them, over the faces peering up at him.

"C'mon and join the party, people! Don't be shy! It's Judgment Day!"

Halfway across the hotel's roof, Slade realized he couldn't just stroll up and watch the street below, in case somebody spotted him up there. Mayfield, Dawkins, and Kilgore would be looking more or less in his direction, as they covered people moving toward the church, and any one of them could see him on the roof, outlined against blue sky.

Reluctantly, he dropped to hands and knees, crawling

that way to reach the northwest corner of the roof. It turned out that the roof wasn't completely flat, as he'd imagined, but it had a little ridge across the middle of it, so that rain or melting snow would drain off into downspouts. Creeping toward the corner he'd selected, then, he slid a little, but the angle wasn't steep enough to dump him overboard.

Slade took his hat off as he reached the hotel's decorative cornice, overlooking Main Street. Rising far enough to see the church, he saw that something like a hundred people were collected there, with still more on the way. Not sure he would have answered to a church bell's ringing, personally, Slade knew that some small towns used it as a general alarm, in the event of some calamity.

This time, it worked against them.

The convicts had their hostages outside the church now, on its slightly elevated porch, two steps above the crowd. Mayfield was saying something to the townspeople, and while Slade couldn't make it out, he had a fair idea of how the rant would go. The people who had captured him and shot his outlaw friends were meant to suffer for it, had to learn their lesson, on and on.

One thing he'd learned, dealing with criminals, was that damned few of them accepted blame for anything they did. Robbing, raping, or killing, take your pick. The lawman who arrested them, the jurors who convicted them, the judge who sentenced them were held responsible. Felons spun fantasies of sweet revenge as if human society itself had been created solely as a means of persecuting them. The thought of "getting even" for some nonexistent injury came as a natural reflex to bad men—and some women— Slade had known.

But relatively few pursued it, even when the opportunity

arose. In Fergus Mayfield's case, he had not only followed through but also sucked four other men into the vortex of his fantasy.

And stopping them was bound to be a problem for one beat-up lawman on his own.

Slade judged the distance from his aerie to the church door as about one hundred yards. From where he sat, there was a good chance he could drill Mayfield, but after that there would be hell to pay. Six seconds for an expert to reload the trapdoor carbine, and within that time, Dawkins and Kilgore could be killing hostages, or firing wild into the crowd. And two more gunmen, likely firing from the hardware store.

How many dead or wounded, by the time Slade was prepared to fire his second shot? Assuming he could even find another target, then?

Too many.

Wait and see what happens next, Slade thought. *But don't wait too damned long.*

"You see there, Tad? It's workin' out jus' like he said."

Earl Mayfield couldn't hide his admiration for his cousin. Fergus was a thinker, always planning things. Granted, his schemes fell through sometimes, like when he'd tried to rob the bank in Gilead, but that was part of thinking big. And here he was, fresh out of jail, come back to make it right.

To make the people who had messed with him regret the error of their ways.

Earl couldn't say exactly what would happen after that. Maybe a fast ride down to Mexico, or out to California, where they'd do whatever took their fancy. Live like kings on other people's money, until . . . what? Earl couldn't see that far ahead, but he supposed Fergus would let him know what to expect from each day, as they went along.

One thing: they'd have to get through this day, first.

Earl couldn't help it; he was worried about all those people in the street. Suppose they took it in their heads to rush at Fergus and the others. He and Tad could only shoot so many of them from the hardware store, before they tore his cousin limb from limb. And then, where would he be?

Another thing that troubled Earl was all the townspeople he *couldn't* see. For all he knew, there could be twice as many folks in Gilead as what were on the street so far. He pictured them in shops and homes, loading their guns or honing knives, maybe getting some courage from a bottle, working up the nerve to strike.

He thought about the dumb kid coming in behind them, then, and started feeling jumpy.

"Tad!"

"Yeah?"

"Go in back, there, and make sure the door's locked."

"With the dead'un?"

"He ain't gonna bite you."

"Jesus, Earl—"

"Just do it!"

"Yeah, okay."

Earl watched the hostages, edgy around the rifles lined up on the showcase, until Tad returned. "All set?" he asked.

"It weren't locked, but it is now," Tad replied.

"Okay, then." No more rude surprises.

Tad edged toward the shop's front window, carrying one of the hardware fella's Winchesters. "What's Fergus tellin' 'em out there, you figger?"

"Hell if I know. You can bet it ain't how much he loves 'em," Earl replied.

"I reckon not." Tad watched the show go on another minute, then asked, "Are we gonna kill 'em all, you think?"

"Can't say."

That made the hardware lady gasp and snuffle, turn in toward her husband when he put his arm around her. Earl had grown up hearing women cry—his mother, aunts, and sisters—and it didn't melt his heart, the way it did some men's. He'd come to see it as the way of life: people were happy, sad, or angry, then they died.

"Whatever," Tad replied, "I wish we'd get on with it."

"You just keep a sharp eye out," Earl ordered. "If the crowd starts gettin' twitchy, lemme know right quick."

"And blast 'em?"

"That's the ticket."

Earl was getting nervous, too, but daren't let it show, for Tad's sake. Fergus was the thinker of the family, but Earl had always been his brother's rock, his anchor, when the pair of them were cut adrift and overwhelmed.

Like now.

Earl felt his knuckles aching, where he'd clutched his Winchester too tightly, and he willed his fingers to relax. A few more minutes, he decided.

Then the party would begin.

"You hear that?" Ed Schultz asked.

"It sounds like bells," Floyd Dooley said.

"One bell," Mike Bowers corrected him. "Like from a school, or a church."

"It's not Sunday," Vance Underwood said.

"No," said Bowers. "It's not."

"Trouble, then?" Jubal Leach asked the group.

They had just caught their first glimpse of Gilead, off in

the distance, increasing the tension among them. Bowers didn't have to guess what they were thinking, each man wondering if there'd be gun work waiting for them in the town and how they'd each stand up to it. Men judged themselves in different ways—by land possessed, or money earned, sometimes the women they attracted—but a killing fight tested their mettle to the core.

"Reckon we'd better see what that's about," said Bowers, nudging his sabino mare into a rapid trot.

The others kept up with him, one or two of them a little hesitant, but no one falling far behind. They'd come this far from home to prove themselves, when others quailed, and none of them was showing yellow now, however shaky they might feel inside.

Bowers was fighting an attack of nerves, himself. Why not admit it? If the clanging bell ahead wasn't a summons to a picnic—damned unlikely in the middle of a weekday afternoon—then Gilead had trouble. Possibly a fire, in which case extra hands would never be unwelcome. Or a gang of killer convicts tearing up the place.

The good news: if it *was* their pack of fugitives, his posse had their number roughly matched.

The bad news: none of those who'd joined the hunt were killers.

Maybe townsfolk would assist them, maybe not. You never knew exactly how civilians would behave, under the gun—or lawmen, either, when it came to that. Some officers, and local law especially, were affable and slow to shoot, while others kept the lid clamped tight, didn't shy away from spilling blood. People in Gilead had captured Fergus Mayfield once before, and killed a couple of his pals, but Bowers had to wonder whether that had been their one hurrah.

If maybe they had nothing left.

A quarter mile from town, Bowers reined in and waited for the others. Dooley rode a little way beyond him, then caught on and doubled back.

"What's goin' on?" asked Schultz.

"Before we ride in there," said Bowers, "I want to remind you that it's *my* job to arrest the men we're after, if they're willing to surrender. You all volunteered to come along, but in a pinch you need to look out for yourselves. Hear me? Your daily rate don't cover funerals or widows."

"What?" asked Leach. "You want us to turn tail?"

"I'm sayin', if you follow me from here on in, do what you have to, to protect yourselves. Don't plan on takin' anyone alive, unless he's dropped his gun and comes with hands held high."

"You're purty sure it's trouble, then," said Dooley.

"Pretty sure," said Bowers. "But you won't know till you're in the thick of it. That happens, keep your head down and your eyes wide open."

It was all he had to say, and Bowers wheeled his mare back toward the town of Gilead, with its incessant tolling bell.

It was a heady moment, staring out at upturned faces, reading fear on most of them, impotent anger on the rest. The bullet graze on Fergus Mayfield's chest was barely an annoyance now, as the adrenaline pumped through his veins, invigorating him. He thought he understood how ancient conquerors had felt, standing amidst the ruins of a city they had sacked. This just might be the moment he'd been waiting for since he was born.

And it was going to get better, yet.

If he could only think of something more to say.

How could he suddenly run out of words, when he'd

rehearsed this moment in his mind a hundred times? Frustration made him grind his teeth, the townsfolk staring at him, waiting, until sudden inspiration dawned on Mayfield.

"You, preacher! You got the good book memorized, I reckon."

"Well . . ."

He jabbed the muzzle of his Colt into the parson's ribs. "Do ya, or not?"

"I know most of it," said the minister.

"Awright, then. Give 'em somethin' good about revenge."

The preacher thought about it for a second, was about to get another jab, when he said, "Romans 12:19, 'Vengeance is mine; I will repay, saith the Lord.' "

"Not *that,* damn it!" growled Mayfield. "Ain't no vengeance from your lord today. It's *my* turn. Hit 'em with a better one!"

"Um . . . well . . . there's chapter 21 of Luke: 'For these are the days of vengeance, that all things which are written may be fulfilled.' "

"Tha's better. Speak some more, preacher!"

The pastor cleared his throat, then told the crowd, "Ezekiel 25:17. 'And I will execute great vengeance upon them with furious rebukes; and they shall know that I am the Lord, when I shall lay my vengeance upon them.' "

"Now you're talkin'. Drop the lord and put in Fergus Mayfield. Furious rebukes, by God, for what you done to me! One more, and put some hellfire in it!"

Another moment while the preacher thought about it, then he told his audience, "From chapter 32 of Deuteronomy: 'For a fire is kindled in mine anger, and shall burn unto the lowest Hell, and shall consume the earth with her increase, and set on fire the foundations of the mountains.' "

Mayfield felt like cheering. "I dunno about the mountains," he declared, "but this damn place is gonna burn, awright. Startin' right here!"

Turning, Mayfield grabbed the nearer of the lanterns Reese had lit, on his order, and hurled it down the full length of the chapel, toward the pulpit. It fell short, smashing against the front end of the dais, but he didn't mind. A lake of burning kerosene began to spread, flames crackling as they ate into the church's floorboards, racing off in all directions.

"One to grow on!" Mayfield cried, and flung the second lamp off to his left, against the northern wall. In seconds flat, fire climbed the dried-out planks and started licking at the rafters overhead.

A wail went up in unison from the assembled townsfolk, music to his ears, as Mayfield shoved the preacher toward the steps in front of him. The minister resisted, crying out, "Oh, Lord! My God!"

Mayfield couldn't decide if he should plug the sin buster or crack his melon, then it came to him. Stepping aside, he grabbed the preacher's arm, half dragging him back to the doorway of the burning church. "You wanna roast for Jesus?" he demanded. "Be my guest!"

Before the preacher knew exactly what was happening, a hard kick to his backside sent him stumbling through the portal, into swirling flames. He panicked, tried to double back, but Mayfield shot one of his legs from under him and put him on his back, just as a blazing timber fell from somewhere up above and pinned him down.

The screaming started, then, inside the church and outside. Mayfield's captive audience was bolting, scattering, despite their fear of being shot down in their tracks. Kilgore let out a rebel yell, Winchester rising to his shoulder—then his head exploded like a melon with a firecracker inside, and Mayfield dived for cover.

Slade had planned on shooting Mayfield first, was ready for the long shot when his target pitched the minister inside the burning church, but then the crowd broke wild and he heard Kilgore whooping, saw him getting ready to unload on the civilians scattering before him. Knowing that he couldn't save the parson, Slade had done the next best thing and tried to help the fleeing townsfolk.

One man down—but now, he'd lost the leader of the pack.

Mayfield had ducked behind the church, taking advantage of the black smoke pouring from door, windows, and belfry. In the time it took to register that he was gone, Reese Dawkins also made his break, diving into the crowd that had begun dispersing, scooping up a slender woman whom he held in front of him, a wriggling human shield, to make his way across Main Street.

Slade had another cartridge in his Springfield '86 by then but couldn't risk a shot at Dawkins with his captive in the way. He looked around for Mayfield, hoping he might surface, but the shops and offices along the western side of Main Street gave him perfect cover if he chose to run the full length of the town. Slade gave it up and swung his carbine back toward Dawkins, who had reached the eastern sidewalk now, outside of Hilker's Hardware.

Where, as far as Slade could tell, the other members of the gang were still holed up.

Slade's rooftop perch was useless now, he realized, as Dawkins and his hostage disappeared inside the hardware store. Unless one of the gang emerged onto the street, the

best that Slade could do from where he sat was shoot holes
through the roof at random, wasting ammunition with no
positive result.

So, time to move again.

But if they spotted him, descending from the roof could
get Slade killed. One of the shooters from the hardware
store could duck out through the back door, down below,
and pick him off the fire escape like swatting roaches off a
wall.

Stop wasting time!

Slade bolted for the east side of the roof, slipping along
the back slope, craning for a look over the edge, to see if
anyone was waiting for him down below. All clear, so far.
The worst bit came when he was forced to turn his back
and worm his way onto the ladder, probing blindly with his
right foot, finding purchase, then beginning his descent.
Last thing before he left the roof, Slade grabbed the Springfield carbine that he'd laid aside, clutching the ladder rungs
in front of him one-handed, while his legs did all the work.

That was the time for someone to pop out and drop him,
but they missed the chance. Slade guessed that Dawkins,
running for his life, had failed to note where Slade's one
shot had come from, or perhaps his cronies in the hardware
store had balked at coming out to hunt a sniper. Either way,
when he was halfway down the ladder, Slade let go and
dropped the last ten feet of so. He landed crouching, with
the Springfield angled toward the back door of the shop
downrange, no targets visible.

Now, it was time to hunt.

18

By the time Mike Bowers led his posse into Gilead, the church bell had stopped ringing, smoke was rising from a building at the northern end of town, people were running wild on Main Street, and the crack of gunfire echoed in his ears. During the time that it had taken him to ride that final quarter mile, it seemed to Bowers that the town had gone insane.

He didn't waste breath shouting any further warnings to his men. If they weren't smart enough to keep their heads down in a gunfight, there was nothing he could say or do to help them stay alive. His focus, now, was on the fugitives who'd left a trail of death across the territory, on their way to Gilead.

First problem: Bowers knew there were five members in the gang, but only three of them were known to him by sight, from seeing them in court or in the lockup, back in Enid. That left two he wouldn't recognize if they were standing right in front of him—that is, until they opened fire.

Not good.

He saw the marshal's office up ahead and to his left, reining his mare in that direction as the street began to clear.
Townsfolk were ducking into any door they found unlocked,
some dodging into alleyways between the different shops,
some of the men tugging their women by the hand, while
others fled alone. Some of the random shots, at least, were
coming from the shattered window of a hardware store,
downrange and to his right.

If he could find the town's lawman—

A pistol blazed at Bowers from an alley on his left. The
bullet struck his mare and brought her down, pitching him
forward, through a tumbling somersault. Bowers heard
something snap inside his shoulder as he hit the ground,
immediately followed by a blaze of pain that left him gasp-
ing in the dust, his right arm limp and useless.

Collarbone, he thought, fighting the throb of agony that
left him dizzy when he tried to stand. Frustrated there, he
scrabbled clear on hand and knees, trailing his dead arm
like a flipper, sparking fresh pain every time his fingers
grazed the dirt. Mounting the wooden sidewalk was a
major challenge, Bowers nearly fainting from the effort,
but he made it somehow, scuttling crablike to the meager
safety of a recessed doorway.

Christ, that hurt!

Pressing his back against the doorjamb, pushing with his
feet, Bowers at last was able to stand upright. Grateful for the
hammer thong that kept his six-gun in its holster, he reached
over with his left hand to release it, no more awkward than if
he had tried to do it with his toes. He'd never practiced with
the gun left-handed, which seemed foolish to him now that
he was in a pickle, but he couldn't turn back time.

Someone had shot him off his horse—but who? A

member of the gang? Or had it been a frightened townsman, thinking Bowers might be one of *them*.

And what had happened to the other members of his
posse? He supposed they'd ridden past him when he fell,
believing they were leaderless and going—where, exactly?

Have to find them, Bowers thought. But that meant stepping onto Main Street, wounded, knowing there were hos-
tile guns on either side of him. Given the choice, he'd rather
find somewhere to hide until the shooting stopped, but that
wasn't an option while he wore a badge.

He was bracing for a lurch into the clear, when suddenly
the door opened behind him and a man's voice asked him,
"Who in hell are you?"

Fergus Mayfield hadn't seen the sniper who'd blown Kilgore's head to smithereens, but he was quick enough to duck
around the smoking church and out of sight before the
marksman put a round through him. Once he was under
cover, Mayfield ran around the back, ducking a gust of
flame that licked out through a window, reaching for him,
and slowed down once he was safe behind the other buildings on the western side of Main Street.

Slowed, but didn't stop.

His mama may have birthed a killer, but she hadn't
raised a fool. Until he knew exactly who had fired that killing shot, his safety lay in movement, staying out of sight
of any townsman with a rifle in his hands. His cousins
and Reese Dawkins were already shooting up the town.
Mayfield could hear it, and the women screaming. That
was music to his ears, but if he wanted to enjoy it, then he
had to find out who had taken the potshot at Kilgore and
make sure it wasn't repeated.

Halfway down the line of buildings, staying in their shade, he ducked into an alley running east-west, jogging down to get a look at Main Street from another angle. If the shooter was on top of any building on the other side, Mayfield hoped he might catch a glimpse and try to get around behind him somehow. Give him a surprise. Instead, he reached the street in time to see a group of riders—five or six, he thought—come roaring into Gilead from southward, guns in hand.

Now, what the hell?

He saw a glint of metal on the leader's vest and knew it had to be a badge. Some kind of posse, damn it, coming in just when he *didn't* need their goddamned interference.

Mayfield snapped a quick shot at the rider out in front, more of a reflex than a planned move, and the horse went down, its rider vaulting forward, landing good and hard. Before he had a chance to follow through, another of the new arrivals pegged a shot at Mayfield, spooked him back into the alley, then swept past and kept on going. By the time he dared to risk another look, the lawman who had tumbled from his horse was gone.

But where?

Mayfield could see he'd hit the animal and not the rider. It was thrashing weakly, spitting blood. A neck wound. He felt vaguely sorry for the animal, but mostly wished it was his human target lying in the street there, bleeding out.

Uptown, to northward, Tad and Earl were firing willy-nilly from the hardware store, at townsfolk still remaining in the street. Looked like they'd dropped a few, which boosted Mayfield's spirits, but it wasn't turning out to be the party he'd envisioned. The other posse men had all dismounted now and run for cover, while their horses milled about, uncertain where to go. The shooting spooked them, and the crackling fire, the people crying out and running.

It was bedlam.

Smoke was drifting down the length of Main Street, getting thicker, and he wondered if the fire he'd set was spreading from the church to other buildings. Mayfield wouldn't mind if that were so—he'd had it in his mind to raze the town entirely—but he wanted to be well clear of the fire himself, to keep from getting roasted. And his horse was at the livery, north end of Main, approximately opposite the church. If sparks blew that way . . .

Damn it! Time to move again.

Slade didn't know exactly what was happening on Main Street, but it sounded like a riot—or a massacre. He still had three more shops to pass before he reached the back door to the hardware store, edging along and watching out in both directions, front and back, for any shooters who might try to spring a trap. The church smoke teased his nostrils, trying to provoke a sneeze, but he resisted it by biting on his upper lip.

Two shops remaining, and he heard what sounded like a group of riders tearing down Main Street, some of them calling back and forth to one another. Was the gang escaping while he crept along through smoke and shadows and tried to flank them?

No. Another fusillade of rifle fire erupted from the hardware store just then, and more cries from the street. Dawkins was still inside the shop, he guessed—and who else? One of them would be the weasel who had come into their camp to spring the convicts, while another ought to be his cohort, who'd hung back to shoot Guy Hampton from the darkness.

Three of them together, and if Slade could take them by surprise . . .

Don't count your chickens yet, he thought—just as a door flew open, almost in his face, and spilled a man in front of him.

Make that a boy, thirteen or fourteen, tops, scared-looking, empty-handed. When the kid saw Slade, he froze and raised those empty hands in front of him. "Please, mister, don't!" he blurted out, and when Slade didn't shoot him on the spot, he squinted, frowning. "Are you one of *them*?"

Slade pulled the left side of his vest back, showing off his marshal's star. "Take off," he told the kid. "Stay out of sight, the best you can."

"Okay!" The youngster bolted past him, running like he'd never stop. Slade stood and watched him go, until the boy ducked down an alley near the southern end of town.

More shooting from the street now, and he almost doubled back to the last alley he had passed, to find out what was happening on Main Street. He could reach the hardware store that way, as well, but going in the front, against three guns, was tantamount to suicide. Slade paused to check the building that the kid had vacated, a butcher's shop with fresh meat on display, reminding him about the knife tucked in his boot.

A last resort, but still there if he needed it.

He'd reached the back door of the hardware store and paused there, trying to imagine the interior layout. The sales room fronted Main Street, obviously, but there'd be another space in back. Storage, an office, something. Slade had never seen a shop without a back room, yet. Two stories, telling him that the proprietor most likely lived upstairs.

Slade pressed his ear against the door and listened, frowning when he picked up nothing from inside. Maybe he'd caught the cons reloading, and whatever conversation they were having didn't carry to the back. He could wait where he was, until the shooting started up again, or—

Slade reached out and tried the doorknob.

Locked.

Goddamn it, *now* what? He could likely shoot the lock off, but it might take several tries, and in the meantime they'd be ready for him. Quicker just to knock, announce himself, and let them shoot him through the door.

Window, he thought and started looking for another way inside.

"I don't like bein' stuck in here," Reese Dawkins said.

"We're s'poseta wait here," Tad or Earl reminded him.

"Says who?"

"Our cousin Fergus," Earl or Tad replied.

"Yeah? Well, he's *your* cousin, not mine," said Dawkins. "An' I'm sick of takin' orders from him."

Dawkins saw the brothers staring at him like a second head had sprouted from his shoulder, or he'd started jabbering some lingo that they couldn't understand. He stared right back at them until they broke eye contact, turning back to watch the street through what was left of Hilker Hardware's plate-glass window.

Shot to hell it was, most of the glass lying outside, with jagged shards around the edges, giving the appearance of a gaping mouth with crystal fangs. Dawkins stayed off to one side, crouching in the shadows, with the town's mayor and his missus close beside him. Tad and Earl were covering the Hilkers and marshal, saving ammo now that most of Gilead's inhabitants had gotten off the street and out of sight.

"Where'd ever'body go?" one of the brothers asked. Dawkins supposed it must be Tad, the dumber of the two.

"You kiddin' me?" he answered back.

"Uh-uh."

Jesus. "You think they mighta gone inside?" he asked the dummy.

"Mmm. I guess."

The other one asked him, "You see where Fergus went?"

"Lit out when Danny got it," Dawkins said. "He didn't leave no forwardin' address."

"The hell you sayin'?" asked the smarter of the pair.

"He left!" snapped Dawkins. "You two wanna wait around and see if he comes back for you, that's your lookout."

"You're goin'?" Tad was visibly confused.

"Damn right, I'm goin'. An' I'm takin' some a these folks with me, for pertection."

"We's s'posed to watch 'em," Tad reminded him.

"I'll leave ya plenty," Dawkins said. "You wanna fight over the rest, then make your move."

Half bluffing, thinking that the pair of them could take him if they tried. Instead of going for it, though, Earl said, "Ya know, Tad, mebbe we should clear out while the gettin's good."

"But Cousin Fergus—"

"We can look for him," Earl said. "How's that? Mebbe he needs our help, and we're stuck sittin' here."

"I didn't think of that."

I'll bet you didn't, Dawkins thought. And said, "Sounds like a smart idea, to me. Bring all these people with us, no one's gonna try'n pick us off."

"So, where we goin'?" nervous Tad inquired.

"The livery," said Dawkins. "Fetch our horses. An' your cousin's, too, o' course. For when you find him."

Earl was nodding. "We can leave these folks inside the stable. Tie 'em up, or somethin'."

"Sure," Dawkins replied. "Or somethin'." No way he was leaving witnesses alive to tattle on him later.

From the street, a creaking, crashing sound distracted him. He turned in time to see the church's flaming steeple topple over to his left, the peaked top of it smashing on the roof next door and hanging there just long enough to let its flames catch hold. In seconds flat, the other building wore a fiery crown, smoke pouring out from underneath its shingles as they burned.

"I'd say it's time to move," Dawkins announced. "Before the whole damn town goes up."

Earl started prodding at the hostages, using his rifle as a goad. "Awright," he ordered. "Ever'body out!"

"Deputy U.S. marshal," Bowers told the portly man who had a double-barreled shotgun leveled at his face.

The glaring stranger saw his badge, lowered the scattergun, and said, "You'd better get in here."

The door had closed behind him before Bowers realized that he was standing in the lobby of a bank—no doubt, the same one Fergus Mayfield had been robbing when the townsfolk rallied with their guns to capture him.

"You're hunting Mayfield and his bunch?" the banker asked.

"That's the idea."

"Rest of your posse's gone to ground."

"They're new at this."

The banker eyed his dangling arm and said, "Looks like you're hurt."

"The collarbone, I think," said Bowers.

"Can you shoot?" All practicality.

"I'm damn sure gonna try."

"You could stay here and help me guard the bank."

"Sounds good," said Bowers, "but my men—"

"They wouldn't have to know."

"I'd know. They need my help."

"You're crippled up."

"I'll pull my weight," Bowers assured him.

"Suit yourself," the banker huffed. "Those bastards think they're coming back to clean me out second time, they'll have to go through me."

"Good luck to you. Is there a back way out of here?"

"I'll show you," said his host, reluctantly.

Bowers followed the banker back, behind the teller's cages, through a smallish private office situated to the left of an impressive-looking vault. There was an outside door, could have been steel, with double locks on the inside.

"Last chance to stay," the banker said.

"Thanks, anyhow. You got a lawman in this town?"

"Beats me," the banker said. "We *had* one, Declan Cooper, but he could be dead by now, for all I know. He damn sure isn't reining in those yahoos."

"I suspect that he's a mite outnumbered. If I see him, should I—"

"Send him here? hell, no! We're closed!"

"Okay, then. If you'd slip those locks . . ."

Grumbling, the banker tucked his weapon underneath one arm, unlocked the bank's back door, and shut it hastily, as soon as Bowers cleared the threshold. Bowers heard the double locks engage, sealing him out.

I shoulda stayed to guard the money, he considered, but he'd lost that play already. What came next? A painful walk downtown to find his posse men, or maybe stumble over some of Mayfield's raiders. Thinking that, he cocked the Colt he clutched in his left hand, its unfamiliar weight there making Bowers feel doubly lopsided, with his broken clavicle.

Fine way to start a fight.

And now, on top of everything, a cloud of smoke was bearing down on him, borne on a warm breeze blowing from the north. He heard the crackling sound of flames—not too close, yet—and wondered if the town would burn while everyone was hiding out or trading shots with one another. That would tickle Mayfield, he supposed, whether the bandit got to rob the fat man's bank or not.

Fighting the fire was someone else's problem, he decided. Bowers already had enough on his hands—make that *hand*—doing the job that he was paid for.

"Roll out and see the famous one-armed lawman," Bowers muttered to himself, and choked a laugh down when the pain of it brought hot tears to his eyes. By God, that hurt! If he got into any kind of tussle with the desperados he was hunting, Bowers knew that he was finished.

Fair enough. Just shoot them, then.

If he could even manage that.

Slade found the window he was looking for—and it was latched, of course. Tried peering through it, but he only saw dim shapes inside what seemed to be a storeroom. None of them were moving, and they didn't shoot him, so he took a chance. Propping his carbine up against the wall, he drew the butcher's knife out of his boot and went to work.

Some fairly quiet gouging at the windowsill produced a gap. Slade worked his blade through there and found the latch by feel, poking and prodding it, becoming more frustrated by the second, until something gave. Its click seemed loud enough to wake the dead, in spite of gunfire still continuing on Main Street, but it prompted no reaction from inside the hardware store.

Slade sheathed the knife and drew the dead farmer's revolver from beneath his belt. The Springfield wouldn't serve him well if Mayfield's cronies caught him crawling through the window, but a blaze of pistol fire might save his life—or hold them off, at least, until he found some decent cover in the stock room.

First things first. He pushed the window up one-handed, thankful that it wasn't sticky in its frame. When it was open all the way, Slade stuck his head inside to get a better look around, seeing where it was safe for him to step as he climbed through, and had a listen toward the sales room. It had gone dead quiet there, which made him wonder if his enemies were poised, waiting to riddle him with bullets as he dragged himself inside.

And there was only one way to find out.

It was an awkward operation, with the gun in one hand, but he managed it, expecting each second he spent half in and half out of the shop's back room to be his last. Reached back, almost an afterthought, to grab the Springfield from its place outside the window. Crouching, then, the pistol leading him, Slade made his slow way toward a door that opened on the hardware store's main room—and found a corpse lying across his path.

Slade didn't recognize the man, no reason why he should,

except to know he wasn't one of the surviving fugitives whom Slade had seen. By logical extension, he ruled out the other shooter from the ambush that had liberated Mayfield and his fellow prisoners. A townsman, then, who'd gotten in their way somehow and paid the price. Unfortunate, but since he couldn't raise the dead, Slade concentrated on the job at hand. He eased around the supine body, toward the doorway, then rushed through it, teeth bared in a snarl of grim determination.

The empty store yawned at him, unimpressed. Slade saw the open door and shattered window, knew his birds had flown, but had to check the upstairs living quarters anyway. Climbing the stairs brought back that sense of apprehension, waiting for a shooter to lean out and blast him backward, but it didn't happen. Slade rushed through the reasonably tidy rooms, found no one hidden there, and peered out through one of the second-story windows onto Main Street.

Where he saw Reese Dawkins, two more gunmen, and a pair of hostages hightailing it through the smoke below, two buildings now in flames, and yet another on the verge of lighting up. Cursing, Slade turned and hammered back downstairs to join the chase.

19

The heat surprised Slade, when he hit the street. Dry, weathered wood burned quickly and intensely, popping in excited competition with the gunfire rattling up and down Main Street. Between Slade and his fleeing targets, just about to enter Gilead's hotel, he counted three sprawled bodies and a fourth still moving. One of those who'd fallen was a woman, skirt and petticoats rucked up around knee level when she dropped. The wallowing survivor was a man of middle age, shot through the hip, dragging a useless leg.

Slade took a rapid mental inventory of his adversaries. Kilgore dead, and Fergus Mayfield in the wind; Dawkins and the remaining fugitives inside the hotel, now. So, who in hell was doing all the shooting up and down the street?

One of the gunmen showed himself, head poking from an alleyway across from Slade. Startled to recognize the man, he called out, "Jubal Leach! What are you doing here?"

After a moment's hesitation, Leach yelled back, "Who's that?"

"Jack Slade." And then, again, "What brings you here?"

Leach showed his pale face in the alley's shadow, answering, "We came with Marshal Bowers."

"We? Who's *we*?"

"Ed Schultz. Vance Underwood. Floyd Dooley. They're around here, somewhere."

"Here!" called Dooley, waving from a doorway two shops down from Jubal's alley.

"Down this way!" Schultz bellowed, from the same side of the street as Slade.

"I'm in the marshal's office!" Underwood called out. "Nobody else here, though."

"Where's Bowers?" Slade inquired, voice raised so all of them could hear him.

"Haven't seen him since his horse went down," Leach answered. "Don't know whether he was hit or not."

"All right, everybody hold your fire," Slade ordered. Adding, "That means *every*body," for the hidden townsfolk, just in case some had their guns trained on the street by now. "I'm crossing over to the west side. Ed, you cover us while we move down to flush them out of the hotel."

"You're covered," Schultz assured him.

It was risky, broadcasting intentions where the fugitives could hear him, Mayfield still at large and lurking God knew where, but Slade saw no way to avoid it. Once he had the scattered posse members all together, they could whisper to their hearts' content, concoct a plan for flushing Dawkins and his buddies out of the hotel.

Unless the fire got there before them.

The shingles of a fourth building were smoking now, just three doors north of Jubal's alleyway. No one was coming out to fight the fire, clearly afraid of being shot, and Slade had no spare time to organize a fire brigade. If

Gilead's inhabitants wanted to save the town, they'd have to do it on their own.

Slade had a job to finish now, before his quarry had another chance to slip away.

He crossed the street with loping strides, braced for a storm of fire from the hotel that never came. Did that mean Dawkins and the others had already slipped out through the back, or were they holed up with their hostages, waiting to see what happened next?

"It's good to see you, Marshal," Jubal said, as Slade arrived beside him. "We were thinkin' something mighta happened to you on the road."

"It did," Slade answered, mindful of his throbbing head. "But I'm still kicking. Are you ready?"

"As I'll ever be," the barber said.

"Okay. We'll link up with the others as we go along. That makes it four to three against them, when we get to the hotel."

Unless the other three had rendezvoused with Mayfield, in the meantime—or escaped while Slade was gathering his posse. And they'd still have to be mindful of the hostages, aside from ducking lead as they went in. Slade thought about Mike Bowers, maybe wounded, definitely missed when there was fighting to be done, then put him out of mind.

He had a plateful as it was.

The hunt went on.

Halfway to the livery, ducking and dodging through the smoke screen he'd created, Fergus Mayfield huddled by the back door of a barber's shop. He could have used a shave, himself, but obviously wouldn't be receiving one in Gilead—

unless the townsfolk got their hands on him and someone had a knife or razor. Some of them would love to shave him good and close, he thought. Down to the bone, in fact, and watch him bleed.

Why shouldn't hate be mutual?

All right, his plan to punish all of them for how they'd treated him had gone to hell. He understood that and was satisfied with what he had accomplished. With a little luck, the fire he'd started might consume the whole damned town—or, anyway, the west side of it—and a few more of the maggots who'd humiliated Mayfield might go up in flames along with it.

The main thing now, for him, was getting out.

The others? What about them? Dawkins was the least of his concerns. Whether he lived or died meant less to Mayfield than a gnat's fart in a hurricane. He thought about his cousins, briefly, and decided they could look out for themselves. They were grown men, able to make their own decisions more or less, and he had left them with a clutch of hostages to use as they saw fit. Some strangers might have said he owed them more, for helping him break out of custody, but what did an outsider know about the debts accrued by family?

Stragglers, by definition, were expendable.

Screw 'em.

Leaving their horses at the stable had been his idea, keeping the animals together for their getaway. Now he could pick the best and freshest for himself. The trick would be eluding angry townsfolk and the posse that had ridden into Gilead after he set the church on fire.

Bad timing, that. He had been looking forward to a long, long night of fun and games.

Oh, well.

He left his hiding place, creeping along with Colt in hand. The livery was fifty yards or so ahead of him, and Mayfield heard some of the horses whinnying in there, excited by the drifting smoke. He couldn't say how smart they were, but fire was something horses understood— enough to be afraid of it, at least.

He entered through the stable's broad back door, where dung was shoveled out at cleaning time, and found one of the hostlers doing what he could to calm the nervous animals. Same youngster that he'd met when they arrived in town, not much between the ears, if looks and conversation were an indicator. Mayfield caught him by surprise when he called out, "I'll take that grullo gelding, son."

The hostler jumped and spun around to face him, obviously recognized him from their meeting earlier, and put it all together from the gun in Mayfield's fist. Instead of sorting out the horse, though, what he did was make a dive to grab a pitchfork standing in the empty stall next door. He brandished it at Mayfield, muttering some gibberish that Fergus didn't catch.

"You oughta put that down," Mayfield advised, smiling— then shot the hostler clean between the eyes. "See there?" he told the shying animals. "Nothing between his ears at all."

There'd been a lull in firing along Main Street, then Mike Bowers heard a muffled gunshot sounding like it emanated from the livery. As luck would have it, he was headed more or less in that direction, anyway, and didn't have to aggravate his aching chest and shoulder with a sudden turnaround. His Colt felt heavier than usual, an unfamiliar weight in his left hand, but Bowers told himself that it would be all right.

Line up your shot. Remember that a fast gun misses more than half the time.

And if he had a chance to shoot one of the convicts in the back, he meant to take it. Bet your life.

Reaching the stable meant he had to cross Main Street, already decorated with the corpses of some townsfolk. Bowers knew the break in shooting might just be the calm before another storm, but if he didn't take the chance, he might as well sit down and stop pretending that he meant to do his job.

Okay.

He stepped into the street, started across, his shoulders tense in expectation of a shot—and even *that* hurt, with his broken collarbone. Each step he took was painful, jarring jagged ends and scraping them together. Mouthing muffled curses, Bowers navigated toward the blacksmith's shop, aware that he was drifting to his right with every second step or so. His pain was like a compass, out of true and misdirecting him.

Bowers corrected for the bias of his aching body, scanning left and right for threats along the way. He didn't like to turn his head, too hurtful, but he had a fair view of the street. If any snipers saw him crossing, he supposed that they could cut him down whether he spotted them or not. Lord knew that there was no way he could manage to outrun a bullet.

No one shot him, though, and in another moment he was crouched beside the blacksmith's forge, eyeing the livery. He'd only heard the one shot, and he wasn't sure exactly what to make of it, beyond the fact that there was someone in the stable with a gun.

Worth checking out. In fact, the only lead he had.

What was the best approach?

He hadn't seen this stable previously, but they normally had doors at either end, for ventilation and convenience when it came to cleaning. Choosing angles of attack would be a toss-up, since the normal layout for a stable would allow gunmen inside it to watch both doors simultaneously. Either pick could get him killed, and Bowers wasn't up to much, in terms of fancy footwork.

The trouble with a single shot was that it could mean anything. From where he was, Bowers had no idea if there was one convict inside the livery, or the whole gang together. hell, for all he knew there might be *none*. The shot he'd heard could just as well have been some resident of Gilead dispatching one of Mayfield's men. The only way to find out was to make his way inside and have a look around.

"Get off your ass and do it, then," he muttered to himself.

Easier said than done, but Bowers struggled to his feet and cocked his pistol, then took the first step toward whatever might be waiting for him in the livery.

Slade felt a little better with the posse men around him. Just a little, though, since he'd confirmed that none of them had any personal experience with gunfighting. Ed Schultz, across the street and covering their moves, came closest as a shooter, from his years of wrangling drunken cowboys in saloons, but that left Slade to lead one barber, one shopkeeper, and one hostler from the livery in Enid. Two of them had actually fired their guns so far, in Gilead, without scoring a hit on anything but real estate. Vance Underwood still hadn't pulled a trigger, and the way his hands were trembling, Slade was tempted to suggest he sit the coming battle out.

He didn't, though. No point in shaming Underwood before his friends.

"We've got three men in the hotel next door," he said. "They had five hostages when they went in and may have gathered more. First thing we have to do is make sure that they don't slip out the back way. Then, we need to go through like a dose of salts and clear the place. Now, hear me well on this: I don't want any of you trying any fancy marksmanship. You get a clear shot, take it, but be damn sure that it's one of them we're after, not some townie. If you see one of them with a hostage, *do not fire*. Call out and let me handle it. We clear?"

He got nods all around.

"Okay, then," Slade continued. "Vance and Jubal, I want you in back, in case they break that way. Floyd, is it?"

"Yes, sir."

"You'll be going in with me. Stick close. Try not to shoot me. You'll do fine."

"Yes, sir."

"Who's got a watch?" Slade asked.

"I do," said Underwood.

"You've got two minutes to make your way around and get in place, then we'll be going in the front. Take off."

The barber and the shopkeeper went jogging down the alley where they'd gathered, then around the corner, out of sight. Slade knew he'd given them more time than was required to reach the rear of the hotel and hoped they'd find some decent kind of cover there. He counted off the seconds in his head, sweating it out, until he figured they should be in place.

"You got that pistol fully loaded?" Slade asked Dooley.

"Yes, sir." The suggestion of a tremor in his voice.

"It's a double-action, right?"

Dooley responded with a jerky little nod.

"Just leave the hammer down," Slade said. "No accidents, that way. If you have a shot, don't jerk the trigger. Squeeze it nice and easy through the pull."

"Okay."

"We hit the hotel lobby, anything can happen," Slade informed him. "Customers may try to run for it. Be crystal clear on any targets, if you start to fire."

"Yes, sir."

"That said," Slade added, "don't hold back so long that you get killed. It's tough to judge sometimes, I know. Just do your best."

"I will."

"Let's go."

Slade rose from kneeling to a crouch and scuttled toward the hotel's entrance, shoving through to see whatever waited for them on the other side. The lobby was deserted, no one at the registration desk to welcome new arrivals. Slade veered off in that direction, checking out the office, finding no one there.

The hotel didn't have a restaurant or kitchen, but they still had storage space to check before they moved upstairs. When that was done, they doubled back to stand before a staircase leading to the second story.

"Here we go," Slade told the hostler. "This is it."

"I don't like bein' stuck in here," Reese Dawkins said.

"Same thing you said about the hardware store," Earl told him.

"An I meant it. All we done is trade one box in for another."

"Bigger box, though," Tad suggested. "Lotsa rooms."

"A box is still a box, dummy."

"You don't insult my brother," Earl advised him.

"Don't I, hell! Your goddamn family got me in this fix to start with."

"Got you outta jail, you mean," Earl said. "Think you'd be grateful."

"Grateful! For the choice of bein' shot or fried alive? Yeah, thanks a lot to you and goddamn Fergus!"

"Where *is* Fergus?" Tad inquired.

"Run off an' left your ass," Reese sneered. "Tha's where your precious cousin is."

"He wouldn't do that," Tad insisted.

"Right. Mebbe he'll swing in on a bell rope when you start to roast and yank you outa here."

"Earl?"

"Never mind what he says. Cousin Ferg'll be here when we need him."

Dawkins thought he heard a creaking on the stairs, just audible from where they'd gathered with their captives on the hotel's second-story landing. Tad and Earl had been for splitting off and manning different rooms, but Reese had argued that they ought to stick together. Now, he wished he'd skinned on out the back and left these idjits to their own devices. He'd have had a better chance alone, but it was too late now to change his play.

"There's someone comin' up," he said.

"You sure?" asked Tad.

"Go have a look," Dawkins suggested.

Tad was going for it, when his brother caught him by the sleeve and reeled him back. "How dumb *are* you?" Earl asked, then turned his glare and gun on Reese. "*You* have a look."

"The hell with that."

Earl cocked his Colt.

"Awright! Jesus! C'mere, missus." He grabbed the mayor's wife, pleased to hear her squeal, and jabbed the muzzle of his six-gun tight against her ribs. "Let's have a little look-see, eh?"

He marched her toward the stairs in lockstep, left arm wrapped around her waist, the hand cupped underneath one ample breast. She suffered it in silence till they reached the stairs, where Dawkins said, "We're gonna take a peek, now. You be nice'n still."

He edged forward, still couldn't see, and had to bend her forward at the waist to peer over her shoulder, down the staircase. Dawkins wasn't sure what he'd expected, but it damned sure hadn't been the U.S. marshal he'd seen lying dead beside the prison wagon, on the night the Mayfield brothers broke him out of custody.

Dead marshal coming back to life and staring at him down the barrel of the biggest rifle Reese had ever seen.

"The hell are you—"

There came a flash, and then his world exploded into crimson, fading instantly to black.

Slade dropped the Springfield, no time to reload it as he hammered up the stairs, pulling the Colt Model 1877 from under his belt on the run. He'd risked the shot at Dawkins, even with the woman standing in his way, because he'd known there was no way around it. Now, he had to leap across her slumping form to face whatever waited for him on the landing.

Two armed men and four more hostages: a woman and three men, one with a badge pinned to his vest, an empty holster on his hip. Slade saw it all and recognized the weasel who'd come into camp before the shooting started—what? Three nights ago? The other bore a close resemblance to him, had to be a blood relation and the shooter from the shadows.

Both of them were shooting now, with Winchesters. Slade hit the floor, wondered if Dooley had the sense to do the same, or if he'd let foolhardy courage push him up the stairs to get his head blown off. Slade's ears were ringing from the close-range gunfire, but he quickly recognized an unexpected stroke of luck.

Choosing to fight with lever-action rifles, rather than their handguns, neither of his would-be killers had a free hand left for clutching human shields. The hostages had either dropped or cut and run the second that their captors started firing, giving Slade a clear view of his standing targets. All he needed now was time, a clear eye, and a steady hand.

His first shot struck the weasel from the camp an inch or so above his belt buckle. The .32-caliber slug bent him double, his next rifle shot drilling into the floor at his feet, while Slade swung toward his kinsman, squeezing the Colt's smooth double-action trigger as soon as the target was square in his sights.

A chest shot, this time—left lung, probably. The second shooter stumbled back and would have fallen, but he hit the wall first, sticking there. The dazed expression on his face seemed normal, somehow, as he worked his rifle's cocking lever, chambering another round.

Slade's third shot pierced his cheek, below the left eye, and his head bounced off the wall before he crumpled, dropping in a lifeless heap. His look-alike coughed up a curse, seeing him fall, and Slade rolled to his left, just as a bullet from the weasel's Winchester plowed up the carpet where he'd been a heartbeat earlier.

Two shots to finish it and put the rodent down, one in the chest, the other through his forehead when he'd already begun to fall. Before he hit the floorboards, Slade was up and standing over them, his smoking pistol ready if they needed any more.

Instead, he heard a hoofbeat clatter rising up from Main Street, coming to him through an open window at the near end of the hall, four numbered doors away. A voice that seemed familiar to him shouted out for someone else to stop, then gunfire crackled from the street.

Slade grabbed one of the fallen Winchesters in passing, reached the window in a sprint, and turned to scan the northern end of Main Street. He saw Fergus Mayfield mounted on a grullo, riding hell-for-leather toward a figure that could only be Mike Bowers, standing with a pistol raised in his left hand. *Why left?* Slade wondered, then both of them started firing through the haze of smoke around them, Bowers lurching, jerking, going down.

Slade snapped the rifle to his shoulder, fired a hasty shot that may have missed, then pumped the lever-action for another try. The next shot lifted Mayfield from his saddle, rolled him back across the grullo's croup and dropped him facedown in the dust. Slade waited for a sign of movement, other than the spastic twitching in his legs, but even that soon faded and was gone.

Floyd Dooley stood beside him at the window, asking, "That was him?"

"It was," Slade said. He turned to find some of the hostages regarding him with stunned expressions, one man helping up the woman who had fallen near the stairs. More smoke was wafting down the street, reminding Slade that Gilead was burning down around them.

"Anybody doesn't want to cook," he said, "should get out while you can."

20

They wound up saving half of Gilead. The fire had moved too fast for anyone to stop it on the western side of Main Street, sweeping through the shops and offices, along to the hotel and then beyond it, burning on into the night. Slade saved his borrowed dapple gray and walked it to the other side of town, while men with buckets full of sand and water tried to fight the flames, but all in vain. A shift in wind almost miraculously kept the fire from crossing Main Street, blowing embers off to westward, where they died without igniting wildfires on the prairie.

Call it Providence or pure dumb luck.

Burning on till nearly midnight, the inferno's light helped Slade and members of his unexpected posse take stock of the human damage Gilead had suffered. Of the townsfolk, three were dead and two had suffered gunshot wounds from Mayfield's raiders. Gilead's physician had his office on the side of town that didn't burn, and he was busy through the night, extracting bullets, stitching wounds, and treating burns suffered by members of the futile fire brigade.

One of the doctor's patients was Mike Bowers, treated for his broken collarbone and two hits scored by Fergus Mayfield in his last wild charge down Main Street. One bullet had clipped his left earlobe; the other wound was worse, a through-and-through on his right thigh that missed the artery but chipped the bone and ripped the muscles something fierce. He'd walk again, the sawbones said, but would be limping for a good long while.

"Better than Mayfield, anyhow," Bowers allowed, on hearing Slade's account of how the convict died. "Wish I'da put him down myself."

"You slowed him up for me," Slade said. "I would've missed him, otherwise."

"I guess that's something," Bowers granted. Then asked, "Is there such a thing as whiskey in this burg?"

The fugitives were all accounted for, two in the street, three cooked in the hotel. Gilead's undertaker would be busy through the weekend, building caskets and negotiating fees with locals who had lost their loved ones, some of whom had also lost their homes and all their worldly goods. Without a church or minister, he reckoned that the services would be abbreviated but respectful. Slade signed off on payment for burial of Mayfield and his cohorts, opting for barest of bare minimums.

Housing the newly destitute in Gilead would be a problem for the mayor, his council, and the citizens who still had roofs over their heads. The posse men from Enid gathered up their horses, walked them to the livery, and settled down to spend the night there, after a late supper at the town's surviving restaurant. Beer all around, in celebration of a sort, although the mood was generally solemn. Slade could tell that they were anxious to get home, a two-day ride still waiting for them, and another night of camping on the plains before they made it.

For his own part, Slade could only wonder what was waiting for him back in Enid. He'd be meeting with Judge Dennison, of course, reporting on the outcome of the manhunt and the doctor's verdict on when Bowers would be fit to travel. Mayfield and the others dying cleared the slate for Hampton, but it didn't balance out the other damage they had done while still at large. Eleven innocents cut down along the way, plus Orville Washington, whose murder by his fellow outlaws wouldn't cost Slade any sleep. A town half razed, and who could say how long rebuilding it would take or how much it would cost those who had lost their homes and livelihoods?

Gilead's marshal had identified the dead man Slade had found at Hilker's Hardware. Name of Wilkins, sent from Enid by Judge Dennison to warn the town, apparently. Slade hadn't known him, wasn't sure why he had stuck around to brace the fugitives, but it had cost him. If he had family at home, Slade planned on letting someone else deliver the heartbreaking news. The judge, for instance, with his famous silver tongue.

On the plus side, Slade had managed to recoup some of his losses from the night the convicts had escaped. Mayfield was carrying Slade's Colt when he went down, along with his gold-plated pocket watch. His lever-action shotgun had been snug inside the saddle boot on Mayfield's stolen grullo, when it finally calmed down and wandered back to downtown Gilead. As for his rifle, he was satisfied to keep the one that finished Mayfield's run.

It was well past two o'clock before Slade found a stall to

spread his bedroll in, and even then, sleep managed to elude him. Finally, inevitably, his thoughts turned to Faith. He wondered how she must be feeling, whether she still planned to leave the territory and go east. It struck him— not for the first time—that he missed talking to her, hearing how she'd spent her days, as much or more than he missed holding, kissing, loving her.

Too late for all of that.

He knew Faith well enough to know that she possessed an iron will most men would have envied. Once her mind was made up on a subject, it was easier to change a river's course than to persuade her that she ought to reconsider. In all fairness, Slade admitted to himself that Faith was usually right in her decisions—which did nothing to relieve his pain at being left behind.

Reluctantly, he had decided not to fight her choice, in this case. There were lawyers, he supposed, who would have championed a father's rights, although they'd never got around to marrying, but what would be the point? If he could somehow force her to remain in Oklahoma for his sake, what would it prove beyond the gross inequity of law? How would he square it with the love he felt for Faith, and knowing that she'd come to loathe the sight of him?

Better to let her go, instead, and focus on his own plans for the future. Should he stay in Enid, with the marshals service, or move on to something else? And if so, what was waiting for him, down the road?

Sleep overtook him sometime after three o'clock—three hours, give or take, until first light and preparation to depart from Gilead. Whatever dreams tormented or delighted Slade, they would be long forgotten with the sunrise and the long ride south.

A blessing in disguise.

The posse made fair time, once they were done with breakfast at the town's surviving restaurant and saying their farewells to strangers they would likely never see again. Mike Bowers wished that he was going with them, even volunteered to ride across the prairie on a horse-drawn litter, but the doctor wouldn't hear of it. As for the residents of Gilead, Slade got the feeling they were glad to see the last of their bedraggled saviors.

There wasn't any big talk on the trail, about their great adventure. Slade supposed they might work up to it in time, a little something to impress the wife or neighbors. Ed Schultz probably could use the outing to enhance his reputation at the Lucky Strike or anywhere he chose to work in future as a bouncer. For the moment, though, Slade's four companions were subdued, perhaps reflecting on their own mortality and how fast everything a person owned could vanish, if their luck turned.

As for Slade, he had a faculty for putting violence behind him. He had been involved in brawls and shootings prior to putting on a badge, and many since, but it had never bothered him to speak of. Lately, when he'd started having nightmares, they revolved around the loss of his relationship with Faith Connover, not the men he'd killed or wounded over time. Slade didn't agonize over a trigger pull or second-guess decisions made when it came down to his life or the other guy's. Lawmen who let that kind of thinking eat at them inevitably hesitated when they shouldn't. Cemeteries nationwide were filled with them.

Slade's sole regret, concerning any of the violence he'd been involved in as a marshal, was the way it had intruded on his life with Faith. He didn't blame the job, exactly, since he'd chosen it with both eyes open—just as Faith had recognized the risks involved. She *hadn't* known a gang of homicidal Danites would besiege her home, of course, looking for Slade and some intended victims of their personal crusade. And no one could have guessed that killers from the Tex-Mex border would show up and turn her wedding day into a massacre.

What woman would rebound from those events and treat them as a normal part of daily life? Who would forgive the man who'd nearly gotten her killed, not once, but twice? And why in hell *should* she? Finding out about the baby only made things worse, of course. One shock on top of others, coming just as she'd decided any hope of settling down with Slade was futile.

His fault, Slade had long ago decided. Not the job's.

The good news, for his posse members, was that none of them had actually shot a man. They'd have no bloody nightmares to contend with, once they got past seeing dead folks in the street. Later, if some decided to inflate their role in wiping out the Mayfield gang, Slade wouldn't argue with the tales they spun. For all he knew, that escapade might prove to be the highlight of their lives.

Which, he supposed, was rather sad.

Slade posted guards, their first night camping on the prairie, working short two-hour rounds without taking a shift himself. In truth, he doubted there was any need for lookouts, but he had the men available and so decided to make use of them. They built a fire—no more cold camping, anyway—and cooked up food they'd brought with them from Gilead. A sort of banquet for the road, with bacon, beans, potatoes, and some biscuits that were tasty, even if they'd started slipping over toward the stale side.

Sitting with the others, warm around the fire, Slade almost

felt that he was part of something, but he couldn't put his finger on it and the moment passed. He knew Schultz from his visits to the Lucky Strike, and Jubal Leach had cut his hair, but Slade did not delude himself that they were bosom friends. They wouldn't meet for drinks in Enid, visit one another's homes, or get together for a big night on the town. Briefly, they'd been prepared to kill or die together in a common cause, but that had not established any kind of lasting bond between them.

Slade supposed he would go back to solitary living for the most part. It had been his way before he came to Enid, solved his brother's murder, and met Faith. It suited him—or *had*, until she'd shown him he could lead a different kind of life. Now that he'd lost the option of a wife and family, he thought reverting to his former lifestyle shouldn't be too difficult. He knew the moves by heart, from long experience, knew how to act, which pitfalls to avoid. He would enjoy himself again, someday, and if it didn't rise to any standard he'd experienced with Faith . . . so what?

He'd heard a man say, once, that no one missed a good thing till he'd lost it. Slade hadn't believed that at the time, and he did not believe it now. Most people, be believed, knew very well when there was something lacking from their lives. They yearned to fill a void—with love, kids, wealth, whatever—but they didn't yammer on about it endlessly, exposing unfulfilled desires to others who might use that weakness to their detriment. Humiliation lay that way, and worse.

Slade would survive without Faith in his life, a fact never in question. He would miss her, certainly, but that would also fade with passing time. It was the notion of their child that haunted him, the son or daughter he would never meet, if Faith moved on. And yet, he thought her way might be the best for all concerned.

If Faith remained in Oklahoma, it would raise a host of problems for herself and for the child. Her relationship with Slade had fueled sufficient local gossip, as it was, without adding an infant to the mix. Faith didn't seem to care what people said or thought about her, but a child was vulnerable—and a mother would be bound to feel the pain her offspring felt from thoughtless insults. If she moved away, though, Faith could spin whatever tale she wanted to explain the absence of a husband and a father. Slade could be a martyred hero or a drunken wastrel, anything she liked, and he would never know the difference.

Her choice.

He wouldn't try to spoil it for her, change her mind, or hold her in a situation that she found unbearable. Love owed that much, at least.

Nearly asleep, he heard coyotes howling in the distance. Most people seemed to think that was a mournful sound, but Slade wasn't convinced. For all he knew, the pack was celebrating a successful hunt, or welcoming a brood of newborn pups. They posed no threat to Slade this evening, and he wished them well.

"I regret that none of them survived for trial, but in the circumstances . . . well . . ." Judge Dennison turned toward his window overlooking an enclosed courtyard, where a gallows built for six cast its angular shadow across paving stones. "Perhaps it's just as well."

"They'll be a while rebuilding Gilead," Slade said. "If they decide to stay, that is."

"Don't underestimate the frontier spirit," Dennison advised.

"No, sir."

"I hope that Marshal Bowers won't decide to quit on us."

"It didn't sound that way," Slade says. "Likely depends on how his leg heals up."

"He's got a job here, either way, if he desires it. I can always use another bailiff."

Slade had no idea if Mike would want to work around the courthouse every day and didn't offer an opinion on the subject. "Sorry that I couldn't make arrangements for your messenger," he told the judge, instead.

"Poor Mr. Wilkins. I suppose he felt the urge to be a hero, at the end."

"Sounds like he almost pulled it off," Slade said. The mayor of Gilead had filled him in on how Lem Wilkins died, facing four guns. The story, futile as it was, made Slade wish that he'd known the kid—enough to miss him, anyway.

"He had no kinfolk in the territory, that I know of," said the judge. "I'll ask around, of course, but if we don't come up with anyone, he may as well remain in Gilead."

"A lot of funerals," Slade observed.

"It's the nature of our business, I'm afraid," said Dennison. "The nature of humanity, in fact. It's why they need us, Jack."

"Good to be useful, I suppose."

"If I may ask without offending, how's your other situation?"

"No change there," Slade said. "What's done is done."

"It needn't be, you know."

"How's that?"

The judge shrugged massive shoulders. "People change. Perspectives alter. You, yourself, are living proof of that."

"I haven't changed as much as some might think," Slade said.

"Oh, no? You were a gambler and a drifter when I met you. Now, you represent the law. You've saved lives and brought criminals to justice. And I dare say that you've learned to love."

For all the good it did, Slade thought. But said, "One doesn't help the other much."

"It's not an easy road, I grant you. If you feel that separation from the service might be beneficial to your situation—"

"No," Slade interrupted. "It's too late for that."

"Well, you know best, I'm sure."

"Don't bet on that."

"Why don't you take some time off, Jack? Let's say a week. Relax a while."

"It couldn't hurt," Slade granted. As to whether it would *help*, he couldn't say.

"Next Monday, then. How's that?" asked Dennison.

"Sounds good. Thanks, Judge."

"Don't worry. There'll be ample work waiting when you come back."

"There always is."

"And always will be. Nature of humanity," the judge repeated. "Mark my words."

Slade left the courthouse, passing lawyers with their paperwork and people waiting for their turn before Judge Dennison, to plead their cases. Downstairs, there'd be prisoners in cages, some also in shackles for the safety of their keepers, biding time until they heard their sentences pronounced. Acquittals were a rarity, though not unheard of.

Most who waited in the cells would be confined in one way or another—work gangs, maybe prison—for a period of months or years, to be determined by the court. Those convicted of a willful murder would be hanged under the judge's watchful eye, a duty that he claimed to owe the prisoners that he condemned.

The hangings were a public spectacle that Slade avoided, unless he was called upon to supervise. Deputies took that job by turns, none of them eager for the duty, but accepting it as one more aspect of their job. While Slade agreed that getting rid of killers was a public service, he had never cared much for the *public* aspect of it, and the gawkers who turned out to celebrate an execution physically repulsed him. They learned nothing from the grim experience, and some appeared to treat it as a form of entertainment, prompting Slade to wonder what was in their minds and hearts.

As if I have a right to judge, he thought.

The noon hour had passed, and he was ready for a beer—perhaps for several. If he was on vacation, why not act like it?

He passed on by the Lucky Strike—too soon for him to see Ed Schultz again—and headed for the Gold Dust, a competitor nearby. Along the way, he saw Blaine Abernathy on the far side of the street and changed directions on an impulse, veering off to intercept the doctor.

Why?

Two weeks before, as he was riding out of Enid on another job, he'd seen Faith coming out of Abernathy's office, lingering beside him briefly on the sidewalk, talking. Faith had seen Slade passing by, he thought, but offered no acknowledgment. Her choice.

Why corner Abernathy now? Slade wasn't sure. He understood that doctors weren't supposed to talk about their patients with third parties, barring a specific grant of leave to speak. Slade couldn't even think of what to ask the doctor, really, even if discussion was allowed. And yet, he felt an urge to share the doctor's space, as if proximity alone would somehow reassure him Faith was doing well, that she was happy with the choices that she'd made. That everything was fine, and he could start to live again.

Stupid idea.

Slade almost gave it up, but by that time, he'd reached the sidewalk and was set on a collision course with Abernathy. Fifty-some years old, a little stooped from carrying the weight of human pain and suffering. The sawbones seemed distracted, steering around people in his path, but not quite seeing them.

Then, he looked up through wire-rimmed spectacles and absolutely saw Jack Slade.

The doctor's face changed, tightening, as if he'd felt a sudden pang of indigestion. Disapproval, maybe? Was he blaming Slade, somehow, for Faith's decision to go on and bear their child alone? Of course, he knew their situation, having tended Faith after the shooting, on their scheduled wedding day. Why *wouldn't* he go grim at sight of Slade, who'd brought his patient so much grief and pain?

Slade had decided just to nod and pass on by, but Abernathy spoke to him, instead. "Marshal, I understand that you were injured in the line of duty. Are you healing well?"

"Turns out I've got a hard head, Doctor," Slade replied.

"Good, good." Distracted sounding. "You have my sincere condolences."

A joke, perhaps? "Not sure I follow you," Slade said.

Doc Abernathy blinked at him, confused, then lost a shade of color from his weathered face. "Oh, my. I didn't . . . um . . . Forgive me, please. I thought she must have told you."

She? *Faith.*

"Told me what, Doc?"

"Mmm. I really shouldn't . . . No . . . You understand my obligation . . . But you *were* the father, after all."

Were?

"Doctor?"

"Marshal, this is very awkward. I'm afraid Faith lost the child."

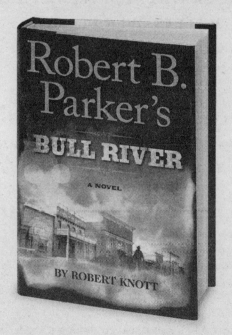

PETER BRANDVOLD

"Make room on your shelf of favorites:
Peter Brandvold will be staking out a claim there."
—Frank Roderus

THE GRAVES AT SEVEN DEVILS

BULLETS OVER BEDLAM

COLD CORPSE, HOT TRAIL

DEADLY PREY

ROGUE LAWMAN

STARING DOWN THE DEVIL

RIDING WITH THE DEVIL'S MISTRESS

.45-CALIBER FIREBRAND

.45-CALIBER FURY

.45-CALIBER REVENGE

"Recommended to anyone who loves the West
as I do. A very good read."
—Jack Ballas

"Takes off like a shot, never giving the reader a
chance to set the book down."
—Douglas Hirt

M32AS1109

Don't miss the best Westerns from Berkley

LYLE BRANDT
PETER BRANDVOLD
JACK BALLAS
J. LEE BUTTS
JORY SHERMAN
DUSTY RICHARDS

penguin.com